Love Ain't No Soap Opera

Love Ain't No Soap Opera

A SHADYBROOK SERIES NOVEL

BY

CONNIE KUYKENDALL

Printed in the United States of America
First Printing, 2016
ISBN-10: 0997027207
ISBN-13: 978-0-9970272-0-4

*Praise for Love Ain't
No Soap Opera*

"This story is clever and witty, filled with memorable characters and snappy dialogue. At the same time, it deals with the universal—and sometimes heart-wrenching—desire for love. Our hearts go out to the main character even as we laugh at her antics, and the eccentricities of those around her . . .

The main character, Selah Morgan, is immediately likeable, and undoubtedly many women readers will identify with her. The reader has a feeling that she's going to laugh and chuckle throughout this story even in the midst of Selah's struggles and heartaches . . .

The ending leaves the reader smiling."

**Winner —Golden Leaf Award
for Best Novel & Best First Page**

~Blue Ridge Christian Novelist Retreat

"People look at the outward appearance, but the Lord looks at the heart."

1 Samuel 16:7, NIV

Chapter One

"*Like sands through the hourglass, so are the days of our lives.*"

Days of Our Lives opening title sequence,
narrated by Macdonald Carey

*E*VERY GUY IN *this town is a certifiable redneck.*

Selah Morgan peered over the top of her cell phone and analyzed the male customers in her family's diner, Good Company.

Momma stepped into view and clucked her tongue. "That was not a Christian thing to say."

Selah jerked down the phone. "I didn't say anything."

Momma smirked and waggled her index finger. "Oh, but I can see them wheels a-turnin'."

"Can I help it if they look like they're on a casting call for some down-and-out in duck country reality show?"

Selah slipped the phone into her electric-blue apron and leaned against a matching booth.

She'd graduated Shadybrook High with a few of these guys thirteen years ago. Table Five was divorced and refused to pay child support for three kids. Tables Six and Seven were unhappily married. Table Three had issues with staring and with displaying his hunting knives, among other things, in public. Most of the men were decked out in Rip Van Winkle beards and camouflage. Sadly, no matter how much Realtree they heaped on, she could still see them.

And then there was her father, who sneaked out the side door while Momma had her back turned. Catching Selah's eye, he put his finger to his lips and left in his roulette-red Dodge Charger, like Santa Claus going up the chimney. Except this jolly old elf was headed for the Shadybrook Speedway, leaving Momma to handle the dinner rush alone. Her parents were a walking public service announcement for why she should stay single. Selah massaged the muscles in the back of her neck.

"You'd get more done if you quit looking at your phone and the clock."

Selah took a deep breath and faced Momma. "I'm self-employed. I need my phone so I can be in constant contact with my clients."

"You ain't got but a handful of computer clients. Maybe you should look for a new employer." Momma began to wipe down the chrome countertop—the restaurant's centerpiece. But truth be told, Momma was the real centerpiece.

Selah shook her head as she retrieved a plate of chicken-fried steak from the kitchen and slid it onto Table Three without making eye contact. Then she delivered a burger platter to a customer sitting at the counter.

Momma was still talking, or preaching, as her father called it. "You're just itching to get home and watch them stories with Frankie."

Selah hated it when she was right, which, according to Momma, was ninety-nine percent of the time, one percent allowing for the day she'd married Russ Morgan. On most days, Selah's soap opera, *The Winds of Change*, and its sizzling star, Cane Ashton, were all Selah had to look forward to.

People who turned up their noses at daytime drama had never laid eyes on him. Cane's wavy, milk-chocolate brown hair and dark eyes set off a rugged jawline that was made for television. Just the thoughts of him had her running to turn down the diner's thermostat.

Selah's phone rang and her fantasies evaporated with the smoke on the grill.

"See? What did I tell you? It's Sherman Miller—a paying client." The country lawyer had hired her to set up his website and office management and billing software.

When she turned, her hip bumped a table and knocked over a glass of water. Her spirits plummeted like the miniature waterfall she'd created.

Momma smacked her dishrag down on the table and attacked the mess. "If your father was any good, he'd be here doing his job instead of doing who-knows-what at the track."

Selah grabbed a mop and bucket and rolled them over to the wet booth.

"Ow! You ran over my foot." Momma reached down,

pushed away the bucket, and massaged her saddle oxfords. "Call your client back and go on home. I can't afford your kind of help."

The tightness in Selah's neck snaked itself around her head and sunk its fangs in her forehead. She jogged to a vacant booth, sidestepping the Wurlitzer and the fun-house mirror that turned every curve into a saddlebag. She smoothed her Good Company t-shirt across her ample hips and sucked in her belly.

"It's no reflection on your work," Sherman said when she returned his call, "but I need to end our contract."

Selah sank into the booth, her head buzzing. Why was the aroma of bacon so overpowering all of a sudden and why didn't somebody put a cork in the Patsy Cline torch song playing on the jukebox? "I'll give you the absolute lowest price I can. Y'all are family."

Maybe it had been a mistake to venture out on her own, leaving the safe, solid company where she'd worked sixty-hour weeks as programmer/webmaster/tech support/ glorified gopher with health insurance and a steady income. Then again, maybe not. She cringed when she thought of the boss who'd taken the company's hands-on training policy literally.

"I remember when our firm had an event at your parents' diner." Sherman chuckled. "You were just a wee little thing, running around with pigtails flying."

Selah pushed her long, raven curls behind her ears and doodled a smiley face on a paper napkin.

"Now that you're an adult, dear, you will understand that my partner and I looked at areas where we could cut costs." He paused. "I'm afraid you're the weakest link."

She changed the smiley face into a frown and gave the head horns. "Can't we work something out?"

Don't grovel. Don't cry. Tech people were supposed to be in demand, turning away work. How could she be so awful at her job?

Selah tugged a pink antacid pill from the pocket of her blue jeans. Would one do the trick? Better yet, was there any chocolate cake in the diner? Momma appeared and set a chocolate shake on the table. Selah smiled up at her and gripped the glass, her hand trembling. Momma patted her shoulder and slipped away.

"My granddaughter is handling our tech support from now on," her defecting client continued.

"Your granddaughter." Selah blinked. "Isn't she thirteen years old?"

"She's smart. Makes straight As. Always talking on that cella-phone of hers."

Selah hung up and laid the phone—and her head—on the table. Some people worried about losing their jobs to foreign outsourcing. Her services had been replaced by a teenager with purple braces and a Hello Kitty book bag.

If Selah had learned one lesson from twenty years of watching daytime soap operas, it was that life was a whole lot easier if you were young, rich, and skinny.

"What is going on with you?" Dorian Forrester tsked and pointed her fork at her co-star, Cane Ashton. "You look skinny and pale, not your usual obscenely attractive self."

"If you're trying to impress me on our date, Dori, you're failing miserably." Cane grinned, but his body felt heavy, as if he'd done a day's worth of drills in his old football pads.

All he'd wanted to do after work was go back to his apartment and crash, not put on a suit and spend the evening at a pretentious Italian restaurant near the studio. "Don't know how much longer I'll be in the business. There's a cattle call for a character who's nothing but a younger version of my character. They're edging me out."

Dori frowned but her porcelain skin didn't wrinkle. "I would never allow them to replace you."

"They forced you to take a pay cut," Cane said. "Even you can't fight it, and you're the queen of daytime."

She adjusted her diamond necklace. "Indeed I am. I shouldn't be made to endure such disrespect, not to mention the monologues and abominable storylines Mason has been feeding us lately."

Cane stayed quiet, letting her fret and grumble for twenty minutes about their head writer, Mason Lord, and the dismal ratings of their soap opera, *The Winds of Change*. Dori, at fifty-five, was one of the most beautiful women in Hollywood. As she leaned across the table toward him, her hazel eyes twinkled. Her full, red lips were moving and she was saying something about a rumor she heard in hair and makeup.

He stirred when she ran her fingertips down his arm and rested her hand on his. This was the perfect opportunity for a mindless good time. Like the old days, back when he partied every night. He didn't have to think. He just found a girl to love for a few hours, which, for a teen TV star, was like shooting fish in a barrel. It was bliss, until it wasn't.

He focused on her mouth to keep his mind from drifting. When he'd started on the show at age thirteen, he dreamed of kissing his sexy, older co-star. What was wrong with him now?

Cane leaned his elbows on the table and rested his chin on his fist, running through his to-do list. He couldn't keep putting off that phone call to the doctor. He wouldn't be able to hide his pain and clumsiness from the cameras much longer.

Dori jerked her hand from his. "I think we should call it a night."

His head snapped up. "Why? We're just getting started."

"You remember that book and movie, *He's Just Not That Into You*?" She retouched her lipstick. "Your mind is everywhere else but on me tonight."

"Dori, I—"

"I had such high hopes for us." She blinked slowly, like a cat. "I've never had a proper boy toy."

He chuckled. "You don't expect me to believe that, after all these years of platonic friendship, you want to cheat on your husband with me. You deserve better than my company."

"I do, don't I?" She raised an eyebrow. "You can tell your problems to Dori. Are you and my daughter an item? Eva follows you around on set as if you were the Pied Piper."

"It's not about her."

"It's always about Eva." Dori rolled her eyes, which was comical on her elegant features. "Maybe you're searching for something more than a fling. Perhaps a family? It's about time. You're in your thirties and never married. Some cultures would call you a monk."

"I appreciate your concern, as you have so kindly conveyed it. But a family is not in my future."

His family was gone—collateral damage.

"Don't waste too much time being a bachelor." She stood and he jumped up to help her with her coat. "One day, a lonely old man will stare back at you from the mirror. Trust Dori."

She touched his cheek and left. Half the men in the restaurant watched her go.

Their waiter returned and jerked his thumb toward the door. "Was that . . ."

"In all her glory." *And I let her get away. I must be losing it.*

Chapter Two

"*Ah, soap opera, the land where women are strong, cherished, and cellulite-free,*
the people you love are never really dead, and irritating people can be recast."

Dorian Forrester, soap actress,
The Winds of Change

"SINCE YOU DIDN'T reply to my texts, Selah, I thought we'd lost you. Figured your mom had finally driven you over the edge."

Selah arrived home from the diner at the same time as her best friend, Francine "Frankie" Newman.

"Let's just say I am in serious need of our weekly soap marathon." Selah kicked off her snow boots and hung her coat and Good Company apron on a rack near the door. She contemplated tossing the apron in the fireplace.

Frankie shrugged off her soggy NASCAR jacket and

dropped it onto the battered beige carpet. "I'm relieved to see the TV and DVR lasted another week."

Selah found the remote and pushed play on *The Winds of Change*. Dori Forrester's character, Leanna, was hosting a fashion show beneath palm trees and sunshine in Beverly Hills. Sleet tapped against Selah's window in Shadybrook, Virginia, a town more reminiscent of Mayberry.

"Only because Momma bolted them down, like the sets in hotel rooms, so my father couldn't cart them off again."

She caught a glimpse of her body in the full-length mirror beside the door. *You and your mirrors, Momma.* She squeezed her eyes shut and turned away. "Let's take a break from reality, forget about him, and focus on the gorgeous fantasy men of daytime. Please tell me you got the stuff."

"Yeah, girlfriend. It wouldn't be a party without it." Frankie relinquished a plastic grocery bag that had stretched so thin, it ripped. Unfastening the top button of her fashionably tight jeans, she plopped down on a squishy pillow facing the television.

Selah eased into a La-Z-Boy like a civilized person—well, a civilized couch potato. She opened the bag and inhaled deeply as the gloriously fried aroma of Chinese food permeated the air. "They should bottle this and call it aromatherapy."

"Hey, if they made it into a perfume," Frankie said, "maybe we could finally attract some men."

Selah threw back her head with laughter. "Eau de General Tso."

"Mmm," Dori purred from the TV, her angelic face and smile shimmering under the lights. "I think I see my next four husbands in this next group of luscious models storming the runway." The audience tittered.

In real life, the grand dame of daytime had been married to the same man for over thirty years, while her alter ego had been married eleven times. Selah would survive if she never married, but the longer she stayed single, the more the rest of the town saw her as desperate or a lonely loser they needed to fix up with another lonely loser.

For instance, that morning, as she waited in a sterile white exam room for a routine physical, in walked the last person she ever wanted to see, especially when the only place to hide was under a paper gown.

"Katie Buchanan." Selah's mouth went dry. "I didn't realize you had become a nurse."

"Well, hello, Selah Morgan. I didn't realize you had become a—" Katie glanced down at her chart, "professional computer nerd. No surprise there."

"I may have been a nerd in middle school, but studying helped me get a near-perfect score on the SATs." She smiled piously, but her cheeks burned as the nicknames Thunder Thighs and Selah Whale-ah paraded through her head—names Katie and her brother, Cody, had called her in the school bus, and the playground, and the cafeteria.

"I have a technology consulting business." Maybe she could convince the small-town doctor to convert to an electronic records system.

"Oh, right. Is that like Radio Shack?" Katie nodded. "So, the doctor may give you a diet, probably this big one." She pulled a stapled packet from a brown folder hanging above a box of tongue depressors.

"Evidently, going to a professional nursing school

didn't make you professional. Maybe we should wait for the doctor. Besides, I already exercise."

"But this plan is so simple." Katie smiled under burgundy lipstick and blue eye shadow. Surely scrubs weren't meant to be skin-tight. "This time next year, you'll be in a bikini on the beach."

Selah bit her lip, thinking that God, in this situation, would allow an exception to His turn-the-other-cheek rule.

Katie persisted. "You'll be sure to land a man then, unless . . . Are you LGBT?" Katie noted something on her chart.

Selah's eyes widened. "No. No. I am not. Is there a code for straight? Like HT for heterosexual? Write that down."

This is the last time I am ever going to the doctor.

Selah shook her head at the memory and downed a cheese wonton. Suddenly, her chest constricted and she felt as if she was breathing through a straw. She fanned herself with a magazine and stood from her chair.

Must have been the fireplace or the MSG. Given that the doctor pronounced her healthy, it couldn't be menopause. Being in her thirties wasn't even old enough for a mid-life crisis.

But when Cane appeared on the screen, all was right with the world again. Selah's stomach went gooey in a good, no-antacid-required way. He had never married in real life. Selah knew that because she had watched *The Winds of Change* and read *Soap Opera Digest* and *Soap!* since she was a teenager. Other women would escape to daytime drama too, if they saw the prospects in Shadybrook.

Cane's character, Dean, had been betrayed. *"In the two*

months I was lying in a coma from a gunshot wound, you had an affair with my brother and got pregnant. Why, Kelli? Why?"

Eva Forrester's character, Kelli, snuffled and turned her face from the camera. *"I, um, was grieving for you. The doctors told me you were going to die, that it was hopeless. Uh, please forgive me?"*

"I can't forgive you for losing faith in me . . . in us."

"Who writes this drivel?" Frankie yawned. "I remember how you cried when they thought Cane's character was dead."

"I do not cry. I have seasonal allergies." He was the only man worth crying over.

Selah frowned and cocked her head to one side. "Speaking of him dying, does he look peaked to you?"

Her friend shrugged. "Who knows what's real, with all their makeup and spray tans?"

Selah helped herself to more lo mein and garlic chicken, which promptly slid off her chopsticks and onto the floor. "Too bad we don't have a dog to clean it up."

The storm door opened with a bang. The wind propelled Momma into the living room like a countrified Mary Poppins.

She halted at Selah's mess and shook her head. "Cain't leave you girls alone for five minutes."

"Sorry, Momma."

Momma trudged to the kitchen, returning to wipe up the mess and vacuum the entire living room.

"You're a regular cleaning fairy, Mrs. Morgan." Frankie chewed open-mouthed on a fried wonton as she watched the undertaking.

Momma flicked a kitchen towel at Frankie's behind before heaving herself into a rocker.

"You didn't miss much on the show," Selah said, but Momma had dropped off to sleep. "She must have narcolepsy. Nobody normal falls asleep that fast, especially when *Winds of Change* is on."

Frankie rooted around in the plastic bag until she found a stray wonton. "Saaaaay-lah, *c'est la vie.* Nobody takes our show seriously anymore."

"The online buzz says *Winds* will soon be cancelled just like *Another World* and *Santa Barbara.*" The demise of two of their beloved shows was like losing a family member.

Selah's childhood dreams came alive in daytime drama. Horseback riding on the beach, playing spy games, and escaping burning buildings alongside gorgeous men in exotic locales—they made her believe in love, romance, happiness, and other fairy tales.

Judging from the glaze over Frankie's eyes, she was dreaming about the same place. "How long have we been doing this? Twenty years of screaming at the TV, eating, and laughing while your mother sleeps."

"I'm awake," protested a voice from the direction of Momma's chair. The voice faded into a light snore.

Selah snickered. She swept her hair into a long ponytail and felt her shoulders relaxing as she lowered her hands.

Curly hair was the blessing or curse of nearly every woman in Shadybrook except Frankie, who splurged on that Japanese straightening business. Most of the women in town believed their curls were brought on by something in the water. Momma said it was God-given, a sort of manna to the Israelites. Selah thought it was *Twilight Zone*-creepy, likely the result of in-breeding on her father's side.

"They can't rescue the show from the bottom of the ratings if they center it on the recasts like Cane's newbie co-star," Frankie hypothesized.

"Does she own anything other than halter tops and boy shorts?" Frankie hopped up and did jumping jacks while Selah fast-forwarded through the commercials and a bit of a monologue from that co-star, Eva Forrester, who played Kelli. "When they have auditions for models like her, the sign must say, 'Body wanted, please leave brain at door.'"

Frankie was a fine one to talk about model-worthy bodies. She was as strikingly beautiful as any model or daytime ingénue, even when her long blonde hair and slender legs were streaked with grease from a stock car at her father's Shadybrook Speedway.

The ladies at church potlucks used to say, "You're such a pretty girl, Francine. Soon you'll have all the boys after you, just like your mother, God rest her soul."

Then, they turned to Selah and cackled. "Curly Sue. What a sweet and smart girl you are. You're going to be a scientist or teacher someday, bless your heart."

Selah turned her attention back to the TV screen to fend off a little earthquake of jealousy.

Chapter Three

"DO YOU EVER feel twelve years old?" Selah sunk into the recliner again and hugged her knees to her chest. "You do adult things like work and pay bills, but your life, your mind, your feelings are still frozen in time?"

"I race cars, which qualifies me as a lifetime woman-child." Frankie grabbed Selah's copy of *Soap!* and sat down. "Speaking of our eternal immaturity, whatever happened to The Book?"

"The Good Book?"

"Not *that* Book. The book you used to write in. Where we put the pictures of our latest daytime loves." Frankie leaned toward Selah. "The one I drew in, that we worked on after school while we were supposed to be doing homework."

Selah sighed. "The men had to be extremely fine to make it into our Hunk O' the Month Club scrapbook."

That was the fad back then: the Fruit of the Month Club, Beer of the Month Club, steak, dessert, books, you name it. "Our club was the coolest of them all. Remember, we called it 'wicked awesome.'"

"Each actor we fawned over had the 'it factor' or nos-tril-flaring charisma," Frankie said as she tapped her index finger on the photographs of male actors in the magazine. "If you put this one's eyes with this one's personality and that one's smile, you have the perfect guy."

Only Cane Ashton is the whole package.

"We put our hearts on the wire for the men of daytime who light our fire and ignite our desire," Frankie recited in a sing-song voice.

"Ugh. Did we really say that?"

"Every club has to have a motto. If only we had gotten the monthly shipments."

In those days, when the soaps were over, Selah once again became the worried, overweight teen who took the world on her shoulders. She squeezed into stretch stirrup pants, hid under a bulky sweater and leg warmers, and trudged off to school. None of the boys there remotely resembled the soaps' handsome heroes. How she dreamed that one of those men would ask her to get on the back of his motorcycle and blow out of this hick town with him.

"Hello?" Frankie waved her hand in front of Selah's face. "Where'd you go just now?"

"Nowhere, unfortunately."

She contemplated the sparse living room in her par-ents' small ranch-style house. The pictures and knick-knacks were gone. Momma had given up on decorating a long time ago. Instead, only the mirrors remained, plus the mismatched couch and recliners that sat against the har-vest-gold walls. It would've been perfect for a disco.

Not that she was complaining. She loved her parents, and living with them again helped pay down her student loans. "Why don't we console ourselves with fortune cookies?"

"Let me get mine myself." Frankie grabbed the bag from Selah's hands. "It's bad luck to hand someone her fortune."

"Oh, for cryin' out loud. Just pick one. They don't mean a thing."

"Some fortunes have deep meaning." Frankie twirled her finger in the air as if she were a mad scientist propounding a new theory. "Mine, for instance, says . . ."

She cleared her throat, then paused dramatically while she cracked open the cookie and unraveled the paper. "'Cookies go stale. Fortunes last forever.'"

At Selah's laughter, Frankie tossed the fortune into the empty take-out bag. "You're right. That one is cheesy. Maybe you'll get one that will forever change your life and bring you peace and happiness."

"I *am* happy. I don't need a crazy fortune cookie to tell me I'm happy." She stared down at the tiny paper from her cookie and crinkled her nose. "It's defective."

"Do what now? It can't be defective." The older Frankie got, the deeper her Southern accent grew. Did Selah's accent sound that bad?

"What's it say?" Frankie grabbed for the paper.

Selah held it out of her reach. "'Faith.' That's all. On the back, it has my lucky numbers and the Chinese word for 'Focus.'"

"Faith." Frankie's tongue lingered on the word. "Maybe it's a sign."

"Are you a Christian or a mystic? God wants us to read the Bible, not look for signs in fortune cookies." Selah felt a twinge in her neck. "Plus, it's from Chinese Willie's, not the Iron Chef. How supernatural could it be when it came from a restaurant owned by a Caucasian ex-Marine who opened a Chinese take-out business during his mid-life crisis?"

"Whoa, Nelly! Slow down that high horse." Frankie stood and struck her Wonder Woman pose, fists on hips. "Fortunes are from Confucianism or Buddhism or some other -ism. But don't you think God sends us subtle signs all the time? He could throw a billboard onto your lap if He needed to tell you something."

Frankie sure was high on Mountain Dew that night. "Maybe He'll drop two handsome, single men into our laps while He's at it."

Or not.

"He's going to have to be more specific than just 'Faith.'" Selah crunched up their bags of trash and tried to pummel the rusting metal waste can into submission when the lid didn't shut. "I have faith. I have a fine, faith-based relationship with God. On the other hand, this is nothing but a mass-produced, generic, defective fortune cookie with no hidden meaning."

"Oh, ye of little faith."

Selah smiled, but her friend's words curdled in the pit of her stomach. *I probably have GERD.* She would not return to the doctor to find out.

"Show's over. Isn't it past your bedtime?" She turned off the television and draped a blanket over Momma.

"I'm going. Even though it's freezing and I have to

walk three whole blocks to get home." Frankie picked up her still-dripping jacket. "Hey, let's see if your mom's really asleep."

Selah grabbed Frankie before she could shake her coat over Momma's unsuspecting little head. Well, little head with big, big hair.

"If you promise to behave yourself," Selah's voice quivered, "you can sleep over and wait out the storm. It'll be a slumber party, just like old times."

"I will never, ever behave myself, and that's why you need me, my friend." Frankie slapped her on the back. "But I do need to get up early to crunch those numbers at Daddy's racetrack. And you have to get up early and write that killer proposal for your computer-hacker, nerd-squad business, or whatever it is that you do for a living."

"Web development and design. I apply my master's in information technology to teach clients how to use social media to their advantage. I'm a jack-of-all-trades when it comes to the computer." Selah's pitch hadn't sounded this flat on paper.

"Right. Defender of the Information Superhighway. Whatever."

"And accounting is magical and rewarding?"

"I moonlight as an accountant only to support my real calling as a racecar driver." Frankie pointed down the hall to Selah's office and bedroom. "You, on the other hand, have no outlet outside this dungeon of dulldom."

"I'll have you know I moonlight as a rogue spy, capturing criminals and aliens bent on destroying Shadybrook." So not true. She'd gladly let the criminals and aliens destroy the place.

"You've been watching too many soap operas." Frankie unzipped a pocket inside her jacket. "I almost forgot. I brought Christmas pictures for you."

"You're behind the times. It's April." She took the damp pictures, then Frankie pulled up her hood and jogged off into the slushy snow.

Selah glanced down at them and blew out a breath. *Great. Just what I need. Pictures of myself.* In twenty years, had she really changed for the better?

***

"How is it that we've been doing these cast photos for twenty years, dude, and every year, we get more attractive?" Shayne Nixon said, grabbing Cane's neck from behind.

"Hey!" Cane flinched as pain burned a trail down his neck and arm.

Shayne looked him up and down. "Correction, I get hotter and you look like you've had reverse Botox."

Cane cracked a smile. "Rotox?"

"Ha! Rotox. Rho No, you're really ugly!"

He smoothed the jacket of his classic tuxedo and assessed Shayne's black suit with white tie and black-and-white spats. "Fashion advice from the junior mobster?"

Shayne snorted and waved a monster cookie under Cane's nose. "These are fantastic. You should try some."

Cane shook his head. Shayne was a one-man three-ring circus.

Shayne crammed one cookie in his mouth and another in his front coat pocket. Standing side by side in the New York City studio, they watched as the crew rolled in a six-foot-long cake that read, "Happy Fiftieth Anniversary, Winds of Change."

"You and I have been through a lot together over the years." Shayne munched as he talked.

"Don't you mean you've put me through a lot over the years?"

"You have no respect for your elders."

As cameras flashed around them, Cane blinked and resisted the urge to squint and rub his eyes. Julia Whitmore, the show's executive producer, came over and hugged him with the force of a sumo wrestler. She punched Shayne on the shoulder before moving on.

"You look like you're fighting to stay awake, bro." Shayne wiped the crumbs from his hands and patted Cane's face.

Cane stepped back. "I'm just feeling under the weather. No big deal." He should call the doctor, but that would involve more medications, injections, and tests. It would mean setting foot in the hospital again.

"I can fix that. I've got a girl I can set you up with, a real vixen. Better yet, take one of these," Shayne pulled a pill bottle from his inside jacket pocket. "Up, down, any way you want to feel."

Cane grabbed Shayne's arm. "Are you crazy? Hide that before someone sees."

Shayne yanked his arm away and returned the bottle to his pocket. "I have valid prescriptions for all ten medications."

"You need help again. You're an addict."

"You need to get a life. All work and no women or booze make Jack a dull boy." Shayne ruffled Cane's hair and trotted off to shake hands with the network executives who had stopped in for the celebration.

He had no idea how much Cane wanted to get a life, one that didn't include Shayne and other reminders of his past. Cane dragged his palm down his face and then rubbed the back of his neck.

But there it was—his past— sitting in front of him in black and white or, in his case, chocolate cake and white buttercream frosting. He was transported to the lowest day in his career, the day he had done a face plant into a two-foot long cake that read, "We'll Miss You, Cane." Yeah, that was a special memory. That and the three-hour plane ride home with mortified parents rescuing their teenager from the evil clutches of *The Winds of Change* and New York City.

He was clean now, but he would always be that guy— the child star who gave in to temptation and torpedoed his career. In twenty years, had he really changed for the better?

Chapter Four

MAYBE I HAVE ADD, or is it ADHD? It couldn't be the adult kind since Frankie had deemed the two of them eternally immature.

That was the only logical explanation for Selah not having written a single word of her proposal before ten o'clock in the morning. She had let the rough draft catch dust on her desk for weeks. Never mind that winning the contract was crucial to jumpstarting her consulting business and moving it out of the converted walk-in closet in her parents' house.

She tapped a pen against her forehead, but the page was still blank, like her tragically uninspired brain. She pointed at the computer. "You are a filthy beast!"

That must work only when *All My Children*'s Erica Kane said it.

Selah reached for Frankie's pictures to take a quick look, but she immediately tossed them back into her desk drawer. Focus. She needed to focus. But how could she when that yellow wallpaper was peeling, the mimosa tree in the front yard had lost a huge branch in last night's ice storm, and the Wallingfords, her eighty-something neighbors, were sitting on their front porch in rocking chairs and matching camo snuggies?

Selah bit into a cheese Danish and chased it with orange juice and Mountain Dew. At eleven o'clock, she reached for her Bible and recited aloud Exodus 4:12 and Deuteronomy 5:22. "'I will help you speak and will teach you what to say.' 'He wrote them on two stone tablets and gave them to me.'"

She slammed shut the Bible. "Look, Lord. You authored the Ten Commandments, wrote on Nebuchadnezzar's wall and in the sand, and inspired the entire Bible through forty authors. How about a crumb for me? I'm spinning my wheels here."

After another ten minutes of drumming her fingers and sighing and waiting for divine inspiration, Selah sent an accusing look heavenward and slammed her laptop shut without saving the epic.

Outside her rain-streaked window, a gauzy fog draped the Blue Ridge Mountains under a gray-smothered sky. Yep, it was definitely the right weather for a pity party. Writer's block and fickle clients could wait.

Selah rescued Frankie's photos from her junk drawer. Even if she was able to escape her mother's mirrors, she couldn't avoid her reflection in this awful picture of her and Frankie setting up an aluminum Christmas tree beside the Wurlitzer at Good Company.

A customer once said that, with her soft, dark curls and olive complexion, Selah favored Catherine Zeta-Jones. Sure she did, when Catherine was pregnant.

Selah surveyed the damage like a magazine editor

deciding how to retouch a model who'd eaten an M&M before her photo shoot: Double-chin: Reduce. Cute dimples and cheerful smile, but cheeks are too full: Reduce. Pink sweater, which Selah thought looked slimming at the time, is pulled too tightly across the "bat wings" under the upper arms: Reduce. Size 18W (W for Wide) jeans cutting off circulation at stomach despite their stretch fabric: Reduce, reduce, reduce! Oh, just go ahead and crop out everything but Frankie and the Christmas tree.

Selah rubbed her arms. If only she could be free of the skin she was in. With a sigh, she stuck the photograph into what Frankie had deemed The Book. The Book, since its inception twenty years ago, was now two albums, brimming with their Hunk O' the Month Club photos, photos from college, Selah's journal entries, and old fortune cookie messages. She hadn't added a hunk to the mix in years. The last one was Cane Ashton.

Selah squeezed in a new journal entry:

It saddens me to look at The Book and see the sweet, hopeful face of my former self—the little girl who believed in unicorns. This girl thought she could be successful and that a man like Cane Ashton, or any man for that matter, could fall for her. I thought by the time I was thirty-something, I would have it all figured out, I would be self-assured and confident, whatever my circumstances, whatever my weight.

Sometimes I feel as if there's a black hole where my heart should be. Food doesn't fill it. Shopping doesn't do it. I'm a Christian. I shouldn't feel this way. I should be grateful for my many blessings.

God promises to satisfy the longing soul and fill the hungry soul with goodness. I have faith in that—I think—but the years go by and things don't change. I feel like a big, fat failure.

Well, she could always write soap opera angst if all else failed. She started to add last night's fortune to The Book but instead jammed it into her jeans pocket. She would throw it away later.

She picked up her Bible to put it away. The Bible, ironically a *Women of Faith* version, was heavy in her hands as she tried to remember the last time she'd felt comforted by the words inside. What she did remember were all the unanswered prayers: "Lord, please help me grow my business." "Lord, help me with my weight." "Lord, help me with my parents." Maybe she needed to be more specific.

Selah flipped to Matthew 17:20. "If you have faith as small as a mustard seed, you can say to this mountain, 'Move from here to there' and it will move. Nothing will be impossible for you."

Heat surged through her. "Move this!" She hurled the Bible across the office. Clearly, she should have pitched for the Nationals, because the Bible shattered a wall-mounted mirror and landed unscathed amidst the broken pieces.

Selah's hands flew to her mouth. She peeped heavenward. No lightning bolts. No peals of thunder. That was a good sign.

Two birds with one stone, I guess. She hated that mirror and she didn't feel much love for that particular Book at the moment either.

Her laptop beeped from behind her, and she startled.

An e-mail from FrankieNewman@shadybrookspeedway.biz displayed a red urgent flag and the subject line, "Exciting News for Your Boring Life."

"Tell me again, Frankie. Why are we friends?"

Before Selah could open Frankie's e-mail, Momma appeared in the doorway of the office. "What was that noise? Wow, you look terrible!"

"Gee, thanks."

"What's gotten you in such a bad mood?"

"I'm not in a bad mood." Selah slapped her hand down on the metal desk, and it quivered.

"What happened yonder?" Momma raised an eyebrow and nodded toward the pile of glass and Bible.

"We had an earthquake—5.7 on the Richter scale. It was horrifying. Didn't you feel it?"

"Mmm-hmm. Don't tempt God, Selah Marie. Virginia has fault lines." Momma patted her enormous brown bee-hive, which would not have moved out of place if they had actually experienced an earthquake or cyclone.

"I reckon that Bible and my mirror musta knocked you clean on the noggin before they hit the floor." Momma procured a broom and dustpan and removed the debris.

"I was going to pick that up eventually." Selah tried to change the subject. "Do you need any help at the diner?"

Momma, the co-owner and cook at Good Company, proudly wore an electric-blue poodle skirt emblazoned with a vinyl record and a matching shirt with "Margo" embroidered above the pocket. She even had the face of a sixty-year-old Mrs. Cunningham from *Happy Days*.

"No. Why? Are you trying to get out of your own work again?" Momma straightened and frowned. "It's not your responsibility to save Good Company. You save your own business. If your lazy father were any good, he'd help me this afternoon, instead of slithering around the track, checking out the new keno girls."

Selah's stomach sank. As much as she hated to hear it, Momma was probably right. "I'm sure he's just helping Mr. Newman install the new keno betting and slots equipment."

"Sprucing up the devil's workshop." Momma pursed her lips. "I've half a notion to call the lotto board and report the track."

Selah popped an antacid. "Frankie's dad claims he's exempt from the illegal gambling law because the track straddles the Virginia and West Virginia state lines. Regardless, a call like that would just hurt Frankie."

"I suppose so. Even if they shut down the track, your daddy would find a game, be it darts or three shells and a pea."

"Anyway, speaking of dirty dogs, you'll be interested in this." Momma threw a folded newspaper onto Selah's desk. "Now, there's a sign if I ever seen one."

"A sign?" Selah straightened the paper, searching the headlines.

"I near 'bout fell over when I saw it. It's the billboard sign you and Frankie were talking about last night."

Selah's brain fog lifted a little. "So, you *were* awake during the show!"

"Of course I was awake. Each week, I tell you that I see every minute of that harebrained show." Momma shook her coif indignantly before slipping out the door, carrying the garbage bag full of broken glass. "All y'all come by the diner and see me later, sugar."

"Y'all? Frankie is allegedly working, Momma. It'll just be me."

But Momma was gone, leaving behind a cloud of Aqua Net hairspray and the latest "Adopt-an-Angel" newspaper listings. These were the pets in the shelter where Selah had volunteered her dog-walking services, well, mostly her cuddling, petting, and squeaky-toy-throwing services.

Momma had circled the picture of a dog whose tangled hair and beard were so straggly and eyes were so covered that it looked like a tiny Ewok from *Return of the Jedi*.

When she read the scraggly dog's description, she gasped and her heart did a little flip-flop. "No way."

Twenty minutes later, Selah was surrounded by twenty-five barking, drooling canines. She walked down each row of kennels in the shelter, searching for one in particular—a mangy little beast named Faith.

"That is one tough cookie." A shelter volunteer frowned as she opened the giant steel door of Faith's cage. "Her owners abandoned her in a storage shed when they moved out of their house. She's fortunate to be alive after all the neglect she's suffered."

The little creature didn't back away but shook on three legs as she peeked up from behind a mass of wiry brown fur.

Selah choked back tears. "What else can you tell me about her?"

"I don't think she likes being penned in. She's ready to run free."

"Join the club, pooch." Selah tapped the cold metal bars. "How soon can we break her out of here?"

Dogs have a lot to teach humans. For instance, Selah learned that Faith, her precious new "angel," not only disliked being penned in, but also did not appreciate any type of restraint. She strained against her hot-pink leash as Selah tried to fill out her paperwork and pay her adoption fee. Although Faith weighed only ten pounds, Selah felt as if she had wrestled an alligator.

Later, her wild little Ewok dragged her through Aunt Ruby's Pet Emporium, Bait-n-Tackle, and BBQ Pit to stock up on all things doggie. Ruby appreciated animals in any form—be they pets, bait, or dinner. Creepy.

Selah's cell phone rang. "Where you been?" Frankie shouted. "I've been texting you and calling all day."

"Sorry. We've, uh, been busy."

"You're never going to believe this, but I won! I won the *Winds of Change* contest."

"What contest? No, Faith! Don't eat those treats off the bottom shelf." Faith had stolen a peanut-butter bone while simultaneously preparing to wee-wee on a bag of kibble. Selah jerked her leash in order to avert disaster. The shelter had assured her that the dog was house-broken, but all bets were off in a pet store.

Frankie was still yelling in a high-pitched voice. "I won a trip to the *Winds of Change* fan club event—airfare, hotel, and tickets to the luncheon. Just like we've been dreaming about for years!"

She stopped mid-stride and Faith slammed into the back of her leg. "That's . . . wow . . . that's amazing, incredible." She clasped her free hand to her chest, and her heart pounded against her fingertips. "Who are you taking with you?"

Frankie stopped to grab a breath. "You, of course, you big dummy."

"Me?" Selah dropped Faith's leash and thrust her fist into the air. "Yes! I'm going to New York City. Woo-hoo!"

A nearby parrot squawked and beat its brilliant green wings. The chain reaction sent Faith skidding across the floor, headlong into a playpen of kittens. A naked sphinx kitten sank its claws into Faith's furry beard, knocking the dog off balance and onto her back. Feathers went flying from the parrot, who hollered, "Let's get ready to rumble!"

"What the world is that screeching? Where are you? What is going on over there, Selah?"

She slipped on the drool-soaked bone Faith had dropped on the floor. On the way down, her phone went flying, and Selah took out an open vat of pay-by-the-pound cat litter.

Aunt Ruby scrambled to gather the kittens into their enclosure. Like her demented parrot, Ruby muttered Selah's name over and over again.

When Selah was finally able to reach her cell phone, she moaned into it. "I can't go to New York. I lost my mind temporarily. My life is a disaster. My dog. My work. My parents. I'll call you later."

"You can't go? You have a dog?" Frankie was still pleading when Selah ended the call.

Selah handed her credit card to Aunt Ruby. As Selah knelt and pried the velvety sphinx kitten from a nearly catatonic Faith, she fought the urge to curl up with the dog on the floor, two whimpering, trembling balls of hair.

Chapter Five

"The catalogue of miseries seems to cry out for commercial spots and a station break:

the stuff of noonday soap opera."
Author Stefan Kanfer

*I*T TOOK A two-hour nap and two aspirin before Faith and Selah recovered from their pet shop *cat*-astrophe. However, Selah feared neither of them would ever fully recover. She was still picking cat litter and feathers out of her curls and Faith's fur.

"Hold still, pooch." Her little terror sneezed and shook as Selah sprayed doggie deodorizer on her coat.

"Let's go meet your new grandparents and see how long it takes Momma to say, 'I told you so.'"

At three o'clock in the afternoon, Good Company was nearly empty. Momma had turned up the volume on the jukebox and was mopping the floor to the tune of "A Little Bit of Soap."

Selah flashed back to the time she tried to moonwalk on a wet floor in the diner and fell into a bucket of sudsy water. Momma had laughed so hard, she'd cried as she rubbed a towel over Selah's matted hair.

They hadn't laughed together like that in a long time. Selah tried not to notice how tired Momma's face looked and how she rubbed the knee that was overdue for a replacement. "Why are you mopping when you pay other people to do it?"

"Now, sugar, you know those boys ain't gonna do it right. And your father," she said as she tossed a look over her shoulder, "is otherwise engaged."

Russ Morgan, the host at Good Company, sat in a booth, smiling across the table at a much-younger woman. Good grief, was she even twenty-one? It was a familiar scene, but it never ceased to stir her mother to jealousy and anger. Selah herself felt some dark emotions simmering in the pit of her stomach.

"This calls for a chocolate shake." To Momma, any occasion called for ice cream or chocolate and preferably in combination. The apple, or in their case, apple pie à la mode, did not fall far from the tree.

Momma threw down the mop and grabbed three glasses from behind the counter. Naturally, she was fixing him a shake, too, after all his strenuous labor.

Selah set Faith's carrier on the barstool beside her.

"Oh, my goodness. Look at that dog!" Momma exclaimed as Faith's curly brown tail thumped against the inside of the carrier.

Suddenly, she gasped. "Selah!"

"What's wrong?"

"Where's her other leg?"

Selah slapped her forehead. "That's what that dog was missing! I'll have to call the pound and see if they've still got it."

"Poor wittle baby with only three legs and a mean, mocking momma." Momma abandoned the ice cream and carried Faith into the kitchen.

"I'll just be here keeping an eye out for the health inspector." Thank goodness he was a friend of the family and lived more than two hours up the road.

When they returned, Faith had something brown dripping from her furry beard. The condiment looked suspiciously like the secret sauce in Momma's famous meatloaf.

"You're not supposed to feed Faith table scraps. She'll get fat and her teeth will rot out."

Momma looked stricken. "I beg your pardon. I do not serve scraps in this fine establishment. Is your mommy starving you, my wittle mangy baby? Don't worry, your Gwama will feed you some real food."

She got a chinful of kisses from Faith and returned the dog to the carrier.

"So, Selah, I heard you and Faith caused quite a stir this morning at the Bait-n-Tackle. Only you would adopt a three-legged dog that could cause so much trouble."

Selah rested her weary head on the counter. "You heard already?" Word traveled fast in Shadybrook, especially when Momma or her sister, Ruby, were involved.

"An old broom knows where the dirt is." Momma smiled smugly and poured a ton of chocolate syrup in

Selah's glass, just the way she liked it. "I knew you'd go get this dog when I showed it to you. You're so predictable."

I think I'm insulted. "I am not predictable. In fact, I'm going with Frankie to New York City."

With a bang, Momma slammed her milkshake on the chrome countertop. Her father looked up from his conversation. "No, ma'am, you are not. I will not have you traipsing off to New York City by yourself."

"I just told you I'm going with Frankie."

"You might as well be on your own for all the common sense that girl has."

"Mother!" Selah's blood pressure was rising rapidly.

"Don't *Mother* me, Selah. I practically raised that girl when her momma, bless her soul, passed away. I know how Frankie is." She shrugged as if it should have been obvious. "Besides, you girls will be talking and laughing up there in the big city and you'll forget your heads. Something awful could happen. You could be kidnapped. I'll have to put your pictures on a milk carton."

"I think thirty-something is a little old for a milk carton."

"You're still my baby, and I worry." She cupped Selah's chin in her hand. The guilt trips from her mother lasted longer than any trip she could take outside of Shadybrook.

Selah's father had torn himself away from his attractive customer and was waiting for Momma to hand him his shake. "She's right. It's not safe. Frankie is part of this family, but she doesn't make the wisest choices. She's spacey and unreliable, not practical or predictable like you."

Again, I am insulted. Selah didn't know who to defend first, Frankie or herself.

Before she could speak, she heard Frankie's voice. "Hello, Mr. and Mrs. Morgan. My ears were burning," she called out a little too brightly.

Selah's nervous laugh made her snort whipped cream up her nose.

When Momma started to set out another glass, Frankie waved it off. "No, thank you, Mrs. Morgan. I wouldn't want the sugar to make me any spacier than I already am."

Frankie paused for effect, smiling with all her teeth at Selah's parents. "I won't tarry long. I've come to take Selah to the dark side."

She looked pointedly at Selah and then at the door, but Selah sat frozen to the barstool, awaiting the wrath of Momma.

Russ spoke first, in the mildly condescending tone he usually reserved for unhappy customers, "Now, Francine, there's no need to be ugly."

Oh, boy. Frankie hated her given name.

"You hafta realize that a trip like this will be expensive. It'll take Selah away from her business. The diner's hit hard times as well, and we need her help here."

The words "hard times" bounced around in Selah's brain. When had her family not known hard times? She stared at her father, seeing him through the eyes of a second-grader, seeing the black eye he sported when he dragged in at two o'clock one Christmas morning. Selah just knew it was Santa Claus who had made all that racket—until she realized it was her father taking the gifts from under the tree.

Frankie brought her back to the present. "It's three

days, Russ." Her voice was no longer perky as she ticked off her arguments like the numbers on a spreadsheet.

Selah took a long hit of her chocolate shake.

"First of all, I won the trip. Second, her expenses are paid. Third, and most important, she needs some excitement, a change of pace in her life. Her clients will benefit from her new attitude."

"Can I say something here since we are talking about my life?" Selah's anxious whisper disappeared amidst their volleys of "listen, young lady" and "with all due respect."

Suddenly, she found it hard to breathe. Faith trembled in her carrier. She patted the dog's head and slipped outside with the carrier, grateful for the cool wind against her flushed face.

"I think we'll go home, Faith. Writer's block, broken mirrors, and fat pictures are looking pretty good right about now."

Chapter Six

*A*FTER THEIR QUICK escape from the diner, Selah set Faith free from her carrier and connected the leash. Gazing up at the darkening snow clouds, she prayed silently. The words sloshed and tumbled in her mind like Hershey's syrup and ice cream in Momma's blender.

Lord, I'm sorry about the Bible thing earlier, but I want to be honest with You. This life, this town, these parents You've given me here . . . I'm not handling them well. This person You've made me isn't someone I like very much. I'm overwhelmed, Lord. Potentially suffocating. Is this what a panic attack feels like? Help me. Show me.

"Wait, Selah!" Frankie called as she ran to catch up. She stepped in front of Faith, forcing them to stop. Her hair splayed around her face like a blonde Medusa. Selah's, no doubt, looked like the Bride of Frankenstein.

"Why did you leave when the fun was just getting started?"

"It's not fun when it's at my expense."

"Don't be a downer." Frankie scrunched her mouth into a pout. "And don't tell me you're not going to New York. We're going to have a blast! Just listen to this."

She pulled out a brochure and read, "'Catch the passion and excitement of *The Winds of Change* whirlwind tour of New York City. Fill your days and nights with individual fan club meetings and with dinner and autograph signings featuring the entire cast.'"

Selah's pulse quickened at the thought of hugging Cane or Shayne or chit-chatting with Dorian. She would breathe the same air as the stars she'd watched all her life. "I want to go, but . . ."

She pressed her free hand against her muffin-top to quell the spasms that had started in her stomach. How could she meet people like that when she looked the way she did?

"You cannot say no," Frankie pleaded. "Cane Ashton and Shayne Nixon will be there. Don't deprive yourself of this."

"Maybe after I lose a little weight. I can't leave Momma behind, chained to a grill and having to save every dime for household and diner bills."

Faith began to growl. Selah looked up to see what upset her and collided with Deputy Sheriff Cody Buchanan. She jumped back.

"Ladies." He grinned a brown smile and spit a wad of snuff directly into their path.

Selah's face flamed, remembering the torment he and his now-nurse sister, Katie, had inflicted on her. She couldn't look at the terrible two without being reminded of the weigh-ins before PE class, the guy friends who asked

Selah to pass notes to her skinny girlfriends, and the polyester band pants that fit like a tutu on a hippo.

This is why people home-school their kids.

"What the heck happened to your dog?" He pointed to Faith's missing leg.

Frankie made a sweeping gesture toward Cody's lower half. "Same thing that happened to your—"

"Frankie!" Selah grabbed her arm.

"Brain! I was going to say brain."

Cody guffawed. Frankie pushed him out of their way and they marched on in silence. They turned the corner from Main Street to Somerset Lane and headed up the stairs to Selah's ranch-style house. Well, her parents' house, where she had a bedroom and a closet-office.

"I hate that guy." Frankie whirled around with fire in her eyes. The wood on the porch creaked under their feet. "That is exactly what we have to look forward to if we stay around here. See any Shaynes or Canes on your parents' front porch?"

Tears pricked the corners of Selah's eyes but did not fall as Frankie continued her rant. "You can't find a man while you're working sixty hours a week out of your parents' home, going to a women-only gym, and living in Redneckville."

"Maybe I don't want a man. Maybe I just enjoy looking at the perfect, gorgeous ones on TV."

"Well, what *do* you want then?"

To be skinny and hot like you. To tell people how I really feel. To take chances. To stop living my life for other people. To let go and breathe.

"If you are trying to psychoanalyze me, we might be

here awhile." Selah stared at her snow boots and sagged against the wooden railing. "I don't know what I want or what God wants for me."

"Well, let's find out, then." Frankie took her by the shoulders and looked her square in the eyes. "You need this trip, whether you admit it or not. I need it, too. I'm bored out of my freakin' mind here. Everybody knows our business. Your parents drive you crazy. They drive me crazy. You've got writer's block, and you're worried and depressed all the time. You just ain't right."

Selah swallowed down her tears. "I want to go, really I do. Hypothetically, it sounds wonderful."

She looked down at Faith so she didn't have to see the disappointment on Frankie's face. Faith scratched at her jeans, begging to go inside where it was warm and comfortable.

"Please. Think passion, think excitement."

"In reality, that life is just a dream, a fantasy, and . . . and I don't have the money to go or the right clothes to wear. Mine are all so tight, I'd need a corset to suck in my gut."

Frankie's face hardened as she released Selah from her grip. "You know who you sound like?"

Selah shook her head.

"Your mother."

Selah shoved her frozen hands into the pockets of her jeans. Her fingers traced the defective fortune she had intended to trash.

"Okay, then. Your mind's made up. I'll call you when I get back." Frankie turned and started down the stairs.

Selah scooped up Faith and hugged the dog's quivering

body against her chest. They stood at the edge of the porch steps, watching Frankie walk at a geriatric pace down the short driveway, her head hanging.

Selah felt someone's eyes on her and realized that her neighbors had listened in on the entire discussion. "Hello, Mr. and Mrs. Wallingford."

The couple had been sitting in those rockers day in and day out for as long she could remember.

Selah had a flash of her future in Shadybrook: she and Frankie, at eighty, sitting in rocking chairs on her parents' front porch, staring at the same view, wondering what could have been, if only—

Panic rose in her throat and screamed, "Run!"

"Get ready to spend time with your grands, little buddy, because Mommy's going to the big city to find herself!"

Faith turned her adoring brown eyes toward Selah's face and let out a burp worthy of a Rottweiler.

Selah laughed and kissed the dog's scruffy head. "I'll miss you too."

"Wait!" she hollered at Frankie, who still had not made it to the mailbox. Her friend turned expectantly. "I changed my mind. I'm ready to follow my fortune cookie!"

Chapter Seven

"We're all fighting a tough fight to stay in the business."

Chris Goutman, executive producer of canceled soap, *As the World Turns*, quoted in the *Richmond Times-Dispatch*, July 4, 2010, "Final Spin for As the World Turns"

CANE ROLLED ONTO his back, savoring the last few minutes of slothfulness before his snooze alarm sounded. When he stretched, his hand brushed the cold, vacant spot beside him on the bed.

As the chill seeped into his skin, so did the feeling he got before he reached for a bottle of pills, when he was frantic for a quick exit out of his body and life.

He pounded his fist against the bed, willing away the craving. He hadn't given in for the past fourteen years. He'd catch a meeting on his way to work, but he wasn't counting on any help from the Higher Power that Narcotics Anonymous espoused.

"I could use a little help down here," he growled at God as he pushed himself up. "Yeah, whatever."

He had to get up early for the fan club luncheon. His limbs felt like lead, but he couldn't disappoint his fans, the ones who scrapbooked his screwed-up career, sent money to charity on his birthday, and named their pets after his character, Dean.

First things first. Why did he have polish on his fingernails and toes? He scratched his head. Had he sent Tiffany, no, Cecile, home? What in the world happened last night? Cane threw his glittering toes over the side of the bed. Pink was his color, though. Who knew?

Despite his pre-coffee brain fog, he remembered sitting on the couch with her in his apartment. Just sitting and talking. She was pretty enough. She seemed normal at the time, gossiping about her sorority sisters and the celebrities she encountered at the swanky New York City spa where she worked as a receptionist.

But when she used "OMG" and "LOL" in the same sentence, he decided to tell her that this date would be their last. Just as soon as he could get a word in edgewise. Her monotone must have lulled him to sleep. And Mom always said he could sleep through a hurricane.

As Cane studied his face in the bathroom mirror, he could hear his co-star, Shayne Nixon, proclaiming Cecile a vixen and encouraging Cane to take her out. Cane was lucky the vixen hadn't knifed him in his sleep. Shayne was in on this somehow.

Instead, she had used her lipstick to draw a handlebar

mustache under his nose. The 'stache wasn't so bad though. It gave him a Wyatt Earp look. Maybe the show would let him grow one for his cop character.

Why had she written the word "God" on his forehead? He'd encountered stalkers before, but this was over the top. Oh, right. The mirror image was backward. She'd intended to call him "Dog," a fair assessment of his former exploits.

He found the living room as defiled as his face. She had kicked over his coffee table and pushed the books from his bookshelf onto the floor. He bent and retrieved Dad's Bible. Holding it to his face, he sniffed and a cobweb went up his nose. What had made him think it would still smell like Old Spice?

He clutched the Book to his chest. How many nights had he peeked in Dad's room to say goodnight and seen him crying over it, praying for God to change Cane's heart and keep him safe? Turned out, Dad should have prayed for himself instead.

🎬

Selah's heart pounded as she looked around the hotel ballroom where 500 other soap fans were gathered to meet 20 actors from *The Winds of Change*. *Lord, stay with me today. I'm a big chicken.*

"Are you still worrying?" Frankie asked.

"We finally made it to New York City. How could I worry?" Just because she had spent the last week listening to Momma's dire warnings of "I have a bad feeling about this trip"? Why should that make her anxious?

"Are you breathing? Then you're worrying. Cut it out. We are fine. We are single—"

"And ready to mingle." Selah giggled.

Selah had traded her sweatpants for a sophisticated navy pantsuit with a lavender-blue scarf that matched her eyes. Frankie had traded her blue jeans and NASCAR jacket for black skinny jeans, a black tee, and a cropped black leather motorcycle jacket.

Thoughts of Momma and Shadybrook vanished as they ate brunch, lost at the charity raffles for soap props and scripts, and made new friends with fans who had flown in from California and Texas. Every few minutes they looked at each other with grins like loopy grown-up teenagers. There were no words.

Once the soap stars were introduced and seated at their signing tables, it was every girl for herself. "They'll never know what hit 'em," Frankie said as they fist-bumped.

By the time Selah secured her place in the middle of Cane's line, Frankie had maneuvered her way to the front of Shayne's. Shayne laughed at something Frankie said and slid his hand a little too low at her waist. Selah shook her head and the muscles in the side of her neck constricted. Frankie could turn a man's head, even when she wasn't trying.

Cane wasn't so handsy with his fans. The onscreen couple, Cane Ashton and Eva Forrester, sat in front of a large black-and-white cast photo of themselves. Eva emptied a martini glass, then leaned her elbows on the table to play on her cellphone.

And Cane . . . how could he look even more attractive in person with his snug black t-shirt and day-old stubble? Selah felt herself smiling when he smiled.

She pointed her new digital camera at him and pushed the button to take a picture, but it didn't click. Blowing out a breath, she inspected the button and lens as if she knew what she was doing. She worked with computers, not small electronics, and trying to take a selfie on her phone without crossing her eyes would have been impossible.

When she looked up, it was her turn in line. Cane was calmly waiting and watching her. Her face flamed, a habit that was becoming increasingly annoying.

She tried the button again. Nothing. Her trembling hands gripped the camera as she pushed the button repeatedly and muttered, "This stupid thing . . . does . . . not . . . work . . . Rrr." She actually growled and stomped her foot in front of two incredibly gorgeous actors.

The fans behind her coughed and whispered. Would this misery never end?

She waved the camera and huffed. "I'm really sorry, I can't get it to work." A big duh. "Where's my Polaroid Instamatic when I need it?"

Cane, whose eyes had widened in either amusement or fear of attack by a wacko fan, said, "Why don't you let my able assistant handle the camera? Come on over here beside me."

He held out his hand and stood to a height that must have been over six feet. At five foot five, she snuggled in at his chest, engulfed in warmth and the scent of cedar and mint. A fleece blanket by the fireside wouldn't have felt that good.

"So, where are you from?" he asked.

"When you wrapped your muscular arms around me, I completely forgot." Her brain was as non-functional as her camera.

He chuckled and squeezed her hand. Then, in a heartbeat, they had smiled for the camera and Cane was thanking her for coming. The moment was over and she walked away, star-struck and humiliated.

She didn't stop to get an autograph from Eva. She thought she heard clapping from the fans behind her. Surely they were saying, "Good riddance, you wacky, camera-wielding kook. It's our turn now."

She looked around for Frankie but couldn't see her through the crowd of mostly middle-aged women and a smattering of men. Selah had forgotten to remind her to turn on her cell.

She slipped out of the ballroom in search of a water fountain so she could splash some ice-cold water on her burning face. *Yes, I am one hot mama.* Frankie would, no doubt, find the camera debacle hysterical.

The long, sterile hallways and beige doors of the hotel's conference center all looked the same. Perhaps she had taken a wrong turn into David Bowie's *Labyrinth* or Alice's Wonderland. When she passed a glass door leading to a garden terrace, she noticed two of the show's stars outside, taking a cigarette break.

Selah stopped to gawk at the actors in their more natural environment. They saw her and waved. She heard footsteps and something slammed into her back. Flashing back to the pet store, she landed on her hands and knees with a thud and an "Oof!"

The perpetrator was attractive, but the furrow between his eyebrows begged for Botox. He snorted and *tsked* as he rooted through the tangled mess of his papers and Selah's fan club materials.

She tried to catch her breath as she waited for his apology. Without a word or an offer to help her up, he jumped to his feet and disappeared down a hallway. The actors out on the terrace jogged to her side and helped her up. They left after she assured them that she was okay.

Her outrage at the "Botox Brute" grew with the red splotches on her hands and the bruises on her knees. She decided to track him down because he owed her a big apology, not to mention he had grabbed her autographed picture of Cane. She heard angry voices coming from the direction of the Brute's escape.

"Curiouser and curiouser." She followed the sound.

Within moments, Selah turned a corner and came face to face with the man who'd run her down. Her assailant appeared to be throwing a tantrum in front of the soap's executive producer.

"Listen, sister. We're all busting our humps here to keep this show afloat. If you don't like it, why don't you see if you can find anybody who will do a better job? Hire a new head writer. Hire a new casting director." He flailed his arms in Selah's direction. "Better yet, why don't you hire her—Calamity Jane?"

"Sorry for the interruption. I wasn't eavesdropping. This guy, the loud one, knocked me down and took my photographs. I was hoping to get them back."

He crossed his arms over his chest, but Selah stood her ground.

The Julia Whitmore started toward her. "I apologize that you had to witness Mason's appalling display of incivility." With piercing dark eyes and a brunette mane like a lioness, she was a commanding presence. When she narrowed her eyes at Selah's assailant, he suddenly looked a lot less cocky.

"I'm Julia, executive producer for *The Winds of Change*." She grasped Selah's hand like they were old friends. "Normally, Mason acts in keeping with a seasoned professional but, as head writer, he is under a lot of pressure to boost ratings."

Julia's designer suit hung loosely on her tall and lanky frame, and her ragged fingernails evidenced that she too was under pressure to make the soap a success. "Are you a fan of the show?"

Am I a fan? Hah! "Of course. That's why I'm here."

Julia's smile seemed genuine, an instant connection. "Since Mason suggested that I fire him and hire you, perhaps I should get to know you a little better, Ms.—"

"Morgan. Selah Morgan."

"What do you think of my show, Ms. Morgan?"

Mason blanched. Suddenly under the microscope herself, she knew exactly how he felt. The air seemed to have been sucked out of the narrow hallway. She stood mute, looking from Julia to Mason. She had never recovered from the grad school professor who'd asked her to stand in front of the class and explain the evolution of the microprocessor.

"Please be brutally honest. You can't hurt our feelings," Julia said.

Need confidence. Now, Lord. "Well, first of all, as a whole, I love the characters on this show." Selah inhaled deeply. "But can y'all please go a month without someone trying to get pregnant, getting pregnant and wondering who the father is, miscarrying a baby, or stealing a baby?"

"Easier said than done." Julia shrugged.

"As much as I enjoy the hot men of daytime, I'd like to see a few normal-looking people. People who look like me.

Can we have some full-figured women who have smoldering affairs with the hot guys? How about some Latinas? Or those who have mixed skin colors? People with disabilities?"

Selah was on a roll now. "Between all the face lifts and the stick figures, I don't recognize any real people."

When Mason frowned and sighed, Selah faltered.

"Pretend he doesn't exist. I do it all the time." Julia turned her back to him. "Your suggestions are valid. What do you think about the relationships on the show?"

"I miss the true romance . . . on location . . . on a beautiful island. Whatever happened to the supercouples? Epic romances with couples who waited more than a week to sleep together." Selah gained momentum, amazed that they still listened. "Not cheesy flings, but a break from the rapes and murders that surround us in real life."

"You make some interesting points. There's a conference room over here where we can sit and I can take notes." Julia ushered them into the vacant room. Sitting at the head of a small table, she patted the plastic chair beside her. Selah took it. Mason leaned against the wall. All his scowling had to be giving him a headache.

"We were discussing supercouples, the romances that survive in spite of all obstacles." Julia's cell phone vibrated in her jacket pocket. She slipped it out, glanced at it, and returned it to her pocket. "Tight budgets and the rapid pacing of our storylines today make it harder to film on location or sustain couples in the long-term. But supercouples are still alive, in part, as couples fall in love, face a conflict or another love interest that tears them apart, and make their way back to each other, often years later."

"What you're saying is that Luke and Laura getting a divorce on *General Hospital* was a sign of the times?"

"Exactly, but there's always a tease that they'll reunite somehow." She poured herself and Selah a glass of water from the pitchers on the table. "Now that we've had a lesson in Soap 101, what were you saying about soaps and violence?"

"Maybe daytime shouldn't try so hard to imitate the language and grittiness of the primetime shows. I'm not preaching a sermon to y'all, but give viewers an escape into something hopeful, positive. I miss the days when the soaps were magical."

Mason checked his watch and gazed at the exit. The corner of Julia's mouth turned up. "And?"

"And why don't you come out from behind the camera and act again? You're still glamorous and beautiful, and you were great on *Generations*. I miss the veteran actors."

Julia steepled her fingers together like Donald Trump in a boardroom. "Your kissing-up abilities will take you far in this business. You certainly have a lot of grand ideas about me and my show."

"I wasn't buttering you up." Selah's spirits fell and she braced herself for rejection. The glint returned to Mason's eyes.

"This is your lucky day, because I'm in the market for fresh ideas." Julia smiled with her eyes. "I want more of your enthusiasm."

"Great!" she said, a bit too much like Tony the Tiger.

"I hate to interrupt this love fest, but the fans do not write this show, Julia." Mason leaned down and banged his fist on the table. "The writers write this show."

Julia ignored Mason's plea and sized her up. "You

look to be in the age of our key demographic: eighteen to thirty-four."

"I am." Although not for long, unfortunately.

"I need to think through this and work out all the details, but I'd like you to return to New York." Julia tapped her chin with a pen as she talked. "This venture will be along the lines of a one-person focus group, but with more publicity and interaction between you, as the show's liaison, and the viewers."

"That sounds wonderful." To put it mildly. This was the best day of Selah's life.

"The other fans will live vicariously through you, see their favorite show through your eyes." Julia stood and paced, peering at Selah, her new pet project. "You'll be the SuperFan. Or, maybe we'll call you the SoaperFan. That might be more memorable."

"Or more meretricious." Mason rubbed his temple with his fist.

The look Julia shot him would have withered a fake flower. "This could work for us."

Selah nodded so vigorously she feared whiplash.

Julia turned to Mason. "And *you* will make this happen. See that Selah gets everything she needs to be our SoaperFan."

He looked like a six-year-old, sitting in the corner, his friends watching.

Selah smiled sweetly. *That's right, mister. You can knock me down, but you can't keep me down. Watch out! I may break into a chorus of "I Will Survive."*

Chapter Eight

SELAH AND FRANKIE squealed and jumped up and down like teenagers at a boy-band concert. The weight of Selah's suck-in undergarments forced her to stop and catch her breath. They made her look ten pounds lighter but crushed her internal organs. She might require garden shears to remove the spandex.

Cane chose that moment to walk through the hall-way where she and Frankie celebrated her surreal encounter with his show's executive producer and head writer. He stopped to stare and was rear-ended by four ladies in his entourage. Selah had heard he was a player. She wasn't inclined to believe everything she read, but Momma would have reminded her, "Where there's smoke, there's fire."

Frankie's back was turned to Cane, but Selah saw him in high definition.

He caught her eye and flashed a wicked grin and a three-fingered wave before moving on. He must have recognized her as the crazy-blushing-growling-stalker-fan from his autograph line. How would she ever look him in the eye when she began her SoaperFan gig at the show's New York studio?

Frankie stopped jumping. "Wow, you're red all of a sudden. Do you have high blood pressure?"

No, just another heart-pounding encounter with her favorite soap star.

"You cannot have a cardiac arrest before you start working for *Winds of Change*."

"I think maybe I've had some sort of episode already, or else I'm hallucinating." Selah shook her head. "I still cannot believe the amazing, talented executive producer just offered me a job, even though it is temporary."

"This is outrageously awesome." Frankie suddenly frowned. "I do have my doubts, you know."

"What doubts?"

"You've lusted after these guys since you were nine years old. What will you do when you get close to one? You might spontaneously combust! Do you think I should call ahead and warn Cane and Shayne?"

When Selah dropped Frankie off at the Shadybrook Speedway, they hugged and laughed, enjoying the last dregs of their New York City adventure. However, the giddy hangover faded when Selah reached her house and found it dark and empty: no parents and no dog.

She went to hang her scarf and coat on the rack by the front door, but the rack was not there. MIA was the brass-plated poker for the fireplace, likely the latest victim of a bad bet on the winner of Dancing With the Stars or some boxing match. She peeked in her bedroom and office to verify that her belongings were safe. Thank goodness, her father had not yet learned to pick a lock.

Selah would never forget the time the burly man in a dark suit came to the house and carried out their TV set. She was twelve years old. He smelled of cigarettes and grape like the lollipop he gave her. The one in his mouth made him look like a bulldog chewing on a bone. When she covered her face with her hand to ward off the odor, he said, "Don't cry, kid," and ruffled her curly black hair. As usual, her father wasn't present for the fallout of his actions.

"I promise I'll get it back," he said when he came home the next morning. His eyes were always wild and bloodshot when his night hadn't gone so well. "I promise."

Selah closed her eyes and stuffed down the memory. Welcome home.

She changed clothes and returned e-mails from clients, then headed to the diner to tell Momma the good news about her new job. A different cook was frying hamburgers in her place behind the grill at Good Company. Dad stood at the counter, serving up a plate of onion rings and southern charm.

Russ Morgan was sixty-five with a growing sugar gut, courtesy of Momma's sweet iced tea and banana cream pie. His cornflower-blue eyes, which crinkled at the corners when he smiled, his full, white Mark Twain hair and mustache, and his arsenal of jokes about hillbillies and farm living made him popular with the customers.

His eyes lit when she set down her coat and hopped on a barstool. "Selah, I'm glad you're home."

He came around the corner of the lunch counter to give her a hug. "How was the trip?"

"Great. How was the track?" She sucked her lips against her teeth.

"Good. Good." He smiled and rubbed his hands on his Good Company apron. He must've turned off his hearing aids. "Fix yourself a Co-cola. I'm going to get back to work."

Funny, she hadn't seen him doing much work when she came in.

"Hold on." She hollered and waved her hands. "Where are Momma and Faith? They're not at the house."

"Aww, right," he bumbled like Columbo. "The dog's at Ruby's. Momma's laid up in the hospital."

"Why is she in the hospital?" The familiar knot returned to her stomach.

"She fell and had surgery on her arm."

As the news sank in, Selah imagined the worst. "I was gone for less than a week! You should've called."

"She's okay now. She didn't want me hovering. Somebody had to keep an eye on the diner." His mouth twitched and he looked away.

"Well, *somebody* oughta be keeping an eye on Momma." She threw him a hard look in an attempt to make him feel guilty and stomped out of the diner.

Jarred by the cold air, she realized she'd forgotten her coat. She was not going back in there and risk having to apologize for getting angry or hear his excuses for leaving his wife alone in a hospital miles away.

I hate dreary, cold weather. I hate getting sucked back into this black hole of a town. And I really hate hospitals.

A half hour later, Mom's sterile hospital room and the frown on her pale, sleeping face gave Selah more of a chill than the low temperatures outside. Her phone rang to the tune of the *Winds of Change* theme song. She whispered an apology to the attending nurse and ducked into the bathroom to take a call from an area code she didn't recognize.

"Selah Morgan?" asked a perky voice she mistook for a telemarketer. "I'm calling on behalf of Julia Whitmore, executive producer at *Winds of Change*. She wanted me to notify you that we sent out your package, including a confidentiality agreement and other paperwork that I need you to fax back before you come next Tuesday."

"So soon? But I thought—"

"Your itinerary will be full. Briefings with Julia, writers' meetings, blogging, online chats, an interview and photo shoot with *Soap!*, and a benefit concert with the cast members. That's just for starters."

"But, next Tuesday—"

"We'll see you then."

When the line went dead, Selah stared at the phone. How had her life turned upside down in such a short period of time?

"Selah? Why are you in the bathroom talking to yourself? Come out here and see your momma."

When Selah approached the bed, Momma reached out with her free arm, and Selah bent to kiss her on the cheek.

"It's about time you got back. I missed you."

"I missed you too." Selah pulled a hard plastic chair over to her bedside. She hadn't seen chairs like those since elementary school. "What happened? You were fine when I left."

"I told you those boys your father hired couldn't clean

that diner floor like I could. I fell on their soapy mess and tore up my bad arm."

"You have a bad arm? I thought it was your knee."

"Knee's wore out too. My arm's been a-hurtin' me for a while. Figured, at my age, it was just arthur-itis."

"Why didn't you tell me about your arm?" Selah inspected the purple and black splotches on Momma's face and the cloth sling cradling the bandaged shoulder. She took Momma's hand on the good arm and clutched it between her hands.

"I don't talk about all my troubles, sugar. I don't want to worry you."

Selah's eyes grew misty. If Momma only knew how much she worried.

After an hour or so, an orthopedic surgeon ducked in to explain that the tendons were already inflamed and that the fall had torn Margo's rotator cuff, requiring surgery. Because of her advanced age, she would likely need six to eight weeks of recovery time.

"Six to eight weeks." Repeating the news out loud, Selah thought she might be sick herself.

"I know it seems like a long time, but I'll be okay now that you're home. I can't drive, cook, and do physical therapy without you."

Selah nodded slowly. "Six to eight weeks." She was Alice in Wonderland as the room's blue curtain divider and white walls bore down on her and she grew too big for them.

"I hate to impose on you, but you can see that your father is worthless." Momma never attempted to mask her disappointment in Russ Morgan.

"I love you, Selah. I can always count on you, my baby," she said, weepy from the pain medication.

Selah rubbed her hand and smiled weakly.

The nurse slipped in to check Momma's vitals.

"May I stay with her?"

"I would say yes, but there's not enough space for a recliner in these short-stay rooms." She'll be fine to go first thing. The doctor wants to monitor her overnight because of her high blood pressure and that goose egg."

Selah cringed, imagining her mother's head hitting the black-and-white checkered tiles in the diner.

Momma opened her eyes again. "Before you go, how does my hair look?"

"It's perfect as usual."

When the nurse snickered, Selah said, "You're right, she's going to be fine."

Winds of Change was turning into *General Hospital*. All Cane ever played these days were hospital bedside or morgue scenes as his cop character, Dean, investigated the serial killings. The constant reminders of death made it harder to bury his own memories.

Sweat trickled down the back of his neck. A day player nurse moved toward Shayne with a blood pressure cuff. If a real medical professional had used the cuff on Cane, she might have pronounced him ready for a triple bypass.

The day player said, "You'll have to leave now, Detective. We're taking the patient to surgery."

He nodded, trying not to stare at her pink and blue scrubs. The nurse taking care of him and his brother in the hospital had worn pink and blue as well, as if they were in a children's ward. How could he recall such an inconsequential detail from that night when he struggled to remember what his mother's eyes looked like?

He had grasped at the nurse's sleeve, pleading for information about his parents until she gave him a sedative. "You'll have to calm down, Mr. Ashton, so we can take you to surgery."

When the scene was over, he jogged off set as fast as he could without drawing attention. In his dressing room, he peeled off his black leather jacket and changed into shorts and sneakers. His friend Justus was in town for a few days and wanted to meet him for a pickup game at the gym. During the cab ride over, Cane focused on memorizing tomorrow's script. He tried to block out the memories that had seeped into his mind and the fatigue that had seeped into his body.

"Why couldn't we meet at a restaurant like normal people?" Cane said ten minutes later as Justus shoulder-bumped him out of the way and nailed a jump shot. Cane caught the ball on the rebound. Taking a shot, he tripped and missed.

"The old gray mare's not what he used to be," Justus caught the ball and held it under his arm.

"Don't put me in the nursing home yet. I'm only thirty-five. The NFL let Brett Favre play until forty." Cane bent over, resting his hands on his knees.

"And look how well that turned out." Justus dribbled the ball and made another basket. "Put a shirt on already. You're making the rest of us look bad."

He retrieved the ball and heaved it at Cane's bare chest.

The impact felt like a missile exploding against Cane's body. He half-laughed, half-coughed.

"Seriously, you okay? You seem more out of it than usual."

"I can always count on you to make me feel better, buddy." Cane threw the ball and made a basket. "I'm fine."

He was better than fine. Nothing to worry about. He didn't need a doctor. He needed sleep after consecutive fourteen-hour days at the studio.

He made another basket. "How are the wife and bambino?"

"Awesome." Justus broke into a grin. He took his phone out of his gym bag and pulled up pictures of his infant son. "That's my boy. Smart and handsome."

What would it be like to have a normal family life?

"I'm proud of you, Justus."

Cane's dad had told him that over and over—after his football games, after he passed trig and chemistry, and after he was baptized. He could still hear his dad's gentle voice. *You survived that soap opera and have been blessed with a second chance.*

Justus put his phone away. "Melissa asked when you're coming to our house for dinner. We'd love for you to stay and go to church with us too."

Like that was going to happen. Cane shook his head and the room began to spin. As a football player, he knew what it was like to have his bell rung a few times. But the shock of his head connecting with the AstroTurf was never this intense. He clutched the basketball to his chest, waiting for the carousel to stop. When it did, he blew out a jagged breath.

"I'm done for the day, man." He tossed the ball to Justus and slapped him on the arm as he left the court. "Tell her I said hello and thanks for the invite, but I'm allergic to lovesick old married couples." And to God.

He shuffled to the locker room, sticking close to the wall for support. Then he pulled his phone out of his shorts pocket, found his neurologist's after-hours number, and dialed.

After a dreary drive home from the hospital, Selah discovered that two prospective clients had, via voicemail, declined her services. She left a message on Frankie's answering machine and picked up Faith from the Bait-n-Tackle. She found the dog dozing inside the kitten pen, her new bubblegum-pink nail polish and matching hair bows indicating that she, Aunt Ruby, and the kittens had made peace since the parrot incident.

Dad wasn't home yet, even though the diner had closed for the night. Mail and stacks of dirty dishes covered the kitchen table. Buried under the newspapers and overdue notices lay a large manila envelope addressed to her mother. The return address label read, "Baldwin & Winthrop."

Selah froze. Mitchell Baldwin was a divorce attorney, the kind of divorce attorney you want on your side when you expect things to get nasty. So, Momma had finally filed for divorce after more than thirty years. Had she fallen because she was distracted by the turmoil? Whatever Dad did this time must have been a humdinger.

When Selah slammed the envelope down on the table without opening it, Faith cowered and clawed on the carpet in an attempt to hide under the sofa.

"I'm sorry, baby girl." Selah picked her up and cuddled her trembling body before setting her back down.

She plodded into the living room, Mountain Dew and dessert in hand and Faith trailing behind. She slumped onto the sofa. The upholstery had been patched three times and the cushions sagged, but it was home. She swallowed her soda against the burning lump in the back of her throat. What kind of person runs off to another state on a pleasure trip when her family and her work need her the most?

Lord, it's me again for the millionth time. Thank you for making the trip amazing. Now that I'm home, I'm overwhelmed and confused again. I'm back to whining and pity parties when I desperately want to change.

"Never fear. Help is here!" Frankie burst through the door without knocking. "I got your message and came as fast as I could get away with."

Selah was mid-sip when Frankie came hurtling toward her. Snorting Mountain Dew up her nose, she sputtered. "I sent you a voicemail, not the bat signal."

Selah covered her mouth with her hand and coughed. Faith sat up and barked at her.

Frankie stopped in front of the sofa, hands on her hips. "Hold on. Why didn't you lock the door? Why are you sitting in the dark? Where is the coat rack?"

She coughed again and cleared her throat. "I'm having a welcome-home pity party. Care to join me?"

"This looks more like a funeral." Frankie lifted an eyebrow at Selah's Mountain Dew and Momma's chocolate treasure pie. "Oooh, with better food, though. I'm in."

She helped herself to pie, digging deep for the crackly peanut butter center, and cackled at Faith. The dog was now lying spread-eagle on Selah's lap, mouth wide open, waiting for whipped cream to fall into it.

"While you're gorging yourself, let me give you a recap." Selah mimicked a TV announcer's sing-song voice-over. "On today's episode of Sorrows in Shadybrook, Selah Morgan fears her business is failing, but she receives a telephone call with an opportunity that promises to change her life. Her dreams are cut short when Margo Morgan suffers a devastating fall and faces a recovery time of six to eight weeks, but not before Margo can file for divorce from Russ Morgan, her absentee husband."

"Mmmm. I heard about your mom. That's what I call daytime drama." Frankie took another bite of pie, eyes half-closed.

With her mouth full, she said, "Thish is fantastic, Shelah. Not your life, the pie. The pie ish fantastic. What's your mom's secret ingredient?"

"It sure ain't love. Whatever it is, she will take it to her grave. Now focus. We're talking about the Sorrows of Shadybrook."

Selah retrieved the pie pan from Frankie's hand and set it on the coffee table. "Julia's office called. She wants me to fly to New York and start the SoaperFan gig next week."

"Why do you make it sound like a bad thing?"

"Being in New York was fun." Selah rubbed figure eights on the soft fuzz covering Faith's belly. "Now that I'm back home, trying to fix things, I feel as if I'm plugging holes on a sinking ship."

"Then jump in and swim. Save yourself. You are getting on that plane next week."

"I don't understand it. I've asked God to help me make

the decision. The more confused I feel and the more I beg Him to show me, the quieter He gets."

"I'm making this decision for you. You have a commitment to *Winds of Change*. I have a commitment to play Nurse Nightingale to Mommy Dearest while you're gone."

"What? No, I couldn't ask you to take care of her. I need to stay and hold my remaining clients' hands, bolstering their confidence in my ability to serve their businesses."

Ever the accountant, Frankie ticked off her arguments. "First, I'm taking your mother to physical therapy or doctor's appointments, whatever Her Royal Majesty requires. Personally, I think she needs therapy for her mental health, but—"

Selah opened her mouth to disagree and shut it again.

"You'll be gone only a month or so. I, being a miracle worker, will have her up and at 'em in a week. She'll be back to her self-righteous, irritating self before you know it."

From the glint in Frankie's eyes, Momma might be facing Nurse Ratchet rather than Nurse Nightingale. Maybe that would motivate Momma to work harder and faster at recuperating.

"Second, Daddy would let me off work anyway for a worthy cause."

"The worthy cause being my mother and my temp job in daytime drama. Sounds like more of a charity case."

"Oh, and I can cook and clean too."

"Cleaning a carburetor does not count, Frankie."

"I'm capable of caring for your mother—and your little dog too." Frankie let out an evil "muwa-ha-ha" laugh and rubbed her palms together. "Your mom loves to remind me that she practically raised me. It's time for me to repay her. Fourthly . . ."

Selah cocked her head and rested her cheek against her palm. "Is fourthly even a word?"

"Fourthly, your clients are potable, right?"

"Potable? Like water?"

"Potable, portable. You know what I mean." She huffed. "You can make websites or programs or hack things, whatever geeks do, on your laptop from a distance."

"I wish you were portable and I could take you with me for moral support."

Frankie was right about one thing: Selah was a computer nerd. She was of no use to an Emmy-winning television program full of beautiful and young creative types. Julia would come to her senses and Selah would be on the next flight home.

"Fifthly and finally, I do not think your parents are divorcing. They enjoy annoying each other too much to give that up. No one else would tolerate them."

"You've got a point. Will that conclude your presentation?"

She nodded and smacked her lips, clearly pleased with herself and her pie.

"You forgot to put a few things on your list: my student loans and the expenses I will have to charge to my credit cards. Everything costs three times as much in the City."

The tightness in her chest and churning in her stomach felt larger than the Blue Ridge Mountains outside her window. If she let this dream die, it would eat away at her gut for the rest of her life. She couldn't give up this opportunity to experience life in the world of soaps, life outside Shadybrook.

Frankie shrugged, deflated.

"Don't worry that perky blonde head of yours. I've made up my mind. Mountain Dew helps me think clearly."

"True." Frankie held up her can and her laughter erupted into a loud burp. "It's the nectar of the gods. That is, if you believe in other gods."

"You are such a redneck. I don't know how I'll ever leave you behind." Selah rolled her eyes.

Frankie jumped up again and threw her arms around her friend, repeating the squealing incident at the fan club weekend. "You're going! I'm so proud of you. You're very weird, but I'm still proud of you."

Her bottom lip quivered as she remembered the day they'd become best friends. That summer afternoon, her mother was scrubbing down the counter in the diner. Selah was filling salt and pepper shakers and rolling napkins.

"Can I please watch *Winds of Change* on the TV here, Momma?"

"Selah Marie Morgan, haven't I taught you better than to idolize that show? You know how God feels about idols. Eleven-year-old girls are very impressionable." Momma carefully polished a gleaming gold statue of Elvis.

A lecture on the perils of television, coming from the woman who named her after Marie Horton on *Days of Our Lives*—not too convincing. "C'mon, Momma, *Winds of Change* is not about idols. And it's not like you haven't watched it with me before."

Selah slid into a booth and groaned when her whopping thighs stuck to the plastic seat. Her feet tapped to the ticking of the second hand on a clock shaped like a juke-box. She shoved a mass of black curls out of her eyes and moved on to filling ketchup bottles.

Looking longingly at the black-and-white set mounted above the counter, she said, "Please, just for an hour? All I want is to watch that wedding on *Winds of Change*. It's supposed to be real romantic, like a fairytale." Plus, there was this cute actor named Cane Ashton.

"A fairytale, is it?" Momma's lips stretched into a thin line. She kicked the jukebox twice to make it stop playing *Love Me Tender*. "Look around here."

Selah's eyes followed her waving dishrag.

"Does this look like the mansion of a billionaire tycoon? See any dashing playboys fixin' to take me on a private jet to Tahiti?"

"No, but—"

"Listen to me good, sugar." Her voice mounted above the hum of the shake machine. "Love ain't no soap opera."

"But it kind of is—"

"If it was a soap opera, you and me would be skinny." She threw her drippy rag into a bucket of brown water. "If it was, your father and me would be a supercouple like Luke and Laura, livin' high on the hog."

Luke and Laura. Now there was a romance made in heaven . . . Wait. Was her mother still talking?

"Don't you cut your eyes at me. I'm tellin' it like it is. You're too smart to fall for that nonsense." She sunk onto a barstool and rubbed her eyes with the back of her hand. "The only things we have in common with that soap opera is heartbreak, cheatin', and pain."

A lump formed in Selah's throat. She shoved out of the

booth and tripped on her high-top sneakers. She caught herself before she hit the black-and-white checkered tiles.

When she looked up, her worst enemy stared back at her through the window. Her tormentor, the sheriff's thirteen-year-old son, Cody, was definitely material for a soap-opera villain. She watched with dread as he puffed out his cheeks and stomach and waddled down the sidewalk in front of the diner windows.

Her father had told her to punch his lights out, but she wasn't like that. She couldn't even get up the nerve to tell Momma she hated grits for breakfast.

Momma muttered something about men and the patience of Job, oblivious to Cody's slow-motion show in front of the diner.

While Selah prayed that she wouldn't cry, she spotted Frankie outside, watching him. Frankie saw her and waved like a princess, her blonde, wavy hair crammed under a beat-up ball cap bearing the name of her dad's speedway.

What Frankie did next sealed their friendship for the next twenty years. She planted a roundhouse kick into Cody's rear bumper. He never saw it coming. He plunged headfirst into Mom's prickly juniper bush. Ooh, that was gonna sting.

Selah threw open the diner doors as Frankie took off running.

At the sound of Cody's moan, Momma said, "Boy, you sound like a stuck hog. What are you doing in that bush?"

Selah used the diversion to make her escape and jogged off after Frankie as fast as her chubby little legs and afternoon Snickers bar would take her. Frankie glanced back over her shoulder, and they grinned at each other.

They made it to that wedding after all.

"Earth to Selah. Why do you have that goofy grin on your face?"

Selah leaned toward her friend. "Just remembering our shenanigans growing up. Your offer to help Momma makes this decision easier. You will never know how much this means to me."

They stood and Selah hugged her.

"I'm taking this fur ball with me, though. I think they're used to celebutantes and their frou-frou dogs in the big city."

"You know what the best part of this trip will be?"

"What's that?"

"The day I kick your decrepit mother to the curb and come visit you on the set."

Chapter Nine

WHEN SELAH ARRIVED at LaGuardia, her driver was not holding a sign, but Selah recognized him instantly by his furrowed brow.

"Hello, Mason, what a wonderful surprise." Perhaps she could kill him with kindness.

He mumbled and took her bag, which was unexpected, considering the ungentlemanly way he knocked her over at the fan club luncheon. When he turned and stalked toward the parking lot, Selah had to run to keep up.

Panting, she slid into the passenger seat of a black Shelby Mustang. "Nice car, Knight Rider. I think it's got enough horses for a country girl like me."

"It's a rental. Nobody drives a car in the city." He revved the engine like a sixteen-year-old boy on a Saturday night.

They rode in silence for fifteen minutes. Selah studied the side of his head, which was about as stony and craggy as Mount Rushmore. Although she had little interaction with men, she was fairly sure there weren't many around like this guy. He stirred up thoughts of Cane with his gooey-chocolate-brown eyes. Was it all an act? Was Cane a self-absorbed, pompous jerk like Mason?

"For a head writer, you're a man of few words."

"You mean a head writer forced to do Madam Julia's bidding?" He glared at her with slate gray eyes, his hands gripping the steering wheel until his fingers turned white. "I dared to disagree with her and, as punishment, I am to babysit you, our fresh-faced SuperFan. Or SoaperFan. Whatever you call it, it's ludicrous."

"I'm kind of partial to the idea myself." No way would she let him put a damper on her excitement.

"What's the point in more publicity? The show's going to be cancelled anyway."

Mason couldn't possibly loathe Julia that much or else he would have defected to another show. It must have been something else.

He darted a sideways glance. "What are you cackling about?"

"Don't you think it's funny?"

"Your appalling southern accent?"

She was too intrigued to be offended. Nothing exciting like this happened in Shadybrook. "You and Miss Julia."

"What?" He blinked.

"You and Miss Julia," She slowly drew out each word. "Mason and Julia. You share the names of one of the most beloved supercouples in the history of daytime television. The way you talk about her has me thinkin' it's not the only thing you share."

He turned three shades of red. A kindred spirit. "You

have known us for all of five minutes. But, by all means, feel free to offer your opinion on our love lives or lack thereof."

"Mason and Julia fought constantly on *Santa Barbara*. They argued to cover up their attraction." Selah's uncharacteristic boldness must have been due to the heady skyscrapers floating high above the sunroof. "Just an observation."

"I know who Mason and Julia were, kid. I wrote for *Santa Barbara* for years. That was another failed show, another wasted effort, just like *Winds of Change*. Mason and Julia died with that show. My career may die with this one."

He shot her a look that said the subject of his relationship with Julia was closed.

"I didn't realize you wrote for SB. I miss that show. The storylines were innovative, even brilliant at times."

With his ego boosted by her praise, he began to open up a bit about why some soaps fail and what elements produce a memorable storyline. He gossiped about his favorite actors and wedding scenes until they reached their destination in a borough outside Manhattan. Just when it appeared his cranky façade was cracking a little, he unceremoniously dumped her at the curb.

"Writers' meeting tomorrow morning. You're invited," he called out the window as he sped off. "It's 'Bring a Beverly Hillbilly to Work Day.'"

So we won't be bosom buddies. She stumbled over the luggage he'd thrown onto the sidewalk. *This is the opportunity of a lifetime. He's not going to ruin it for me.*

She paused at the red door of a production "bungalow" down the street from the *Winds of Change* studio. She could hear Dad saying, "Bungalow? Cottage? Is that what they're calling their mansions these days? Sounds like hog heaven to me."

After entering the security code, she stepped into the "dressing room" of the show's resident diva, Dorian Forrester. Dori, as she was known to her fans, thought the studio dressing rooms were too cramped and sterile, so she decided to renovate a production bungalow near the studio. She was rarely in residence, however, as her contract allowed her six months of "outs" every year. During her current sabbatical, she was graciously allowing Selah to stay rent-free in her home.

Wow, this place is fabulous.

The entryway and living room were decorated with Japanese cherry blossoms in reds, blacks, and whites that were as bold and daring as Dori. When Selah descended into a sunken living room, she spotted a bouquet of purple sweet peas, a striking contrast to the black marble table on which they were arranged. Her name was on the card attached to the flowers.

Dear Selah,

What a beautiful name, darling. Welcome to my humble abode.

Unfortunately, I won't be able to meet you during your visit. I'm off to Italy, promoting my "aDORIng" line of cosmetics and skin-care products. I left you a sampling in the master bath. Be sure to watch my special on QVC.

From the high praise I've heard about you from Julia, I think you'll have a wonderful experience at Winds of Change. The cast and crew are like a big family. Enjoy the love that family brings, but be wary of the black sheep, like my daughter, Eva.

Ciao, Dori.

She waved the card at Faith, who had snuggled in a fluffy, frilly dog bed, which probably belonged to one of Dori's teacup Chihuahuas.

"It's official, little Muppet. God is good."

She read the card again and tapped it against her temple. What did she mean about Eva? Who calls her own daughter a black sheep? Selah and her mother had their challenges, but she knew Momma loved her more than life. *She would never say such things about me to my face, let alone to a stranger.*

She smiled, thinking of Momma. Absence made the heart grow fonder. She pulled out her camera and began to document Dori's not-so-humble abode. She couldn't wait to show them how the other half lived.

But first, she would do what any reasonable guest would—snoop through the cabinets and drawers, luxuriate with a bubble bath in the Jacuzzi, and take a flying leap onto the satin sheets.

Chapter Ten

"A good head writer knows and is tolerated by his audience. A great head writer knows his characters' history, their routines, their darkest secrets in a way that his audience might label multiple personality disorder."

Mason Lord, Head Writer, *The Winds of Change*

HEN SELAH ARRIVED at the *Winds of Change* studio at nine the next morning, she was shepherded through three levels of security worthy of the airport TSA. At an outside gate station in the parking lot, she shivered against the wind for thirty minutes as a guard checked that she was on "the list." His call to Julia confirmed that Selah was not a stalker preparing to wreak mayhem on the stars. If they only knew how crazy she and Frankie could get about their soap hunks!

At a second security desk, she opened her purse for viewing and walked through a metal detector. At the final checkpoint, a security guard seated behind an imposing metal desk eyed her ID carefully and then held it up to compare it with her face. *I knew I shouldn't have fibbed—well, outright lied—about my weight on that driver's license.*

"Be sure your sins will find you out," Momma would say. Why did she have to be right about everything?

Minutes ticked by. Would the guard expose her as a fraud and poser?

At long last, she chuckled and said, "Come on through, Selah. Your hair is gorgeous, girl. It's like a big ol' Cher wig, but real."

Selah had to suppress the urge to hug the guard, in spite of the Cher remark. Selah got that hug from Julia, who surprised her at the door.

"Welcome. I'm glad you made it here safely. I was a little leery of Mason picking you up at the airport. He drives like a cabbie running the Daytona 500."

Energy radiated from Julia as she briefed Selah on the day's activities. "As you can see, we're up and running already. The camera operators have been setting up for hours and most of the actors had six-thirty call times."

Julia led her through a maze of beige elevators, beige doors, and beige walls that weren't attached to the ceiling. Was this a giant warehouse or a theater without seats?

When they walked onto the main soundstage, the perpetually chagrined Mason paced and gesticulated wildly with his coffee cup as he talked on a cell phone.

"Put that thing away. You know the rule about cameras and phones during taping." Julia slapped his arm from behind. "Flip phones have gone the way of the dinosaur, by the way."

He startled and whirled to face her, sloshing coffee on the floor. He narrowed his eyes at them but kept right on talking.

"Mason, since you're here early, why don't you take Selah on a tour of the studio before the writers' meeting?" Julia smiled sweetly, the tension between them as entertaining as the show.

He slammed shut the phone and saluted her with a flourish. "Yes, your majesty. I am eager to serve as your loyal subject, your lackey, your whipping boy."

Just like a writer—way too descriptive.

"Great! Have fun." She trotted off, speaking into her walkie-talkie.

"Tour guide!" Mason spewed in Selah's direction and started power-walking through the sets. "Seven days a week I answer to network executives, advertisers, and actors. I plan storylines six months in advance, all while making allowances for actors who want to do primetime or movies, or go on maternity leave, or feed the children in Botswana. Now she wants me to play hospitality host to our superfluous SoaperFan? What have I done to deserve this?"

He turned suddenly to face her. "Don't answer that."

Selah raised her hand silently.

"We don't raise hands to ask questions around here, SoaperFan. We just butt in when there's a lull in conversation."

"*We* didn't hear any lulls. *We* only heard 'wah, wah, wah.'" She tapped her fingers against her thumb, imitating a yakking mouth.

"Just ask the question." He breathed in and out sharply through his nostrils, like a bull.

She whipped out her notebook and clicked a pen to

write. "I've heard that most head writers don't hang around the set as much as you do. Does the executive producer have something on you, or do you think it's something else?"

His mouth set in a straight line and she imagined smoke coming out of those flared nostrils.

"Something else then, I guess."

"No more questions," he growled as he stomped off, leaving her to run to catch up again. She would get plenty of exercise here. Good thing too. Dori had left dark chocolate bon-bons in the freezer, and Selah had been munching out like crazy, trying to soothe her anxiety. Mason's attitude only made her nerves coil more tightly.

Selah had to remind herself to keep her mouth shut as Mason pointed out eight permanent or "standing" sets, including a fictional coffee house, a bar, a mansion occupied by Dori's character and family, and a hospital nurses' station. Temporary or "swing" sets, such as an alleyway or a rooftop, were broken down and rebuilt by stagehands on a daily basis, depending on the needs of the scene. She fingered a vintage vase filled with fresh tulips.

Selah spotted one of her favorite actresses. Liza, who had been with the show for twenty-five of its fifty years, sat hunched on a barstool in the coffee house set, cramming her lines.

Selah slowed her pace. "May I say hi to her?"

"Of course not. She's working. Think of the actors as animals in a zoo and yourself as a child on a field trip. Observe, but don't feed the animals."

Liza looked up and put aside her script. "Here comes the king of the jungle. And you must be the SoaperFan."

She walked over and hugged Selah like an old friend, and they took a quick photo together.

"I read your autobiography."

"Oh, that's the censored version." Liza's laugh was low and gravelly. "Come by my dressing room later and I'll fill you in on the juiciest gossip."

Mason tapped his foot.

"That means the monkeys have to get back to work now." She revealed that the show taped at least two-hundred and fifty episodes a year and often gave actors more than forty pages of dialogue to memorize a day.

"It's hard to learn lines in advance," she said, shooting a pointed look at Mason, "because our loving writers make frequent script revisions at the eleventh hour."

"Some actors should learn not to antagonize their loving writers." Mason snapped his fingers at Selah. "I just remembered that your tour today will mercifully be cut short because they are filming a love scene. Visitors are limited for the privacy of the actors."

"Ironically, one of whom has posed in *Playboy* and *Maxim*," Liza said and returned to muttering her lines.

"Come, little lamb." Mason waved Liza off and led Selah to the dressing rooms. "Let's find an empty janitor's closet where I can park you while I attend to real business."

Before she could protest, a doorknob rattled to her right. Someone rushed out of a dressing room and ran into her, knocking her onto her back. It couldn't be Mason again, could it?

No. This time, the view was much more appealing. Cane dropped to the floor beside her.

Chapter Eleven

"Interacting with actors up close and personal, outside of the television screen, is a bit like sneaking into the zoo after hours."

Selah Morgan, SoaperFan

FRANKIE WAS NEVER going to believe this.

Cane Ashton was down on all fours, leaning over Selah. As she debated whether getting conked on the head by the cold floor was a curse or a blessing, she realized he was in a bathrobe and boxer shorts, his bare chest peeking through.

Definitely a blessing.

"Are you hurt?" His long fingers brushed her hair out of her face.

She stared up into eyes the color of falling autumn

leaves in the Blue Ridge Mountains. "If I say yes, will you give me mouth-to-mouth resuscitation?"

The autumn eyes widened momentarily before crinkling up as Cane broke into laughter. "I might consider the offer if I wasn't in such a hurry to get to the set." He helped her up gently.

She groaned, more from embarrassment than pain. "Don't worry, temporary lapse in judgment. I think my brain and mouth are reengaged now."

"Are you sure you're all right? Your face is red."

"That's normal. Well, normal for me, not other people, although they would probably say I'm not normal compared to them . . . I'll just stop talking now."

He squinted at her. "Are you positive you don't need a CT scan or something?"

"Go. I'm fine. Truly." One look at his chiseled features and her words turned monosyllabic.

"I hate to leave you like this, but if I'm late again, they might write my character off." Cane gave her a final concerned look and, with a wave, jogged away.

She stared after him, smiling and touching her hand to her cheek. *I am such a stalker-fan. I am the Soaparazzi.*

Cane's scene called for a polite kiss, but Eva pressed her lips so hard against his that he took a step back to balance himself. The image of the woman he had just knocked over popped into his head. Her big hair and bigger Southern accent made him smile.

"Your line, Cane," someone said.

He startled. "Sorry, guys."

Eva's blood-red lips were parted and her breathing shallow as she gazed up into his eyes.

He swallowed and braced himself. This was going to be a long day.

Selah looked around and realized that Mason had abandoned her once again. Although she was sure he would have offered no assistance other than a grunt of disdain.

A production assistant, a.k.a. "PA," noticed her wandering the halls alone and graciously showed her to the conference room where some of the writers were meeting. PA Heather explained that the writers compiled the storyline breakdowns more than a month before taping and the scripts at least three weeks ahead.

"Although we have twelve writers in all, including Mason, the head writer, only one or two of the scribes work on each script. Typically, they work from home and communicate through telephone conferences or e-mail."

"Why are some of them meeting in person today?"

"To talk about the big changes brewing. Maybe they're just curious about the SoaperFan." Heather grinned from under thick, black spectacles and straight brown hair. "Selah, I love your hair. When I lived in Connecticut, I had a horse with soft, dark curls like that."

She blinked. How should she respond when her hair was compared to a horse and a Cher wig in the course of one day? After Shirley Temple, natural curls must have died out in Hollywood. Selah's black spirals were a novelty.

"Forget something, Mason?" Heather asked as they interrupted his meeting. Mason nodded at the PA but barely acknowledged Selah as he mentioned her presentation and quickly moved the discussion to the next storyline arc.

After the meeting, she sat quietly at the table, completing her notes.

"What are you complaining about?" Mason barked.

"I'm not complaining. I haven't said a word." He was like her mind-reading Momma in male form. She gathered her papers and purse and followed him into the hallway.

"Exactly." He stopped and crossed his arms at his chest. "You haven't said a word after the meeting. You're not babbling like you usually do. That can only come to no good."

After all the criticism, she couldn't wait to get back to Faith's kisses and wagging tail. "Why did you feel the need to shoot down every idea I had?"

"It's not personal. The writers think the producer is taking the show in a new direction and that you have been brought in to take their place secretly."

She laughed. "I'm here to generate publicity as the SoaperFan. That's all. I didn't realize writers were so insecure and paranoid."

"Just cautious. Consider all the things professional writers have to worry about."

She gave him a blank look.

He sighed loudly. "Writers first must answer to the Powers That Be. We have to appease viewers with short attention spans, plus make our ideas budget-proof. Then we write a contingency plan for every actress who is negotiating to make it big during pilot season or jump to *The Bold and the Beautiful* or *General Hospital*. Sometimes we plan for Thanksgiving and Christmas in July."

"What's the worst thing about your job?"

"Coming up with fresh ideas in an industry that has already had seventy years of love triangles, evil twins, cloning, vampires, mobsters, murder mysteries, spies, and aliens. What's left?"

"Family connections, love, relationships, character. The staples."

"Run along, Selah. I think you can still catch *The Waltons* in syndication."

"What used to make soaps special was a little magic, a fairytale quality."

"I'm all for escaping reality." Eva, who was Dori's black-sheep daughter in real life and played Kelli, Cane's on-screen love interest, swished toward them in her signature boy shorts and flip-flops. Eva's ratty Cowboys t-shirt exposed impossibly taut abs with a butterfly tattoo.

On reflex, Selah smoothed her blouse over her impossibly plump muffin top, where her dress slacks cut off her circulation. She looked away quickly when she realized she was staring at Eva's stomach while sucking in her own. *Lord, forgive my insecurities.* But they came in waves . . . *Hawaii Five-O*-sized waves.

"Eva, would you deposit Selah at the main sound stage?" Mason asked. "I have work to do."

"You're in luck. I've got a few minutes before my call time."

Selah stuck out her tongue when he turned his back. Eva laughed and motioned for her to follow. When Eva smiled, she bore an eerie resemblance to an adult JonBenet Ramsey and virtually no resemblance to her mother, Dori, the show's matriarch.

"Is Mason always that rude?"

"I've heard he is, but I rarely see him on set. I just finished a love scene this morning, so I've been a busy girl."

So, Eva was the actress who posed for a girlie magazine. Interesting. "What did you do before *Winds of Change*?"

"Commercials. A little modeling here and there." She flicked her hair over her shoulder and used a pocket compact to touch up her foundation. "Honestly, I thought acting would be more glamorous than it is."

Maybe it wasn't glamorous to her, but Selah's skin was tingling and her heart hadn't stopped pounding since she got here.

"Right now, Cane is taping a scene with Shayne Nixon and my baby," she said with pride. The baby was the child Eva's character, Kelli, had with Shayne's character, Ned. For a while, Kelli passed it off as the child of Cane's character, Dean. It was difficult to separate the real person from the character.

Eva put her finger to her lips as she opened the door to the soundstage. They tiptoed across the hardwood. A cute stagehand introduced himself in a whisper and set up two metal chairs in the shadows so they could watch the taping.

Selah's mouth fell open. *The Winds of Change* was a giant playground of beautiful people where the scenery, clothes, and hair changed throughout the day. Three large studio cameras on pedestals skirted the set. A photographer snapped pictures of the taping, careful to stay out of the actors' eyelines.

When Selah's chair scraped the floor, Cane looked up. He shaded his eyes to see out from the lights and waved at her. She returned the wave and then covered her cheeks and mouth with her hand, knowing her hot face must be emblazoned with scarlet.

"It's okay now." Eva patted her leg. "They're between takes."

The stagehand came back with ice cream cookie sandwiches.

"How thoughtful. Thanks." Selah took a piece and smiled up at him.

"That should cool you off." Eva said, waving away the dessert.

Cane returned to the task at hand, which was catching Eva's "baby" in mid-air. The baby he was rehearsing with was a medium-sized doll he and Shayne were throwing back and forth like a football.

"Pay attention now, boys." The director, a burly fifty-something woman in a brown aviator jacket and gauze skirt, chastised them lightly. "Cane, there's a shadow on the baby's face when you make your entrance, so I want you to move about two paces downstage. Closer to the sofa. There, that's perfect. Draw out your last lines a bit too, Cane. Then, Shayne, I'll cue your entrance after Cane's monologue."

The rapid pace left little time for turning to face the wrong camera or forgetting lines. Gone were the days of cue cards.

The live baby and her mother arrived to much fanfare and cooing from the actors. Cane regaled the infant, whose twin brother was used when she got fussy, with funny faces and noises. The baby flashed a drooly grin and reached for his nose.

Selah smiled and felt a twinge in her stomach. She

quickly squelched it. *That had better not be a maternal twinge. Cane would be a natural as a parent, but the world ain't ready for me to pass on my DNA.*

"Okay, this is the real thing, everybody. Quiet on set." All eyes focused on the director as she called out the names of the cameras and cued the actors with "Five, four, three, two." Cane began his monologue, which included ad-libs to allow for precious reactions from the baby. Selah wanted to clap at the end of the scene. She darted her eyes at Eva, who was still engrossed in Cane and "her" baby.

"Do you and Cane get along well?"

"Mmm-hmm." She licked her lips. "Walk with me back to my dressing room. I want to know more about the infamous SoaperFan."

Eva peppered her with questions about the blog and social media feeds and what Selah planned to write about her. She even offered to show Selah around the city. Selah and Frankie had been wrong when they labeled this starlet another vapid model.

Why had Dori warned her against her daughter when Eva was so friendly and welcoming? The black sheep appeared as gentle as a lamb.

Chapter Twelve

SEVERAL DAYS PASSED before Selah worked up the nerve to visit Cane in his dressing room.

Holding her breath, she knocked lightly on Cane's unadorned door. It slid open, unlatched, with the weight of her hand, which was still sore from playing Xbox with two teen actors taking a break from schoolwork. The adults waiting for their call times joined in, laughing and trash-talking over the video games.

"Cane?" she called tentatively. "It's just me, Selah Morgan. You know, we ran into each other in the hallway this week. Literally. Accidentally, though, of course."

She took a few tentative steps inside and glanced around.

"Cane? They told me you'd be in here." *Wow! I am standing in Dean's dressing room. I mean, Cane Ashton's dressing room.*

No, she was not one of those fans who called her favorite stars by their characters' names even after being corrected by the star himself. She took her role as SoaperFan seriously. It was her responsibility not to pry into the stars' personal lives, but—

Oh, my goodness, is that a picture of Cane with Dan Marino?

Beside it stood another photo of a bearded Cane and an older couple, who shared the same dark brown eyes and warm smile. Parents, maybe? Selah was careful not to touch anything, as if CSI would come by later to dust for fingerprints.

She shot a glance at the door. "I'll just wait for Cane here," she said aloud. No answer. *Excellent, that means it's safe to snoop some more.*

On the table beside the couch lay a stack of papers covered with a yellow sheet and dated the next day. She lifted the cover page. It was tomorrow's script. Perhaps she could take a little peek.

A thump caused her to suck in a sharp breath. A glass shattered against the wall.

"Cane?" she called, edging toward the light in the bathroom. She felt like all those stupid, doe-eyed victims in the slasher movies, who just had to explore the sounds coming from the basement. Like a moth to a bug zapper.

What she found in the bathroom was equally disturbing. Cane sat on the floor, his back pressed to the wall. His wet head rested in his hands, his knees pulled up against his bare chest.

Did this guy even own a t-shirt? As she tiptoed around broken glass and shut off the dripping faucet, she noticed he wasn't wearing shoes.

"Cane, are you okay?" Duh. Evidently not. "Did you step on the glass?"

He lifted his head, looking up at her through lidded eyes. "What are you doing here?" His voice carried no emotion.

Please don't let him be drunk or high. She wouldn't have known if he was. Shadybrook didn't exactly have an AA or a liquor store, unless you counted the beer sauce for Ruby's barbecue.

"I came to introduce myself and my plans for the fan websites and chats and the door was open and I . . ."

He didn't appear to have heard any of her nervous babbling.

She kneeled awkwardly beside him. "What's wrong? Can I do something for you? Do you need medical attention?"

He snorted a laugh and shook his head.

"I'll go. I'm sorry to intrude or trespass, but when I heard the glass—"

"I was scrubbing off my makeup." He sat up and rubbed his face with both hands. "I took a good look in the mirror, and I—"

"Realized how fine you are?" She finished his sentence. "As if it wasn't obvious."

Her crush on this man had her blurting out all kinds of inappropriate things.

He blinked and then let out a deep chuckle that sounded like a muffled sob with no tears. She laughed a little too, hopeful that he was not having a nervous breakdown.

Even under the tiny bathroom's harsh fluorescent light, with no makeup and with dark circles under his brown eyes, he took her breath. She had to keep her eyes averted because, despite her bold words, looking at him sent a flash of unworthiness through her body. She felt like a whale squeezed into a bathtub, but Cane seemed oblivious to their cramped quarters.

"Who are you?" he asked.

"I'm the one who's going to call 911 for you." She reached for her cell phone.

"No." He grabbed her hand. "Please."

Seeing her surprise at his touch, he explained, "I'm sorry. I didn't mean to scare you. There's no need for 911, because I'm okay physically. I'm just a little shell-shocked."

He looked her straight in the eye. "Wait, you're the lady I plowed into in the hallway." He spoke slowly as if coming out of a fog.

"That's me, the lady." *I am so not a lady.* She was staring with abandon at the hard flesh that outlined his six-pack abs.

"I apologize. I was in a hurry to run a scene with Eva and it's been—I've been . . ." He paused. "Let's just say it's been a long week."

She moved from kneeling to sitting Indian-style on the cool white tile, directly across from him. This day might have been a trial for him, but if she had much of a life, this would be one of the highlights.

"You helped me out with all that rolling around on the floor we did." He grinned slyly.

"I did?"

"Yeah, I didn't have to do pushups to make my muscles look buff for my love scene with Eva." He pounded his chest in a Tarzan gesture.

"I thought you guys used spray tan and shimmer to get a contoured six-pack."

"No, but I'll remember that for next time." He stretched his neck. "I bet you wonder what I'm doing in here."

"It's your bathroom. You can do what you want. I'm just worried about you."

"But you don't know me."

"I'm sure I'd like to, in a different setting, of course." Boy, did that sound like a pickup line or what?

"I'm Cane." He scooched toward her and held out a tanned hand. When she took it, he pulled both of them up and off the floor. Their faces came so close she could smell the mint from his mouthwash and see a tiny scar beside his left eye.

"I'm Selah," she said breathlessly. "I know y'all do things differently in the big city, but that bathroom sit-in stuff is pretty weird. When my family has a sit-in after a nervous breakdown, it takes place at a table laden with fried chicken and buttered rolls." She hesitated, hearing her own awkward words again in her mind and cringing. "Not saying that you were having a breakdown or anything or that I would judge you for it." She dug the hole deeper.

He grinned. "I understand. Let's sit on the couch. Much more comfortable."

He seemed back to normal now, and her discomfort began to ease. She handed him his tennis shoes.

"I'll clean up the glass for you if you show me to the broom." Momma would be so proud.

Her throat closed up as she remembered Momma's voicemail message that morning: "Sugar, I wish I was on vacation with you and Faith up there. Somebody has to stay here and handle your father and the diner. Don't you worry. We'll make it somehow."

"Nah. I'll get the glass later." They seated themselves, facing each other from opposite ends of his couch.

"It's biblical, right?" He bent and slipped on his shoes.

"What is?" Her sudden yearning to be close to him was certainly not biblical.

"Your name. It's something from the Bible, if I recall."

Hmm. He knew the Bible. That was a positive sign. "Yes, Selah comes from Psalms. It means a reflection. Cane is a pretty well-known biblical figure as well, different spelling."

"It's short for hurricane. Hurricane Brock blew through Texas while Mom was in labor."

"Texas?" She pointed at him. "You're secretly Southern."

"After the storm, she packed up our Stetsons and moved up the Mississippi as far as she could get from the Gulf of Mexico."

"The name suits you."

"Oh, yeah. I've lived up to the name." He leaned back and stretched out his legs. "I can't apologize enough for being a little out of sorts today."

"A little?"

"All right, I can't apologize enough for acting like a nut. That should cover it."

"Since we're on a couch, would you like to tell zee doctor a leetle about what prompted your strange behavior?" Selah gave her best German accent.

"Having a shrink certainly couldn't hurt me. After I got a call about some troubling, uh, medical issues, the show dropped me from contract to recurring status. I didn't tell anyone about these issues, but I suspect somebody leaked it."

He dragged a hand through his now-dry hair. "I heard Eva was dropped to recurring too, but she's as good as fired. The show is in turmoil right now."

Oh no. A sickening sensation clawed at her stomach as she recalled her suggestions to the writers about Cane's abominable storylines and lack of chemistry with Eva. Her big mouth and brilliant ideas may have cost two actors their contracts.

"I'm sure it's temporary." Her heartbeat drummed in her ears. "Your storyline has been meager lately, but you're a great actor, you've been on the show forever, and everybody loves you." *Especially me and Frankie.*

"Thank you for that. What you don't know is that, during May sweeps, another beloved character will die at the hands of the serial killer."

Eva and Cane are toast and it's all my fault.

"Anyone is expendable if the storyline dictates. I'm thirty-five. I've peaked in the soap business. I'm not the young stud of the show anymore."

He'd hate her if he found out her part in the firings. Mason had explained to her that the key to soap-story longevity was secrets and lies. She was a terrible liar.

"From what I heard when I was in on some meetings, your medical problem did not cause this firing. Also, it can't be your age or looks. You're gorgeous, and age can't touch charisma."

The muscles in his face relaxed. "Maybe I should fire my publicist and hire you instead." Suddenly, he eyed her strangely. "I know who you really are, Selah."

She gulped, wondering if he could see into her soul. "You do?"

"You're the SuperFan."

"SoaperFan."

"What did you come to see me about, SoaperFan?" He crossed his ankle over his knee.

"Julia suggested that I get to know the cast members personally since I'm blogging about y'all and giving media interviews about my all-access pass to the stars."

"How much access are we talking here?"

"Don't worry. What happens in the dressing room, stays in the dressing room." She smiled at her own corny joke, blanking on anything intelligent to say.

As his dark eyes studied her, she became immensely uncomfortable. Thankfully, she had put on lipstick and cute clothes today. Her curly black hair, her best and most talked-about asset, may have been worthy of a Clairol commercial. However, big hair and bling could not disguise the double chin, rolls under her bra, and the thighs that spread when she sat down.

Her eyes scanned his dressing room, desperate for something to take the attention away from herself. "Are those gifts from fans?" She pointed to a table next to the couch. It held a giant "Cane's Babes" button and a pencil drawing of Cane.

"Yes, they are. The fans are very talented and loyal. I don't deserve such adoration." He picked up the drawing to admire it. "Remember when Peter and Jenny got together on the show? Their cutesy name was Penny, so the fans sent them banks of pennies. The actors donated the money to charity. That was cool."

"See, there's where the show went wrong in pairing your character, Dean, and Eva's character, Kelli. There's no cutesy fan name for you. Dean and Kelli do not go together. Their fan name would be Deli. Not romantic at all."

"As sexy as a slab of salami." Cane laughed, displaying gorgeous teeth that were not perfectly fake or blindingly white. He was more rugged than manicured.

Quit it right this minute. She scolded herself for dreaming about the finer points of Mr. Cane Ashton. No way could he be interested in her when he was surrounded by beautiful, skinny, scantily-clad women on a daily basis.

"Is something wrong?"

She swallowed and averted her eyes as the heat rose in her cheeks. "No, of course not."

He glanced down at his bare chest. "I totally forgot about putting on a shirt. I am so sorry."

I am so not sorry.

Stop it, naughty thoughts!

"No problem."

"The show has me going shirtless a lot lately."

Ratings boost, I'm sure.

Stop it! Stop it!

He jumped up and looked around, for his clothes, she assumed. He found a black Jets hoodie and pulled it over his head. "The reason I asked what was wrong was because you looked hot."

Now it was his turn to fumble and blush. "I mean, you looked like you were a little overheated, upset, exceedingly warm. Judging by your red face, I thought maybe I'd scared you to death in the bathroom."

"I told you already not to worry about it. I was just concerned. I was not afraid of you."

"You should be," he said under his breath. But the look in his eyes was more spooked than venomous.

She cleared her throat and tried to lighten the mood. "So, Shirtless Wonder, how do you keep those abs in shape?"

He smiled as she'd hoped he would. "Is that what the fans are burning to know about? My exercise habits? Is that what you're writing on your blogs?"

"Actually, it's more along the lines of . . ." She pretended to type rapidly. "'Soap bad boy Cane Ashton enjoys running around the studio clad only in tight jeans and flexing his guns. Believe me, ladies, there's even more firepower in person than you'll ever see on your high-definition TV.'"

Cane threw back his head in easy laughter that filled her with warmth. It was un-self-conscious and masculine, with just a hint of goofiness.

"Love it. Especially the bad boy part. Definitely include that. Just in case the fans want to know the truth though, I do a little boxing so it looks more natural in all those fight scenes I have with Shayne Nixon." He scratched his head. "Oh, you can tell them I used to play football and still work out with a few of the retired players."

She motioned to a picture behind the couch. "You were drafted by the Jets, right?

"You've done your research. Enjoy football?"

"Love it. Live it. Breathe it come September." Plus, there was nothing else to do in Shadybrook than work and watch TV.

"I was drafted to the NFL straight out of the University

of Minnesota." He flicked his hand as if it had fallen asleep. "The first week of training camp, I landed on my neck the wrong way. Bruised my spinal cord and broke a few vertebrae. By the time I recovered, my season was done."

"You must have been disappointed."

"It was a mixed blessing." He shrugged. "*Winds of Change* had decided to bring back the role of Dean, so the end of football meant the rebirth of my acting career."

"That's an amazing story. You're a man of many talents. I hear you're even singing at the cabaret charity function later this week."

"I dabble a little. My brother was always the better singer. A regular choirboy." The muscle in his jaw quivered.

"You have a brother?"

He shot up off the couch. "Well, I guess I should head out of here and go home. It's getting late."

"I didn't mean to pry."

He smiled but his eyes didn't crinkle at the corners. Why had he turned cold and guarded at the mention of his brother?

Secrets and lies were not just the stuff of soap operas. His abrupt change in attitude told her that Cane was hiding something, and it was big.

Cane shut the door and leaned his back against it. What was that scent that lingered after she left? Strawberries? No. Cotton candy. He shut his eyes and breathed it in.

The summer before he landed *Winds of Change*, his mom had dragged her teenage sons to the county fair. She insisted that they eat cotton candy with her.

"We're too old for that, Mom," his brother Tanner protested.

"Nonsense." She took a handful, waved it at them, and draped it like silk across her tongue.

Hands in jean pockets, the brothers watched her while keeping an eye out for their friends.

"You try it." Her eyes shone as she sucked on a piece of strawberry cotton candy and handed each boy his own spool.

After she rode the wild hayride coaster, she claimed motion sickness, which necessitated that they put their arms around her to steady her. They were so concerned with her health, they didn't worry about the friends they passed on the walk back to the car.

Cane felt a punch in the gut as he came back to the present. The scent of cotton candy was gone, and so was his mother.

He clapped his hands together and reached for his jacket. Time to hit the gym. Maybe he'd go out afterward. Nothing like good music and a beautiful woman to banish the memories.

Chapter Thirteen

"It is taking everything inside of me not to scratch your eyes out!"
Lauren Fenmore (played by Tracey Bregman)
"Well, make no mistake, the feeling is mutual."

Sheila Carter (played by Kimberlin Brown),
The Young and the Restless

"CUT! WHAT ARE you doing, nurse?"

"I don't know. Did I come in at the wrong time?" Selah gulped. Why had she agreed to this? Julia said it would be fun for her to experience life as an extra for a day, but this was not as easy as it looked on TV.

"Yes, you did." The director's voice boomed like her geometry teacher's. That was the lowest grade she ever received. Where was the motherly director who had coddled Cane and Shayne in their scenes?

Cane winced too. He and Eva stood beside Shayne's

hospital bed. Shayne's character, Ned, was recovering there from a violent encounter with the show's serial killer. Cane caught Selah's eye and winked. She smiled back and exhaled the breath she had been holding.

"Let's try it again. Do not look at the camera. Do not move until I cue you."

She nodded, trying not to jolt her French braid out of place. The show's hair stylists were magicians. She might need the makeup people STAT to wipe the sweat from her brow.

Instead, Eva, wielding her compact of powder, stepped in. "Let's put some of this on you before they think you're the patient."

This time, Selah waited for the director's cue to open the door to the hospital room. *Please help me with these two lines I have to deliver.*

"I need everyone to leave. Visiting hours are over," she said, smiling at Cane, Eva, and Shayne. *Yes! I nailed it.*

She turned to make a triumphant exit and tripped on her clunky white nurse's clogs. The medical charts she held clattered to the floor.

"Cut!"

Shayne pulled the white sheet over his head and moaned. "I'll be in a coma before she gets through this scene."

Eva pointed at Selah's feet. "Just pretend those ugly shoes are Louboutin stilettos and you're working the runway, girlfriend."

Selah blinked.

"She speaks country, not couture, Eva." Shayne yawned.

Selah squatted down to pick up the charts, thanking the Lord that her pink scrubs were loose and comfy.

Cane's muscled arm wrapped around her shoulders. "Let me get those for you."

"We've got to stop meeting like this," he whispered, his breath searing her ear. She raised her gaze to meet his, and the other people in the room faded away.

Yeah, right. And next, she and Cane would run toward each other on a beach with Air Supply playing in the background. *Momma, get outta my head!* She was ruined. Momma's dark view of the world, men specifically, would forever play in Selah's head like a viral video of a kitten playing piano.

The director gave Eva the line about visiting hours and ordered Selah to stand beside the bed and pretend to check vitals. Cane scooped up the charts with one arm and pulled her up with the other. She opened her mouth and closed it again.

"Never mind," the director sighed, "let's just move on."

When Cane's fingers brushed the inside of her wrist, she melted like Hershey's ice cream under a molten flow of hot fudge. How could anyone move on after being touched like that?

⬛

Selah's girl-bonding with Eva Forrester didn't last long. Eva met her in a dressing room hallway, pointing a finger and an unlit cigarette at her head. "I thought we were friends. How could you do this to me?"

"I don't know what you're talking about. We are friends." Although, a true friend would advise her against wearing a lace bra and Daisy Dukes in public.

The absence of makeup highlighted Eva's splotchy skin and the dark circles imprinted under her eyes. Selah was mesmerized by her transformation, a split-personality storyline up close and personal.

"A friend doesn't get another friend fired."

"But I didn't—"

"You know what I'm talking about, SoaperFanatic. You trashed me to the writers, and I got fired."

How would Eva know what Selah said to the writers?

One word . . . Mason.

"The show isn't renewing my contract, so my character's probably going to be murdered by that serial killer." She sagged against the cement wall.

"Let's take this into your dressing room, Eva. Someplace private."

"The hallway is just fine, thank you. I want everyone to hear what kind of person you are—a backstabber. Look at the damage you've done, and you've been here for like two weeks. I'm afraid to see what you'll do for an encore."

"I never meant for you to be fired," Selah stammered. "I . . . I was offering constructive criticism for the way the writers portrayed your character. I suggested they were writing you and Cane into a corner."

Somewhere comedian Jon Lovitz was saying, "Yeah, that's the ticket!"

Eva erupted into full-blown hysterics. Her eyes blazed and she wiped her nose with the back of her hand. "You think you can just come up in here from your little hick town, live in my mother's house, and ruin everything I've worked for?"

"Work" being a relative term.

Her voice was so high-pitched, Selah expected her dog to come bounding through the door. "You think you can mess with me? Think again, you . . . you . . ."

Eva clearly attended no ad-libbing courses in modeling school . . . er, acting school.

"You . . . you big, fat, stupid Scarlett O'Hara."

The fat comment would have hurt if it hadn't been so, well, so stupid. Selah put her hands on her hips. "Well, fiddle dee-dee!" she said in her most exaggerated Southern drawl, "you ain't nobody's pretty thing."

Eva's head jerked back as if Selah had smacked her. Selah suddenly got the feeling they were on the verge of a Krystal and Blake cat fight, a la *Dynasty*.

"If you had shown this much emotion in your acting instead of flaunting your assets and parading around in your underwear, I reckon you wouldn't be fixin' to get canned." Selah braced herself for Eva's retort.

Instead, Eva burst into tears and ran into her dressing room, slamming the door behind her.

"Wait! I'm sorry. I didn't mean to hurt you." Selah called after her, but Eva couldn't have heard her anyway over Eva's bawling.

Selah slapped her hand to her forehead. *Why didn't I turn the other cheek instead of being hateful and making things worse?*

Shayne Nixon sauntered out of his quarters. His smirk let her know he'd heard the whole argument. "Hello, Selah. Remind me not to get on your bad side."

He thrust a clawed hand into the air. "Me-ow!"

Selah had gone to college for years and managed a 3.98 GPA. She'd earned a master's degree and defended a thesis.

But today she felt like the dumbest person ever to walk the planet. How could she have thought she was up to this task? She looked heavenward for assistance.

It was time for a station break.

"Did you get any pictures of Eva rantin' and ravin'?"

"No. This is not a joke, Frankie." Selah tried to collect her thoughts as she collapsed on the leather sofa in Dori's bungalow. Faith climbed onto her chest and turned her back so that Selah could scratch it.

"Video?"

"Video just would have shed light on my own brand of bonkers."

"You could have put this girl on YouTube or on the blogs you're writing. Ooh. Wait. Twitter would be the best. The headline would be, 'Anorexic, chain-smoking soap star's public meltdown over firing.' It's better than watching the actual soap opera."

Her next blog did present a challenge. She had to portray the show in a favorable light and, as much as she might want to, she could not name names or detail her betrayal by a head writer or her near-catfight with Eva.

"You are not helping. I feel terrible about this." She was beginning to regret her decision to call her best friend for advice.

"She's a bully. Why do you care what she thinks about you?"

Twenty years ago, Frankie had asked her the same question when they were in middle school and it was now-nurse Katie doing the bullying. Selah shook off the memory as quickly as it had come to her.

"Don't you realize what I've done?"

"Exposed a phony? Stood up for yourself for once? Faced your fears head-on?"

"I got the daughter of the show's highest-paid star, who is also my landlord, fired. Then I insulted the girl's acting abilities."

"What acting abilities? You spoke the truth after she blessed you out. At least you didn't stand by mute and take it like you always do with your parents and everybody else back home. I think this new job is good for you."

"Frankie, I . . . Hold on, is that Momma I hear in the background?"

"She's holding me prisoner. Please come home. I'm in misery." Momma pleaded.

Selah's heart lurched.

"She keeps calling me Annie from that *Misery* movie." Frankie laughed. "Don't worry about her. You have proof of life now."

"She left me three voicemail messages today. I'm assuming they are about you."

"I am a wonderful nursemaid. Forget Melodrama Momma and focus on your drama. What are you going to do next?"

"I'm going to fix the damage I've caused. As for you, Nurse Ratched, go play nice with my mother."

Selah's plan to apologize to Eva faltered when the actress avoided her at every turn and did not answer her phone or the door to her dressing room.

Equally troubling was the "Guess Who?" gossip page in the latest *Soap!* magazine. The "Fortunate Fan" interview she and Julia had with the magazine turned out beautifully. However, a few pages over, a late-breaking rumor read: "A curvy newcomer on an East Coast soap has been busy. Setsiders say her entrance paved the way for the firing of another newbie and that she's been canoodling with the ousted ingénue's on-and off-screen love interest."

The setsider had to be Selah's uptight mentor, Mason, who'd witnessed her and Cane rolling around on the floor.

The bright side was that, while Eva called her fat to her face, the magazine article had labeled Selah as "curvy." A definite compliment.

Since she couldn't get Eva to listen to her, she proceeded to plan B.

Julia waved Selah into her office. "I can't talk long. I'm overseeing the blocking for a fight scene."

"An executive producer's work is never done."

"I am nothing without my cast and crew. By the way, I'm pleased you're part of my team." Julia flashed a reassuring smile. "The buzz you and the marketing department created in just a few days exceeded my expectations. And here Mason thought this SoaperFan experiment was going to be an epic fail."

Selah took a seat in front of Julia's desk. "Thank you. I'm honored to be here and to help you. I want this show to thrive."

"But . . . ?"

"But I think I may have overstepped. To be honest, I screwed up."

"Why is that?" Julia stood and leaned back against the

front of her desk. The wall behind her displayed a glass cabinet of golden Daytime Emmy statuettes.

"Eva told me y'all dropped her contract. She's right upset."

"That's the business. Sometimes a romance or a character catches fire and sometimes it fizzles. Soap actors never truly get comfortable in their dressing rooms."

"I understand, but I feel responsible. I didn't like her character with Cane's, but that didn't mean I wanted her to be let go."

"Your concern as a viewer about the pairing of Dean and Kelli merely validated what we already suspected—they had zero chemistry. Anyway, we've got too many characters on the canvas right now and needed to make some changes." Julia patted her shoulder. "I'm the EP. I make the decisions around here. You are not to blame in any way."

"There's nothing I can do to make up for getting this girl axed?"

Julia's face softened. "You're serious about this, aren't you?"

She turned and reached for the pen and paper on her desk. She scribbled something and handed Selah the note. "Take this to Eva. It's not a guarantee, just a lead on a role that may be a better fit for her."

Stripper? Call girl? Catty shrew? Selah imagined the roles that might be a better fit for Eva and her hateful attitude.

"You amaze me, Selah." Julia cocked her head. "Mason told me Eva started some rumors about you with one of the trade magazines. Yet you still want to help her?"

She smiled. "Revenge is for soap operas."

Chapter Fourteen

"Making things better for an hour (a day on The Young & The Restless) is evidently what I was meant to do."

(March 25, 2013, *Soap Opera Digest* interview with Jeanne Cooper on her nearly forty-year career in daytime)

CANE AMBLED TOWARD the set while he reviewed the day's script. He'd read the last paragraph four times and had no clue what it said.

It wasn't as if he was asking her on a date. He'd known her only a few weeks. She was part of the cast and crew now, so she was entitled to an invite.

Selah was . . . He couldn't put it into words. That would have been like trying to describe the tornado that blew through your house while you were sleeping. His life had been comfortable drudgery: Get up, go to work, work out, study lines, go to bed, repeat. But Selah and this illness had knocked him off balance.

He'd never been just friends with a woman other than Dori, and she was more of a boyhood crush. As for the rest of the women he'd known, he'd hurt every one. On second thought, maybe it would be better if he put some distance between himself and the SoaperFan.

As he walked by Julia's office, he heard Selah laugh and then footsteps. Selah, cell phone in hand, rushed out of the office door and plowed into him.

So much for keeping his distance.

He caught her by the shoulders. "Whoa. I got ya this time, twinkle toes."

Her eyes widened. "Sorry. I wasn't watching where I was going."

"With your track record, you should give up talking or texting while walking." He smiled down on her, enjoying the view as her full lips parted and lifted in return.

He released her and she leaned back against a wall. He stood within inches of her, resisting the urge to brush back the spiral curls that splayed across her cheeks.

"You've been a bad girl today," he teased. She was anything but bad. He bent toward her, breathing in the scent of strawberries, vanilla, and cotton candy all rolled into one.

"Why's that?" She wrapped her arms around her abdomen.

"Because you're coming out of the principal's office looking guilty."

"I heard that, mister." Julia hustled out of her office and swatted Cane on the behind with a rolled-up script. He yelped and sidestepped out of her way. She trotted down the hall, her high heels clacking with every step.

He jerked his thumb in the same direction. "I should get to the set before she gives me detention." *Hurry up already and ask her about tonight.*

"I read today's script. That fight is intense."

"You never know what will happen when Shayne's involved. He's like family to me, so—"

"So, you're going to knock him out and enjoy every minute of it."

"Exactly." Cane cleared his throat. "Since you're part of this happy, dysfunctional family now, come join us tonight. A few of the cast and crew, Shayne and Eva included, are hitting the hotel skybar after the cabaret benefit."

Her mouth twisted. No woman had ever hesitated when he'd asked for something.

"That's mighty sweet of y'all to include me, but I wouldn't know how to act in a bar."

He cocked his head. "Are you, sweet Southern belle, telling me you're afraid you might lose control and dance on the tables? Or maybe something more sinister?"

Her cheeks flamed. "That's not what I meant. I'm just not . . ."

And there it was. The Ashton charm that got women so flustered. Cane licked his lips. *I've still got it.*

"We're just going out to eat." He lifted an eyebrow. "Sometimes it's the quiet ones you have to worry about."

Selah rolled her eyes and shook her head. Clearly, he was enjoying himself at her expense.

"I need to check my jam-packed social calendar. You'll have to stay tuned, Shirtless Wonder."

He caressed his chest in a sexy, self-deprecating way.

His brown eyes and long eyelashes were like a chocolate fountain she could dive into. The easy smile that had kept women tuned in to *Winds of Change* for years flashed a warning in her soul.

"You are crazier than a June bug in May."

"Does everybody talk like you where you come from? I love it," Cane said.

The ever-glib Mason interrupted. "They're probably worse. Like them Duke boys screaming 'Yee Haw!' from the General Lee."

He heaved a stack of papers into Selah's arms. "I've got an errand for you, if you can drag yourself away from Boy Wonder."

"I prefer Shirtless Wonder." Cane slapped Mason so hard on the back that the scribe coughed. "Don't you ever leave the studio?"

With a wave, Cane said, "Good luck, SoaperFan. You'll need it."

She skipped after Mason but glanced over her shoulder.

"See ya tonight," she summoned her deepest Southern drawl, "if the good Lord's willin' and the creek don't rise."

The echo of Cane's laughter followed her down the hall. It was the same masculine, slightly goofy laugh she'd heard when he knocked her off her feet on her first day at the studio.

I'm loopy over this guy, and I barely know him. Lord, guard my heart.

Maybe you need to let someone into your heart for once. The soft voice came like the wind touching the corners of her mind. She felt raw and exposed, but she would try.

Chapter Fifteen

"When you're in an unfamiliar environment or situation—a new job, home, or city—there's nothing more reassuring than turning on the television (soaps) and being visited by your 'old friends.'"

As My World Still Turns by Eileen Fulton,
who played Lisa on *As the World Turns*
for fifty years

"EXCUSE ME."

"Oops. Sorry."

"If I could just squeeze through here. Thank you."

"Pardon me, please. Excuse me."

Selah felt as if she was line dancing as she sidestepped and pivoted her way through the crush of soap fans at a theater near Times Square. The soaps were a shrinking industry, but the fans remained legion and loyal.

She giggled, squelching the teen-girl-spots-teen-heartthrob squeal that bubbled up in her throat when she flipped through the event's program and saw the names of the soap stars in attendance from *Winds of Change, The Young and the Restless,* and four recently-cancelled soaps. Most of them were already in the VIP section, where Selah would be seated. If only Frankie were here to share in this feast for the eyes.

Selah noticed Eva standing a few rows over and waved. Eva looked straight at her and turned her head.

"Don't mind Eva. She doesn't speak to anybody in the cast but the guys." Sophia, one of the show's teen beauties, wrapped her arms around Selah from behind and squeezed.

"This must be how the Pillsbury Doughboy feels." Selah twisted to face her and received another hug from the front.

She could barely see the girl's blue eyes under long, blonde bangs that reminded her of Frankie. Why hadn't her best friend come when she texted and invited her for the weekend? Aunt Ruby could take care of Momma for a few days.

"You are so cute, SoaperFan." Sophia took her cell from her jeans pocket and started typing. "Hold on. I have to tweet what you said."

The flash from the phone's camera momentarily blinded her in the darkened room. "That photo will be lovely."

"Not so much, but it sure is funny." Sophia snickered. "Come, sit with me. When you want to take a break, there's a green room in the back hallway where you can chill and get refreshments."

She led her to the front row and Selah sat beside her. Selah's eyes grew misty when the sweet young actress introduced her to her circle of friends. At least not every-one on the show thought Selah was a backstabber. Only Eva, Shayne, and Mason.

If the gossip was true, Sophia's character would fall vic-tim to SORAS, Soap Opera Rapid-Aging Syndrome, and this fourteen-year-old cutie would soon be replaced by a twenty-eight-year-old who looked twenty. Selah prayed it wasn't true.

Deafening screams filled the air as the Five Hot Hunks of Daytime, including Shayne and Cane, sauntered onto the stage and pulled up barstools for a Q&A with the fans. Cane spotted Sophia and Selah and winked. The Incredible Hulk came to mind at the sight of his muscles straining against the tight green t-shirt he'd thrown together with jeans and cowboy boots.

A pre-teen giggled and took a microphone to ask the first question. "I just want to say, Shayne, that my mom and grandma and me have been watching you on this show for years and years and we just really love you."

A shadow darkened Shayne's features at the suggestion that he was old enough to excite someone's grandma.

He recovered with a huge, toothy grin and an "I love you too. What's your question, sweetheart?"

The girl brightened. "Um, is it weird, like, having to kiss really young actresses like Carly and Eva?"

Out of the mouths of babes.

Shayne twitched and coughed. "It's one big happy fam-ily around *Winds of Change*, so it's like kissing a little sister. Except not creepy."

The audience laughed, except for Cane, who narrowed his eyes at Shayne.

The next fan, a larger lady about eighty years old, leaned on her cane while she huffed into the microphone. "My name is Ada. Cane Ashton? Cane, can you hear me? My docta says I have to stop watching you on *Winds of Change* because you're giving this old lady heart palpitations."

Cane slid off the stage and jogged down the aisle. He took the microphone from her hands and said huskily, "Somebody grab the defibrillator."

Then, he gently hugged her and moved to kiss her cheek, but Ada turned her head and planted one on his lips. The look on his face was priceless. Selah applauded and hooted along with the crowd.

Most of the questions that followed were insightful, although there was the inevitable "boxers or briefs" inquiry that made her groan. To her surprise, Selah had a blast—that is, until the final question of the night. "Cane, is it true you're dating that SoaperFan chick in real life?"

Selah's mouth went dry and her cheeks seared like Momma's pancakes dropped on a too-hot griddle.

Cane shaded his eyes with his hand as he pretended to peer out into the audience. "Ada, is that you again? I thought you and me were going steady."

The audience tittered and Ada, now seated, waved her cane in the air.

"Isn't the SoaperFan super?" Cane asked to a smattering of applause and a frown from Shayne. "The concept shows how innovative our producers and writers can be. This has been a hugely successful experiment. If you read her blogs, it's clear that she offers fresh insight into the show, what fans believe is wrong with soaps in general, and what's right in this industry."

Sophia patted Selah's leg and beamed. Selah fanned herself with the paper program.

"So, in answer to your question," he said diplomatically, "any relationship with the SoaperFan is strictly professional."

Cane's words and smile were kind, but they felt like a knife twisting in Selah's gut. What did she expect? She could kick herself for allowing this crush to fester. Just because they'd shared a tiny bathroom while he was having his mental breakdown did not mean he would ever see her as more than a friend.

Her mind drifted as the hunks left the stage and she listened to the harmonies of the Divas of Daytime and a Broadway tribute. She needed to e-mail a client about the social widgets on his business website, but couldn't use her phone while she sat on the front row.

As the show wound down, she slipped out of her seat and headed for the green room. Surely they wouldn't paint a modern theater in an avocado green like her bathroom at home.

She found a room with soft lighting and a long table of water bottles and snacks. An actor and actress from *The Bold and the Beautiful* were chatting on one of two oversized couches. She blanked on their names. Just another beautiful couple flaunting well-controlled hair, bright white teeth, and tanned skin with no visible fat or flaws.

"Excuse me. Where is the green room?"

They exchanged looks. "You're standing in it," the actress said.

"But it's blue."

No response.

"The walls are blue, not green."

"You're not from around here, are you?" The actress pointed her finger at Selah. "You're that country girl from *Winds of Change*."

"Yes, I am, thank y'all kindly." If she wanted country, Selah could do country.

"I'll be going now, out of this blue, er, green room." She grabbed a bottle of Evian water. "These are free, right? Of course they're free. This is Hollywood, or the NYC version. Bye now."

They watched her with raised eyebrows and open mouths. She backed out the door, leaving them with a comical story to tell their friends.

She made her way through the darkened hallway. This was not the way she had come in. She passed an office where a few people moved around. People who looked like . . . Shayne Nixon locked in a kiss with the younger costar, Carly, who played his sister.

So much for his on-screen family relationships not being creepy. She briefly considered taking Frankie's advice and using her cell phone to videotape their make-out session and upload it, but thought better of it and turned away. She had prayed for excitement in her life, and God had delivered.

When she returned to the seating area, the show had ended, and fans were mingling with the actors who stayed behind to take pictures and sign autographs. Warm air grazed the back of her neck and caused the hair on her arms to stand on end. Shayne planted himself shoulder-to-shoulder with her, with his hand on her mid-back. He must have seen her in the hallway and followed her out.

He crooked the corner of his mouth into the sly smirk he'd patented on the show. "You look a little pale, honey child. Aren't you having a good time?"

He crushed her to his side in a one-armed hug. The smell of beer, Binaca, and musk cologne assaulted her nose and flipped her stomach. She turned her face away from his and began to breathe through her mouth.

"Cane sure is." Shayne flicked his free hand toward the stage area, where Cane was talking to a group of slender, attractive women.

"Let go of me." Selah broke free and backed away from him. His eyes shone from too much free booze. Or was it a side effect of his rumored prescription-drug habit?

Shayne kept talking. "Soap actors are a lot like politicians, don't you think? Instead of shaking hands and kissing babies, we sign autographs and press the flesh . . . literally."

"What is that supposed to mean?" She hugged herself. *Is he flirting with me or messing with me?*

"Look at him, simple Selah. Cane is The Man! He always has a little action going on, if you know what I mean." Like a heat-seeking missile, Shayne honed in on her insecurities. "Just ask Eva."

"What about her?"

He chuckled and reached out to caress her shoulder. "Don't worry about Cane's infamous exploits. Just concentrate on us, baby."

"I'm not your baby or your sweetheart," she choked out.

Her new friend, Cane, had engaged in "exploits" with her new enemy, Eva. Eva and Cane together. The air went out of the room. The chatter grew tinny and distorted as if she was in a house of mirrors, not knowing what was real or who to trust.

"Are you ill, baby?"

"Something like that." She pushed her way out through the crowd and onto the street, away from Shayne, away from Eva—and away from Cane. *I can't do this anymore. I might not know exactly who I am, but this isn't it.*

The lights of Times Square had seemed welcoming and exhilarating when she saw them for the first time with Frankie during the fan club weekend. Now, standing alone in the gritty air, amidst honking taxicabs and crowds of people shouting in strange languages, she felt small and inconsequential under the glare. How could she have thought she would make it here, that she would belong?

Maybe it was time to give up and go home to her own bed, friends, parents, and diner. She wasn't even sure she could count on those things to be the same. When she needed Frankie most, why had she avoided her invitations to come to New York? Faith was a good listener, but Selah's best friend was the only person who could put chaos into perspective. When Selah stepped off the curb at the next pedestrian crossing, she heard a shout to her left and found herself eye-to-eye with a street vendor. She tried to scramble out of his way but caught her foot in the wheel of his cart.

He cursed with an accented word that she assumed was "witch." "Watch what you are doing! Stupid tourist."

Her eyes pricked with tears. "I'm very sorry."

"That you are. You are very sorry," he hollered and pushed the cart around the corner.

A wave of indignation washed over her. "I didn't do anything to you," she shouted back, but it was too late. The angry man selling "I heart New York" t-shirts was gone.

The vendor was so hate-filled, he would likely have another tantrum and suffer a heart attack or stroke, but all she could think about were his words—how sorry she was.

Just this morning, I asked You to build up my self-confidence and faith, and this is the answer I get? I feel more wretched than ever. Will I ever do anything right?

Chapter Sixteen

SELAH STUMBLED ALONG with a crush of Japanese tourists and the drumming of a steel band until she reached a rolling hotel marquis. Maybe she could rest her feet in the lobby before catching a taxi back to Dori's cottage. How did soap actresses survive in stilettos? She would ask Eva—if Eva was speaking to her.

Selah reached for the revolving door and the wind helped push her into the bustling lobby. Suddenly, it hit her. This was the hotel where Cane and the *Winds of Change* cast planned to meet in the skybar after the show.

Taunting words from the vendor and Shayne continued to mock her. There was no use in joining the group. Selah wasn't in their class. Cane didn't care about her. She was a novelty, a country bumpkin in a big city of sophisticated actors. Like the Beverly Hillbillies, a Connecticut Yankee in King Arthur's Court, a little fish in a big, shark-filled pond.

She shook her head to dislodge the runaway negative thoughts. "You're gonna keep testing me on this faith thing, aren't You, Lord?" She took a deep breath and headed for the hotel elevators.

On the ride up, her phone vibrated. A missed call from Dori, her absentee landlord. Dread ran icy cold through her veins as she listened to Dori's voicemail:

"Buongiorno, Selah. I'm calling to talk about my daughter and about your living situation. Ring me up soon. Ciao."

Make that her soon-to-be ex-landlord whose daughter was fired because of her.

The elevator door opened into a revolving restaurant and bar draped in amber shadows. She squinted through the grit in her eyes, and the first person she saw was Eva smiling across a small table at Cane. Shayne was right about them.

A waiter knocked Selah in the arm with a tray, and she stumbled, wishing death and destruction upon her high heels. With all the commotion, Eva spotted her and crooked her finger for Selah to join them. That couldn't be good. The spaghetti straps on Eva's low-cut black dress hung limp against her slender arms. Selah refrained from waving back with bat-winged arms.

Cane looked up and smiled. Was that relief brimming from his warm, brown eyes? Shayne, sitting on the opposite side of Cane, flashed his smirk. Her favorite video gamers sat at an adjoining table. They gave her a high-five when she walked by.

"I want a rematch. You're going down this time, boys."

"Well, if it isn't our very own backwoods black widow!" Eva said too loudly, raising an empty martini glass.

At least her insult skills were improving. "I see you've been practicing your sweet talk."

The actress lay hold of Cane's arm, marking her territory. Cane shook free of her and stood.

"I can hang out with the guys if there's not enough room," Selah said.

"By all means, come take a load off," Eva said. "Take our chairs and table. You've taken everything else."

"You're being ridiculous." Cane's voice was low and measured. "Our jobs were in jeopardy and you and I were on our way out long before Selah arrived, and you know it."

Eva's face fell at his reprimand. Selah felt a stab of pity for her.

"You're right." Shayne slapped his flat palm on the table, rattling the glasses and silverware. "We shouldn't be mad at simple Selah. She's here to save the show by getting rid of some deadweight."

Eva looked pointedly at her. "The only weight I see is—"

Selah gasped, holding out her arms and looking down at her body. "What are you saying? Am I overweight? Are you telling me that I am fat?"

Eva and Shayne sat open-mouthed.

"Golly, thank you, thank you so much. You've changed my life. I would never have known the truth if you and Shayne hadn't rubbed my nose in it."

Cane, eyes twinkling, covered his mouth with his hand.

Selah's arms were shaking when she put them down. That felt awful good.

"Now that my intervention's over, Eva, I want to speak with you privately."

"I'm not doing anything with you. You're insane." The actress huffed but eyed her with curiosity.

Selah stalked to the enormous glass windows surrounding the restaurant, knowing instinctively that Eva would follow.

"Wow . . ." Selah took in the illuminated masterpiece that was New York City after dark. It was like looking out from the inside of an aquarium.

"If you're planning to throw me out that window, you'll never get away with it." Eva swayed beside her, arms crossed at her chest.

"I wanted to give you this." Selah handed her Julia's note that recommended Eva to a casting director.

"What is it?"

"A peace offering. An apology. A job opportunity. I hope you'll know what to do with it."

Eva's eyes widened as she read the note, but she covered her excitement by whipping out her compact and checking her makeup. She looked back at Cane, who strode toward them, oblivious to the women ogling him.

"Everything resolved here?" he asked.

Now that she had repaid Eva, how could she make it up to him for putting his job in jeopardy?

"I hope so." She smiled at Eva, who turned away. She must have become an actress just to please her mother. Selah knew all about trying to please your parents.

"Let's get out of here." Cane took Selah's arm and nudged her toward the door.

"But we just got here," Eva said, pouting.

"Eva," Selah called over her shoulder in one last attempt to make peace, "Get in touch with your mom. I bet she misses you."

When Cane and Selah were back on the sidewalk in front of the hotel, he let out a low whistle. "You warned me that you wouldn't know how to act in a bar, but I had no idea the trouble you could cause."

She elbowed him. "I was just getting started before Captain Caveman showed up and dragged me away from my BFFs, Eva and Shayne."

He chuckled. "All I wanted was some fresh air. Now, tell me where you ran off to after the show." He inhaled and exhaled deeply.

"I wanted some fresh air."

They strolled side by side down Broadway, although she was tempted to throw herself down on the benches they passed and never move her swollen feet again. Those shoes were going into the fireplace at the end of the night.

"What a city," Cane remarked. "It's different than Virginia, right?"

"How did you know that's where I'm from?"

"The accent . . . and the grapevine."

"New York has a few million more cars, people, buildings, and irate street vendors, but Virginia has more green grass and livestock."

"I saw a potbellied pig on Madison Avenue last week."

Selah laughed and took in a big gulp of ice-cold wind. She turned up the collar of her jacket, wishing she had remembered to bring her hat, gloves, and cozy fireplace. Spring was certainly taking its sweet time.

"You seem like you're adjusting. I was overwhelmed by it all when I came from Minnesota."

If he only knew how close she'd come, twenty minutes before, to flying home to Virginia and never looking back.

"So you went from Texas to Minnesota to New York? You have no accent and you root for the Packers."

"You betcha!" he teased. "My agent made me take voice lessons to get rid of the accent, something I thought was incredibly vain at the time. I also had a football-crazed mother. No other team was allowed in our household but the Packers."

"Smart woman." She noticed that his face had hardened at the mention of his family.

She looked away from him briefly to see a rainbow-colored blur hurtling toward them. Her ears filled with the sounds of laughter and bike horns, then they were suddenly surrounded by a large group of clowns. Where had they come from?

Cane grabbed her hand and steadied her as they passed. A wave of heat shot from her hand through her body. He didn't seem bothered that his face hovered within inches of hers, invading her personal space. The cast and crew—except Eva—were so huggy, shattering her pre-conceived notions about stand-offish New Yorkers. Maybe it was all the kissing scenes or the love scenes that made them so comfortable with each other and with themselves.

When the madcap group had passed, she reluctantly let go of his hand. "Clowns, pigs, soap opera actors—you never know what you'll get in New York City."

"Case in point." Cane motioned toward a hole-in-the-wall called PieParazzi.

"I'm intrigued, but isn't it closing time?"

"The owner will make an exception." Cane opened the door for her, and she stepped up to an old-fashioned lunch counter.

"We're closed," someone shouted and an attractive man emerged from the kitchen.

He grinned broadly and wiped his hands on his apron. "I was mistaken. We have reopened."

She thought of her father standing in front of the chrome counter of Good Company, wiping his hands on a white apron that reached his knees and read, "Kiss Me, I'm Hillbilly."

"Well, Mr. Hollywood, finally you bring me a beautiful woman from your show." The man took Selah's hands in his and turned his back to Cane. "I am Julio. Just one name. Like Madonna."

She returned her host's smile. "I'm Selah Morgan, a friend of Mr. Hollywood. Or, as I like to call him, Shirtless Wonder."

"Welcome then, lovely Selah, to my humble establishment. I will make something special for you, and when you tire of him, I will throw him out, sì?"

Cane pushed in Selah's high-top chair. "It's a good thing I like the food here, because the service is sorely lacking."

Julio shouted in his ear, "Two cheeseburger platters!" and headed back to the kitchen.

"I can't believe you brought me to a diner."

"Are you vegan? We can go somewhere else."

Selah shook her head.

"How about vegetarian? Gluten-free? Lactose intolerant? Peanut allergic? Shellfish allergic?"

"Nope. Food and I get along just fine." A little too well.

"Whew. You're the first woman I've eaten with that wasn't one of those."

"It's perfect." When the cheeseburgers arrived, they dripped with Velveeta and grease, just like home.

As they ate, Selah confessed, "I want you to know that, when I did a phone interview for *Soap!*, the magazine asked me if you and I were an item. Another magazine insinuated it as well, but I had nothing to do with the rumors."

Cane shrugged. "The past ten years, they've had me dating lots of women, mostly co-stars, sometimes simultaneously. The people who watch us fall in love on the show want us to fall in love in real life too."

"Like Eva?"

"What about Eva?"

"She has serious feelings for you."

"We went out once," Cane said matter-of-factly and ran a French fry through a mountain of ketchup.

"What happened?"

"I like Eva, but she's a chain smoker and too clingy and insecure."

Too insecure? I might be in trouble.

As they finished their meals, he said, "You're eyeballing that wall of pies. Find one you like?"

"It reminds me of my parents' diner, Good Company, and my mother's chocolate treasure pie."

"And here I thought it was *my* good company putting that big smile on your face."

Julio didn't wait to ask what they wanted, bringing them slices of a chocolate Oreo pie. It was so rich, Selah could manage only a few bites.

"I have to take some pictures of this place." She pushed away from the table, and Cane stood up to pull out her chair. "May I, Julio? I want to show Momma her big-city competition."

Julio mugged for the camera, displaying a mouthful of brilliant white teeth and one gold one against his tan skin.

Cane frowned and cocked his head. "Do you think it's safe for you to operate a camera, Selah?"

"I can operate a—" Her mouth dropped open. She pointed at him. "You sneak! You remember me from the fan club luncheon. All this time I've been at *Winds of Change,* and you've pretended as if you'd never seen me before."

"I am an actor, after all." He shielded his face with his hands, palms out. "How could I forget you? I was afraid you were going to beat me to death with that camera!"

Cane was breathless with laughter while he reenacted her mini-meltdown for Julio.

"Did you know that when you left our autograph table, you accidentally hit Eva in the back of the head with your purse? That . . . was . . . p-priceless."

Her hands flew to her mouth. "I didn't know I did that. No wonder she hates me."

"And then," he huffed and swallowed, "and then, I go to leave and Selah and this crazy blonde are out in the hallway, screaming and hugging and jumping up and down. And—"

"I know two tired wittle boys who need to get in their jammies and get to bed before they crack up." This time, Selah held her camera steady and started videotaping two grown men reduced to snorting laughter.

"I cannot believe you knew this whole time and didn't say anything, Cane." She pretended to be mad and hurt but was having a hard time controlling her laughter.

"I didn't want to embarrass you."

"This laugh-fest with Julio isn't embarrassing?"

"You are among friends here, Belleza."

"Don't worry, Julio." She patted her camera. "I have this videotape of you two fools to console myself with. Or to put on my blog, Twitter, Facebook and, of course, my YouTube channel."

"You wouldn't." Cane held out his hand for the camera, but she shook it overhead.

"I bet *Soap!* will especially like the part where you snort and your eyes bug out. Whatcha think?"

He grabbed the camera with one hand and wrapped the other arm around her waist to steady himself. Their faces were so close, she could feel his breath against her skin.

"You have something on your face," he whispered. "Looks like chocolate."

"Where?" She reached for her face.

He dragged his thumb lazily across her cheek. "Right there," he murmured and held her gaze.

He was one sly dog.

"I know this storyline. It's the one where the hot hunk of daytime pretends to rub something off a girl's cheek."

"Oh, really? What happens next, SoaperFan?"

"Next, the hot hunk of daytime leans in close."

He leaned in. "Then what?"

She batted her eyelashes. "Then the plucky stalker fan rescues her camera and escapes unharmed." She grabbed her camera and ran for cover behind Julio.

"You lose, my friend. The beautiful lady chooses me."

Julio turned and pressed a piece of paper into her hand. "For your mama."

It was his outrageously sinful pie recipe. She smiled and patted her stomach, which fluttered with all manner of sweet things, her faith in the people of New York City restored.

Chapter Seventeen

THE NEXT MORNING, Selah came face-to-face with another New Yorker. She peered through the peephole of the bungalow door to see a city delivery driver knocking at the door. His car and his jacket said: "Flower Heaven. Call for deliverance."

She hesitated when she noticed the tattoos on his neck. Confident in her mace and the latched security chain, she opened the door a crack.

"Got some flowers here for a Selah Morgan."

Suddenly, Faith growled and barked so loudly, Selah's eyes vibrated. The deliveryman plunked the bouquet of flowers down on the doorstep and ran back to his car.

Selah scooped up Faith and unlatched the door. "Wait. I'll get you a tip."

Faith continued to growl. The dog who had been paralyzed with fear at the sight of a kitten now looked ready to take on the six-foot driver.

"Dat's okay. No tip today. Little dog make big bite."

She shrugged and took the flowers inside. "Can't judge a book by its cover, can you, girl?"

Faith wagged her curly tail. Selah set her on the floor and gave her a treat for successfully defending the bungalow.

Frankie must have sent them. Momma would never give such an extravagant gift.

Selah scanned the card, but could barely keep her eyes open after spending most of the night awake, reliving her dinner with Cane. Rubbing the sleep out of her eyes, she read the card again.

"Thanks for saving me from the men in white coats and from Eva and Shayne, who can be scary too. Cane."

She inhaled and the scent of roses filled her with the urge to write his name in hearts all over her notebook. Since she wasn't twelve and didn't have a Smurf or Strawberry Shortcake notebook or Trapper Keeper handy, she'd have to settle the flutter in her belly with chocolate. What did other grownups do to calm these kinds of feelings?

Knowing she shouldn't, she threw open a kitchen cabinet and pulled out a box of bonbons. She was going to owe Dori a case of them. Selah popped a piece of chocolate in her mouth and let it melt on her tongue. It tasted creamy and rich, but her pulse still raced like the fat that sped toward her arteries.

She had heard people say that, in times of fear, their past life flashed before their eyes. But her future—the life of her dreams—now flashed before her eyes: the ring, the wedding dress, the kiss—

Whoa! Where had that come from? The flowers were only a token of friendship. He would never see her as more than a friend. If a man had romance on his mind, he sent red roses, not innocent white daisies and lavender roses.

If she ran into him today, she would calmly thank him for the flowers. She couldn't show her hand and go all giddy on him. Dad had taught her the power of a poker face. It was better that she keep her heart the way it was before she arrived in New York—hermetically sealed.

She gaped at the box on the counter. Had she eaten five pieces already? Determined to get some distance from the chocolates, she grabbed Faith's leash and they headed for the studio.

Cane turned up his overcoat collar and hefted a sign that read, "Keep Our Soaps Alive!" As he plodded along a picket line in front of the studio, he tried to ignore the protests of his joints. It was thirty degrees, but the high humidity and wind made it feel like minus ten.

His doctor said this disease was more common among people living at cold northern latitudes or of northern European ancestry. He frowned up at the dark clouds strangling a sliver of sunlight. Maybe those factors had played into it, but speculation was pointless. He had it and he would have to deal with it.

He caught sight of Selah striding toward him. The oddball dog she was walking had a face like a miniature Chewbacca from Star Wars.

Her smile widened as she got closer. The sunshine broke through and won the battle against the storm clouds.

"What a pleasant surprise to see you." She hugged him and then jumped back as if she'd touched a hot stove. "Faith and I were out for a walk. I forgot about the rally."

"You're just in time." Cane grabbed a sign that said "SOS Soaps!" and handed it to her. He rubbed the furball behind its ears, and it licked his hand. The three of them joined the line of fans challenging the imminent cancellation of *Winds of Change*.

"Thank you for the flowers. They were so stunning, they outshone the vase of Dori's I transferred them to, probably something from the Ming Dynasty."

"I knew you would enjoy them, SoaperFan." He ruffled her hair with his free hand, his fingers tangling in the soft curls. The only thing that felt more natural in his hands was a football.

"Tsk. You actors and your egos."

She patted her hair back down. It must have been better than a ski cap at keeping her head warm in the April chill.

He raised his cell phone and took a picture of himself holding the sign.

"Is that for your diary, Shirtless Wonder?"

"Twitter. My fans can't get enough of me."

"That so?" She raised her eyebrows. He pulled her to his side, picked up the dog, and turned the camera on the three of them. She squirmed out of his grasp and took the dog.

"The flowers reminded me of the color of your eyes and all the times you roll them at me." He brushed away a few rogue curls, then he ran his thumb down her temple and dimpled cheek and rested it on her chin.

Protestors began chanting and broke the moment. He unbuttoned his coat. He was plenty warm now. He also took off his scarf and draped it around her neck. "Your cheeks were frozen."

Her eyes darted away from his. "Thanks. Are you working today?"

He could barely hear her shouting above the crowd.

"I didn't have a call time until late afternoon, so I came early to show my support. I've been here for half an hour, and I've already got icicles on my nose. The protestors have been here for three hours."

As they walked side by side, Selah sneaked a glance at his profile. He had such a kind face. Not just his obvious hotness, but something deeper.

What if she was misreading his signals? He was a master at flirting. Maybe Selah's adulation stroked his ego. Maybe God had put her on the soap to be a witness to him and Eva, not to be his real-life love interest.

Or maybe it was a fat fetish. She had seen it on a talk show—guys who liked only large women. Otherwise, why would he want a friendship with someone who was not a size six or a size eight or a size ten?

She imagined the headlines: "Are superstud and supersized SoaperFan dating?"

Forgive me, Jesus. This is the part where You tell me that life is more than the body and that my body is a temple, which is not the way I've been treating it. How am I ever going to shake that monkey off my back, that gorilla ravenous for peanut butter pie, bonbons, chocolate shakes, and Mountain Dew?

"Hey, SoaperFan!" He nudged her shoulder with his elbow. "What in the world are you thinking about so seriously?"

"Oh, just monkeys, temples, and milkshakes."

He blinked. "You are . . . I have never met anyone quite like you, Selah Morgan."

"Don't Southern girls say the darnedest things?"

Her phone vibrated in her jeans pocket. Faith woofed. Cane took the leash while Selah answered the call.

"Mason, hi. No, I wasn't aware that your assistant quit after six months. I can't imagine why she would want to leave."

It was Cane's turn to roll his eyes.

"Of course, I'll come make your copies and coffee for no pay. Your demands are my priority."

She held the phone away from her face and glared at it. "He just hung up. No goodbye. No thank you."

"No surprise. Although it was a surprise that his assistant worked for the jerk this long."

A camera truck rolled up. Selah groaned, imagining how her parka and sweatpants would translate to TV. "Here comes the media. I should go."

"Don't run off to Mason just yet." Cane rubbed his hands together and looked at her sideways. "I have an idea. It's time for lunch."

He punched a fist in the air and hollered, "Hey, everybody, how about some hot pizza?"

The protestors cheered.

"I know you love the fans, but are you taking this entire crowd to Pizza Hut?"

"Nope. I've got delivery on speed dial," he said as he launched his cell phone. "I'd like to order a hundred pizzas. Uh-huh. The name?"

He smiled down at her. "Mason. That's right. Mason Lord. L-o-r-d."

She bounced up and down on the balls of her feet. Faith danced on her hind legs and stretched to put her paw against Selah's knee. "He is going to explode!"

Cane cupped his hand over the microphone. "That's the beauty of it. It'll blow over once he realizes how good he looks in the press. What's the worst he can do, write a horrible, painful death for my character?"

"Mason Lord here," he spoke gruffly into the phone. "I'm still holding. Don't forget my senior-citizen discount."

Chapter Eighteen

A FEW DAYS AFTER the rally, Cane felt more like a senior citizen than the "Hot Hunk of Daytime." He gritted his teeth as another wave of pain and dizziness assaulted him. He watched the clock tick down inside Radio City Music Hall, his head throbbing in time with every movement of the second hand.

At least he wouldn't have to fly in this condition. The network had decided to bring the Daytime Emmy Awards home to New York after previous broadcasts from Vegas and Beverly Hills.

"Congrats on your nomination." A voice floated through the haze in his pulsating head.

"Thanks, Eva." He squinted, trying to focus on her face.

His co-star apparently took his gravelly whisper as a sexy come-on, because she leaned in, stroking her hand across his Hugo Boss lapel and batting false eyelashes that looked like two spiders stretching their legs.

Suddenly, alarms sounded and an announcer warned the audience members to take their seats for the show. A spotlight flashed across Cane's face. As always since the accident, the harsh light morphed into headlights. Then his mother, father, and brother's faces appeared. The pain seized him again like three baseball bats hitting his head out of the park.

"Cane? Are you listening to me? Cane?"

It's all about Eva. Still disoriented from the lights, he pushed her out of the way and mumbled, "Sorry," as he stumbled down the aisle.

"You can't leave now." The pout in Eva's voice set him more on edge. "The show's getting ready to start. I want you to sit beside me."

He nodded at the volunteer seat-filler, who had temporarily taken Cane's chair to help the audience look like a sold-out crowd to the viewers at home.

It was better that Selah hadn't come. He would've gotten a kick out of her offbeat first impressions of the show, but he didn't want her to see him like this.

The bathroom was empty when he staggered in, and for that he gave silent thanks. Cane steadied himself against a marble sink and splashed cold water on his face. He tried that deep breathing, relaxation stuff, more acting-class mumbo-jumbo, but all he could think about was the throbbing, boring, searing pain. It occurred to him to ask God for help, but that would have been as futile as his woo-woo acting exercises.

Finally, he scooped up a handful of water and gulped down the migraine pills his doctor had prescribed. This was no migraine, but he needed relief and couldn't take the narcotic pain meds anymore. He couldn't risk it.

Cane turned to see an usher staring at him. *Great, this guy probably has his cell phone camcorder rolling. The video of me popping pills will soon be on YouTube. Then people will start asking questions about my past.* They could never know about his past.

He stood to his full height of 6'1" and squared muscled shoulders that once blocked running backs on the football field. He narrowed his eyes at the gawker, who quickly shuffled out.

Cane didn't know how long he stood there, leaning against the sink and staring at his reflection in the mirror. Unfortunately, his pounding head was still attached, but at least he didn't look like death warmed over. He was camera-ready, every hair in place. His eyes weren't bloodshot or puffy, but they were drawn with emotion his acting skills could not erase.

He sighed raggedly and gathered himself together for the show. Feeling less pain but more grogginess, he took a wrong turn and ended up in the lobby. When he spotted Selah, the fog hovering over his mind lifted as if his brain had taken a caffeine shower at Starbucks. He moved closer, observing her from behind as she watched a television monitor and talked on her cell.

"Eat an extra wonton for me," she was saying. "There's a lot of yummy Chinese food here, but I must confess that I miss Willie's. Yes, I miss you, too, Frankie. Listen, Cane's category is coming up next. I need to get inside."

"There you are, SoaperFan." He touched her elbow.

Selah gasped and turned to face him.

Frankie's voice rose. "Is that him? Put the speakerphone on so I can listen to his sexy voice."

"I can hear you," he chuckled. "She had you on speaker already."

"Oh, right. Hi, Dean. I mean, Cane. Awkward," Frankie said and disconnected.

"My best friend," Selah said.

"I figured. I'm more interested in you. You dress up nice." He took Selah's hand and twirled her around. She was a goddess in a Grecian one-shoulder dress in deep purple. "Nice and hot."

Her blush exploded like a supernova against the pitch-black curls encircled by gold bands and swept loosely to one side.

Dorian Forrester's voice brought him back down to planet Earth. "From *The Winds of Change*, Cane Ashton and Shayne Nixon."

"You're missing your award." Selah gripped his hand and her wide eyes shifted from Cane toward the monitor. He swallowed and leaned against her, feeling at once as if he could collapse or throw up. Her hand was a lifeline.

The smiling faces of Shayne and the other hopeful nominees were boxed in a row like the *Brady Bunch*. Months before, when Cane had received the phone call informing him of his Emmy nomination, all he could think about was winning and the accompanying perks—more exposure, a better contract, and respect from his peers. It was his shot at redemption. But now he struggled to muster up any feeling for it.

"I'm not going to win."

"Hush yo' mouth."

He didn't deserve the nomination. He had coasted along for years on his looks and body, never bothering to continue his acting classes, perform live theater, or audition for other roles, all the things he needed to hone his acting chops.

"And the winner is . . . Oh, my. It's a tie! That means

we have two winners!" The audience murmured as if that was a revelation. "The judges have picked two nominees to take home the Emmy for Best Supporting Actor."

"You're better than the Supporting Actor category, Cane," Selah chided.

"And the winners are . . ." Another dramatic pause.

Dorian's face fell as she read, "From *The Young and The Restless* and *General Hospital*—"

"You gotta be kiddin' me!" Selah released his hand from her death grip and yelled at the screen like a football fan protesting a penalty on a touchdown.

Shayne clapped gamely, but his strained smile said, "Wow. A tie. How wonderful that I lost to not just one, but *two* other actors."

Shayne's contorted, "not impressed" face made Cane snort. Or maybe it was the medicine making him dopey. The vibration in his shoulders grew into shaking and his snort exploded in a belly laugh. Selah's raised eyebrows made him laugh harder. When he wheezed and loosened the bowtie on his tux, she put her hand over her mouth. He clutched his side with one hand and wiped the moisture from his eyes with the other.

"I was about to tell you how sorry I was and offer a shoulder to cry on, but I can see you've come to grips with losing."

"Lost my grip, you mean." He coughed and waved at a couple of rubberneckers passing through the lobby. "I don't know what came over me."

The stabbing pain in his limbs and head subsided to a dull ache. *She's good for me.*

Chapter Nineteen

"I FEEL LIKE CINDERELLA after the ball," Selah confided to Frankie after the Emmys. "I had to return the borrowed dress to wardrobe and my enchanted hair turned into a Chia Pet again. I am trying to convince one of the show's stylists to move to Shadybrook."

"Aww. What's that sound I hear?"

"The wind is picking up. We've got a pretty bad storm here." The lights flickered and Selah flinched.

"No, not that. Your voice. You sound like you're enjoying yourself in New York."

"Who wouldn't enjoy themselves?"

Selah wasn't ready to confide in her best friend about her relationship with Cane when she wasn't sure what to make of it herself. Was their dinner a date or were they just friends? What about the flowers and the Emmys?

"I had a front-row seat to see Cane and Shayne at the cabaret and the Emmys. I also met Cameron Mathison, formerly of *All My Children*."

Selah held the phone away from her ear as Frankie squealed like that pot-bellied pig facing down a taxi in Times Square. She couldn't wait to surprise her buddy with the album of photographs and autographs Selah had collected from the soap stars.

"Listen, I need to go. I'm doing an online chat tonight, and then I've got to take some time and work on a real client's website." She massaged the muscles in her neck.

"Well, there went that spark in your voice."

"This show is my fantasy. The bills for my loans and the diner are my reality."

Her father had left a voicemail complaining about Momma and begging for money. She scrolled through her other messages. Wow. Why had she thought that teaching Momma to text was a good idea? Momma had sent ten texts in one hour about Dad's shenanigans, a busted heating unit at the diner, and a broken-down car at home.

"I need something to fall back on when the fantasy ends."

"Don't talk like that, Selah. Something more will come of this SoaperFan adventure."

"We'll see. How is everything going with you? How does Momma seem?"

"Nutty as ever. Your mother has cabin fever. She's desperate to get back to the diner, if you can believe someone would enjoy cooking that much."

"And my father?"

"Nothing to worry about."

"The fact you said there's nothing to worry about makes me worry."

Frankie sighed. "He's gambling heavily and the breakfast

and lunch business has slacked off since Margo's been away. It's just a minor setback."

"The place was barely holding on as it was. How will we make it after another drop-off in business?"

"Your father can give up gambling away the money you do have."

"Yeah, right."

"Then your parents can sell the diner."

"They love that place. It's the one thing they agree on. If I come home, I can help."

"Don't you dare come home! I did not work that hard to get you to the fan club weekend just to see it all end now. "

"Whoa, what?" Selah frowned. "How did you work hard to get us to the fan club weekend? I thought you won the tickets."

Silence on the line.

"Frankie?"

"I'm driving into a tunnel. I think we're losing the connection." Her voice faded.

"There are no tunnels in Shadybrook, Einstein."

Silence.

"People play enough games around here. I deserve to hear the truth from my best friend."

"I lied to get you to New York City, okay? I lied about the whole thing. I'm not perfect like you."

"You *are* the perfect friend, but I still don't understand why you lied or what you did."

"I knew you would never let me pay for the trip. I pretended to win it so we could have some fun away from Shadybrook and our families."

A lump formed in Selah's throat.

"I wanted you to relax and not be anxious. I wanted to spend time with the Selah I knew when we were kids."

"Neither one of us was happy and carefree when we were teenagers."

"Yeah, but we had big dreams. Now you've found your dream again, and you did that part all on your own. I had nothing to do with the SoaperFan thing. I got you past the grandstands, but you got yourself into the driver's seat and started the engine."

"Oh, Frankie!"

"'Oh, Frankie', as in 'Oh, Frankie, no more lame racing metaphors,' or 'Oh, Frankie, you're the most thoughtful friend a girl could ever want'? Please don't tell me it's 'Oh, Frankie, I'm disappointed in you.'"

"It's 'Oh, Frankie,' as in 'The lights just went out, but I want to continue this discussion later.'"

"Are you safe there? Do you have a flashlight?"

"Yes, but do not tell Momma about the electricity going out. She's liable to call in the National Guard."

She hung up the phone and inched her way toward the kitchen counter, where she had left a flashlight. She felt calmer in the glow of the "aDORIng" scented candles Dorian had lining the windows. That is, until Faith jumped out of her dog bed and throttled toward the front door.

"No, you cannot go outside in this storm, baby dog."

As Faith's whining grew louder, Selah's heart beat faster. Sirens pierced the air. The house was so fabulous she had forgotten there were bars on the windows and she was a woman living alone in the city.

Faith's whines escalated into barking. She scratched at the door.

"What's the matter?" She scooped up the dog. "You're freaking me out, girl."

Selah peered out and saw a dozen emergency vehicles surrounding the studio. Lightning flashed, illuminating a shadow on the bungalow's front porch. The hair on her arms stood on end. She dropped the blinds and followed her flashlight back to the kitchen.

She rummaged through the cabinet drawers. "Where is that gun? I know it's in here somewhere."

Someone pounded at the door, and her heart stopped for a moment.

"Hallelujah, there it is!" She grabbed the realistic-looking prop gun she'd found while she'd been checking out, well, snooping around, the bungalow. Even the rich and famous had junk drawers.

As the pounding and Faith's howling grew louder, she clutched the toy gun in her right hand, the flashlight under her armpit, Faith under her other arm, and prayers in her chest. She inched her way toward the dark living room. In hindsight, it would have been so much easier just to dial 911.

She squinted through the peephole. The dark figure pounding on the door looked familiar.

"Selah? Are you in there? It's Cane."

Thank You, Lord. She tucked the gun into the elastic band on her pants. Her gut would hold that sucker in place. Opening three deadbolts with one hand was a struggle in the dark, but when she finally succeeded, Cane burst in with a rush of rain and wind and the sweet scent of cinnamon buns.

He threw his arms around her and Faith. "I came to make sure you were okay."

She set Faith on the floor and the dog went to work smelling his knees, ankles, and tennis shoes. Selah took his soaking jacket.

He froze. "Why do you have a gun?"

"Because I was alone in a thunderstorm and a madman was pounding at my front door."

"I'm sorry I scared you. There was a lightning strike and an electrical fire at the studio, so we had to shut down taping for the night. I was afraid you had lost power too."

"I bet Julia is ballistic."

"You're right. She hates to get behind schedule." He handed her a bag of candles, flashlights, and pastries. She had to restrain herself from tearing into the buns.

"Looks like you've got things under control, but I brought you some supplies. The prop guys are going to kill me. They always keep plenty of candles on hand for the love scenes."

At least he couldn't see her blush. "Um. Thanks. You can dry off on the couch. I covered it with blankets and towels in case Faith jumped on the leather with mud and claws. So, come on in and set a spell, as we say in the South. Actually, we don't say that, except when we're making fun of the way other Southern people speak and . . . I'm babbling again, aren't I?" She clamped her lips shut.

He chuckled and offered his arm. "You lead the way. I've never been inside Dori's compound."

She took Cane's arm lightly, and they shuffled down

steps to the sunken living room. As they edged toward the couch, he stumbled. He tried to recover his balance but did a face plant on the couch. Rolling over, he punched his leg with his fist. "Clumsy idiot."

"Are you hurt?" Selah dropped to her knees beside him and grasped his hand, rubbing his cold fingers. Faith jumped on his chest and licked his chin.

"If I'd known I'd get this kind of reception, I'd have dropped by sooner." He patted the dog and raised Selah's hand to his lips and kissed it.

She pulled herself away, sucking in a breath that then escaped as a giggle. She shined the flashlight in his face. He was smiling, but something was off. "Be serious now and tell me if you're all right."

He shaded his eyes and sat up against a sofa pillow. "I'm fine. Forget about it."

She sat beside him on the couch. "It's my fault. If I'd lit the candles you brought instead of obsessing over how soon I could eat one of those cinnamon buns, you'd have had more light to see the furniture."

"It's not the dark that made me fall. It's the MS."

"Goodness gracious, you can see my mess in the dark? How embarrassing." She shined the flashlight on the sticky notes and print-outs strewn across a glass table and gathered them into stacks. The amount of paperwork Mason assigned to her had doubled in the wake of Cane's pizza prank. "I'm not the greatest housekeeper, I know. Please don't tell my mother about the mess."

"The only mess is me, Selah. I was talking about multiple sclerosis. I stumble because I have MS." His words hung in the air as if a mallet had struck a gong.

Sitting beside him on the couch, she draped a blanket across his lap as if it could shield him. "This is what you were upset about when I found you in your dressing room bathroom, isn't it?"

"I got my diagnosis and my pink slip on the same day. I was afraid the higher-ups had figured out I was sick."

She retrieved an antacid tablet from her pocket and popped it in her mouth. "How did you know it was MS?"

"I was in a car accident a few months ago. I got a concussion. I started to have fatigue and these explosive headaches. I thought it was either the accident or the old football injury."

Accident, concussion, headaches. How had he managed to keep this a secret?

"The doctors sent me for an MRI. I never suspected they'd find anything, let alone lesions on the brain. The lesions indicate MS."

"Like an alien invasion." She remembered an old horror movie in which aliens turned humans into zombies by leeching onto their brains.

"Exactly like that." The tension in his voice melted a little. "Except it'll be a while before I know what kind of damage the aliens will do."

"What's the prognosis?"

"It depends how well the medicine works. I take injections weekly. At best, it won't get worse than the pain I've been having. I can lead an active life."

"At worst?"

"I lose the ability to walk and speak and see. But the risk of death is rare."

Cane hadn't moved since Selah covered him with the

blanket. How could such an awful illness have any place in this perfect man?

"Is it genetic? Does anyone else in your family have it?"

"I hadn't considered that. I'm still learning about it. I only have one brother, Tanner, and I haven't seen him since … I haven't seen him in seventeen or so years."

"You don't know where he is?"

"No." He turned to face her. "You're the first person I've told about this."

"I'm honored that you would confide in me, but why me?"

"After I mowed you down in the hallway, you helped me, and you've been a friend to me. When I'm around you, I laugh, I feel peaceful, I spill my guts to you. I don't feel sick."

Her defenses, the ones she'd vowed to maintain, split wide open. She edged closer to him, each movement feeling as if she was hurtling toward a precipice. Her mind sent up danger signals all over the place, but her heart didn't care. "Even in the dark, it's not hard to see that you're hurting deeply."

"It's nothing less than I deserve."

"You don't deserve to be sick or die."

"You don't know me or the things I've done." He clenched his fist, and Faith whimpered.

"I know you're an amazingly strong person. You've carried this secret all these months without going crazy."

"Someone who causes death should die, though, right? Isn't that what your Bible says? An eye for an eye?"

"But the Bible also says Jesus is merciful and faithful to forgive our sins." Why did this feel so uncomfortable?

It was supposed to be easy to share Jesus or your testimony with someone in need.

"This one's unforgiveable." He shook his head. "Because of it, God abandoned me a long time ago."

"Nothing is unforgiveable."

"I killed my parents."

She backed away a fraction. Maybe it hadn't been smart to invite him into the house.

The lights flicked on then, and the house filled with the sounds of appliances restarting. Cane drew back too, as if he had touched a live electrical wire. He rose, knocking the blanket and Faith to the floor. Faith barked and scratched at his jeans for attention.

"I should go."

"Why don't you stay until you're dry? You can help me with my online chat tonight. The fans would love to have you as a special guest."

"No, I have to get out of here. I shouldn't have dumped all this on you." He looked around as if he wanted to be anywhere but here. "I'm glad you're okay after the storm, Selah."

"Please don't go like this. You're safe with me."

But he left, taking all the air in the room with him.

Chapter Twenty

A S SOON AS this wedding was over, Cane never wanted to see the inside of a church again.

The fire that shut down the studio two nights ago caused a last-minute location shoot in this shoebox of a chapel in Jersey. Cane tugged at his bowtie, but it wouldn't give. He had little room to breathe in this tux, in front of an audience of three-fourths of the cast and crew, Selah, and a life-sized Jesus staring down at him.

He took his place at the front of the church as Shayne's best man. As sunlight streamed in through the stained-glass windows, he began to sweat and itch in the polyester tux.

When Cane shook hands with the actor playing the minister, he could hear Selah saying, "Jesus is faithful to forgive our sins." The pastor at Mom and Dad's funeral had urged healing and forgiveness too.

He scanned the sanctuary, the center aisle, and the open front doors, careful to avoid looking toward Selah's pew, seeing the hurt in her eyes.

Julia, brandishing a bullhorn, charged in through the

chapel's entrance. Eva dragged along behind her in a short, lacy dress that looked like something out of Madonna's music videos in the '80s.

"Come alive, people! Where is Shayne? He was here a few hours ago. We need a groom for the wedding."

The last time Cane had spoken to Shayne was at the Emmy after-party. He had seemed normal, too normal, especially after losing his coveted statuette.

Julia paused, getting only shrugs in response. "The longer he is missing, the longer you will be here."

Judging by the volume of groans from cast and crew, this was bound to get ugly.

"Your jobs are all on the line." Her eyes flashed as she shouted into the megaphone. Like a televangelist, she paced the center aisle, placing her hand on the shoulder of the person sitting at the end of each row. "This is the epic wedding that will save *The Winds of Change* from cancellation: A Luke and Laura, Cruz and Eden, Bo and Hope, larger-than-life kind of wedding."

Cane snorted along with a few others in the crowd. The flaw in Julia's plan was that the happy couple—Shayne's character, Ned, and Eva's character, Kelli—were not star-crossed like the soap supercouples of the past. Rather, they were in love with other people.

When Julia crooked her finger at Cane, he jogged down the aisle to meet her. "You, find Shayne."

Eva sidestepped Julia and sidled up to him. Before Cane could make a move, Selah's dog crawled out from beneath a pew, planted itself in front of Eva, and began to bark and growl up at her.

"Get that rodent away from me!" Eva ducked behind Cane.

"No, Faith. Come back here." Selah jumped out of her chair and swayed. She bent to remove her high heels and padded toward them in stockinged feet.

Cane willed himself not to smile at her, but he had never excelled at self-control. He scooped the dog into his arms, and it stopped barking.

"Eww. Don't touch it, Cane." Eva shuddered.

Julia, who had been watching the exchange like a spectator at a ping-pong match, intervened and took Faith from him. "This girl yours, Selah?"

Selah held out her arms, but Julia kept the dog, stroking its belly. Cameraman Rick came over and fed Faith a piece of doughnut.

"Yes. I thought no one would notice if I brought her, but she jumped out of her carrier. I apologize. This is the first time she's ever broken free and growled at someone like that." From the glint in Selah's eyes as she asked Eva's pardon, Cane suspected that the dog would be eating steak and gravy for a few weeks.

"That performance was priceless. We've got to work her into the show somehow." Julia turned to Cane and snapped her fingers. "Go now."

He nodded and hustled out as Eva sputtered, "You're making that ferret an extra in my wedding?"

Cane exhaled as he shut the chapel doors behind him. This wedding was turning into an out-of-control reality show.

Now, to find his MIA friend. Shayne couldn't have gotten far on foot if he was drinking heavily. Cane turned the corner at the back of the building and spotted him sprawled out on a bench in the garden. Cane stood over him, watching him thrash and snore. How much longer before he hit bottom and asked for help?

Cane smacked him on the back of the head. "Rise and shine, bonehead. It's your wedding day."

Shayne might be vulnerable, but Cane wasn't going to let him ruin the day for Julia, Selah, and even Eva and drag the show down with him.

Shayne jerked awake and rolled off the bench onto the dirt. "What'd you wake me for?"

"To keep you from losing your job." Cane bent down and helped him stand. "You can't pull off your scenes when you're lit, man. Can I call your sponsor or something? After you make it through this wedding, I will drive you to rehab myself."

He should have gotten tough with Shayne years ago, made him get help. When Shayne swayed, Cane held him up by his armpits and dragged him toward the church. Cane's back and knees screamed for mercy under Shayne's weight. It was going to take an extreme makeover to get Shayne camera-ready again. He smelled like a dumpster and looked like a six-year-old after church, his white dress shirt hanging untucked, his hair sticking out in five directions. Yep. Just like a reality show.

"Get off me!" Shayne flailed and pounded his fists against Cane. "I already have one mother."

"You're a lucky man then. She needs to take you over her knee and remind you that you're screwing up your life royally."

"Look at you, raggin' on me about my life when you're

wasting your time on that big, fat groupie of yours." Shayne puffed out his cheeks. "She's ruining your image, dude."

Sucker punch.

Cane grabbed him by his lapels and shoved him hard up against the wall at the back of the building. "You watch your mouth, *dude*. You and Eva are going to show Selah some respect."

"Aw. Sweet. Superman takes up for his SoaperFan." Shayne screeched like a chimpanzee. "Should I let her in on all the lies you've told about your past?"

"You're on your own." Cane released him and he slid down the wall.

Then Shayne popped back up and sprayed Binaca in his mouth. "Thanks for the assist, SoaperMan. But I've got a wedding to crash." He staggered off.

He rounded the corner and crashed into Selah. "Howdy there, Blunder Woman! You look as lovely as does your wee wittle guard dog."

Cane caught up to Shayne, grabbing his shoulder and pushing him away from her. Cane's stomach rolled as he watched her face crumble. He didn't have to ask how long she had been standing there, listening to Shayne belittle her.

Her eyes were filled with tears, but she jutted out her chin and narrowed her eyes. "I thought you liked me. You're a better actor than I gave you credit for, Shayne."

Faith growled at him as if to back her up.

Shayne's shoulders drooped and, for a moment, Cane saw the guy who opened his home to a homesick kid from Minnesota, the guy who started using after his estranged father died in prison. Then Shayne's mouth reverted to a sneer as he shoved past her.

In a heartbeat, Cane's arms were around her, and she rested her head against his chest. He inhaled and let her scent of strawberries and vanilla float over him. He closed his eyes and squeezed her tighter, unable to put a label on the feeling that gripped his chest and made it increasingly hard to let her go.

"Is that how everybody sees me? Is that how you see me, as a big, fat groupie?"

"Absolutely not." Cane pulled back to look at her. "Number one, Shayne is a drunken fool."

Selah's eyes welled up again as she thought of Frankie and her habit of turning life into a list. Selah might have hopped the next plane home if she hadn't committed to making an "After the Party" webpage with exclusive photographs and video from the wedding. She had played resident SoaperFan for five weeks. It was time to go.

"Number two, Shayne is blind, because you are stunning, inside and out."

Oh, my. "Thank you," she whispered, her cheeks growing warm. Maybe she'd been too hasty in deciding to leave town.

"Let's sit for a minute." He led her to the garden bench. When they sat side by side, Faith promptly jumped up on his lap.

Selah shifted on the cold stone bench. She couldn't cross her legs in this sundress for fear of sharing excessive thigh and calf flab. Instead, she crossed her ankles and pulled her cloak around her shoulders.

"Shayne is a little jealous of the time I'm spending with you."

Selah tried to wrap her brain around these developments. "Does he need medication, do you think?"

Cane smiled. "No, he's got that covered."

"The gild is off the lily."

"What does that mean? Another Southern saying?"

"You know, the blush is off the rose, the blinders are off, the truth comes out. You see celebrities onscreen and think you understand them, but you have no clue about what lies beneath. Nothing is as it seems."

"I get it. If nothing is as it seems, then you're Alice, he's the Cheshire Cat, and I'm Wonderland?"

"Mm-hm. Something like that."

He fished a wrapped box from the inside pocket in his coat and handed it to her. "This is for you, to protect you while in Wonderland."

She started to unwrap the purple paper, then realized that the top lifted off, paper intact. "How fun, a soap box."

"I admit to borrowing that from the set."

She turned the pre-wrapped box over and inspected it.

"You're like a kid playing with the package and not the gift inside. Open it."

She reached in and lifted out a pink mace container on a keychain.

"Works better than a prop gun every time. Just don't shoot your eye out with it."

"Thank you." Unprepared for the tsunami of emotions that washed over her, she kept her head bowed, her hair hiding her face, as she cradled the gift in her hands. No man had ever cared about protecting her before. *Get a grip, Selah.*

"Have I put you to sleep? We should get going. Julia has probably reached nuclear meltdown stage by now." He set Faith on the ground and brushed his hands back and forth across his black dress pants.

When he started to stand, Selah raised her head. "Wait. I have something to tell you." She didn't touch him. If she had, she wouldn't have been able to corral her emotions again.

He turned.

"Resistance to dog hair is futile."

"You always know how to make me laugh, my friend."

Selah opened her mouth to crack another joke and shut it again. It went against her nature to make waves and speak her mind, but something was pushing her to move beyond her comfort zone.

Lord, as usual, my feelings are all over the place, but I trust You. Give me the courage to ask him the questions You've placed on my heart.

"I want more than a few laughs." She swallowed. "I want you to trust me. Please, what is it that puts that haunted look in your eyes whenever you talk about your family or Shayne or God?"

Chapter Twenty-One

WHERE HAD THAT come from? The question hit him like a blind-side tackle by a 300-pound defensive lineman. They'd been talking about Shayne's drama, not his. He darted a glance at the building. Julia or one of her PAs should have come for him by now.

"I prefer to leave my demons in the past."

"No better place for an exorcism than here at church." Her tone was light, but he could feel her eyes on him, boring into the parts of his soul that were too dark for a woman like her to see. That mutt was staring up at him too.

"I don't believe you are a murderer, Cane, but I can't stop thinking about what you said when you left after the blackout. Are you on the run or under an assumed identity? Are you a convicted felon? My brain can generate a lot of scenarios in a short time."

He turned to look her in the eyes. Those eyes, darkening from blue to lavender like a mood ring, should have carried a warning sign. He swallowed. What were they talking about again? Right, his insurmountable sins.

"It's not any of those scenarios. I apologize for scaring you. I am an actor, prone to melodrama." He flashed a toothy grin and patted her knee. Judging from her raised eyebrow, she wasn't buying it.

"Now you're lying." She said softly.

He flinched. "I've shared more of myself with you than anyone in my life. I cannot go down this road with you."

"What road? I can see that you're in pain. Don't shut me out."

"I can't keep dumping all my stuff on you." He glanced at his watch, then stood. "We have to get back to the set. I won't bother you again."

"You are never a bother." She grabbed his hand and clutched it between hers.

One touch of her hand and he was back there again—the scene of the wreck, the place he had successfully blocked from his mind.

He panted as he paced the pavement slick with gasoline and freezing rain. He must have crushed his ribs when they smashed against the steering wheel. Who had pulled him out? Tanner sat propped against a tree, his head between his knees and his hands grasping the back of his head. Where were Mom and Dad? Cane spun around, his eyes searching, blinded by the flashing blue and red lights.

He stopped breathing for a moment. The car was in the ravine, the back half crushed by a red pickup. He had to get to them. Pushing through tree branches bent with icicles, Cane ran toward the edge. A fireman grabbed his shoulders and pulled him back.

"Let me go. Why aren't you helping them?" His throat burned from his screams and the stench of burned rubber.

Someone grabbed his hand and squeezed it between hers. He turned to see a white-haired woman. Her lips were moving, but no sound was coming out. Where had she come from? She wasn't a rescue worker. Maybe she had witnessed the wreck.

"Hey! What are you doing?" He tried to drop her hand, but she squeezed harder.

She fixed her steel-gray eyes on his. "Praying for you, Cane."

His chest seized again and he doubled over, crippled by the weight of what he had done. She had stayed with him, holding him until the ambulance took him and Tanner to the hospital.

"Are you feeling all right, Cane? Cane?"

He heard Selah's voice and his eyes fluttered open as if he was waking up from a nightmare. His eyes darted from her face to her hands, which had turned white from gripping his. He had never had a flashback so intense before, and he hoped to God he never did again.

As he extricated his hand from hers, strains of the bridal march floated out of the church.

"Is the 'Here Comes the Bride' song upsetting you? I hate it too. If I ever get married, it will be to the Monday Night Football theme song or something."

He ran his hand through his hair. "I have to go inside. For your own good, stay away and don't pray for me again," he rasped and walked off without even a backward glance.

Chapter Twenty-Two

"I've finally figured out why soap operas are, and logically should be, so popular with generations of housebound women. They are the only place in our culture where grown-up men take seriously all the things that grown-up women have to deal with all day long."

Gloria Steinem

SELAH GAPED AT him, rubbing the hand that still burned from the heat of his. Cane had left her alone with Faith and the firm belief that God was the only Man who would never hurt or leave her.

Selah looked heavenward at the dark clouds that bore down on her, threatening to crush her. *What's the plan now, God? Why did Cane tell me not to pray for him?* Just for that, she was going to pray for him three times as much.

When raindrops began to fall, she picked up Faith

and her shoes and padded in torn stockings to the front doors of the church. She slid into the back pew beside Liza, who had earned her eternal adoration by publicly putting Mason in his place.

"Witness the final destruction of our show," Liza muttered and motioned toward the altar, where Shayne stood facing his "bridezilla," Eva. Shayne dropped one of the wedding rings, bent over, and split his pants, right down to his Sponge Bob boxer shorts.

She turned to Selah and whispered, "I hate to break it to Julia, but this wedding is more epic fail than epic."

Selah smiled and determined to keep smiling as they sat through take after take of hollow vows of love and forever. Cane stood at the front of the church, beside Shayne, never once looking her way. She thought of her parents' marriage. Had they ever loved each other?

During a break, she asked Julia, "Have you ever been engaged or married?"

"You and Cane haven't gotten engaged, have you?"

"No. No-o. I just wondered why you stayed single. You're intelligent and witty, a great catch."

"I'm terrible at relationships. I am the cliché Type A workaholic. I'm set in my ways and I like my independence."

"A lot of men are the same way." Mason came to mind.

"But the men who are interested usually aren't interesting." She lowered her voice. "Don't tell Gloria Steinem this or I'll forfeit my "liberated woman" card, but I have been brainwashed by the soap ideal of undying love, the fairy tale."

Given today's run-ins with Shayne and Cane, Selah was opting to keep her liberated woman card.

After ten hours, Julia mercifully called it a wrap. "Thank you, everybody. I will see most of you bright and early Monday."

Liza groaned as Selah helped her to her feet. They joined the bottleneck at the exit doors.

Selah's phone rang to the tune of the *Winds of Change* theme song. She answered it while she walked to the van that would take them back to the studio.

"It's me, sugar, your momma."

"I know who it is."

"I thought maybe you'd forgotten. You've left us for so long."

Let the guilt trip begin. Momma wasn't even going to ask how her daughter was faring in New York. "Gosh, how I've missed you and your pep talks."

"What is there to be peppy about?" Momma tsked. "I have bad news, as usual. It rained hard here while we were at the diner. The rain's coming your way. I hope you have an umbrella and—"

"Tell me what's wrong, Momma."

"The roof leaked at the house. It liked to have ruined the entire living room, kitchen, and your office."

"My office." She squeaked and sagged against the van. Had she returned the Book and her photos to the filing cabinet or left them exposed?

"I rescued as much as I could, but your computer equipment . . ."

She rubbed her temple. The pc, printer, fax, peripherals, diplomas, all left uncovered.

"You have to come home and help me clean up. Your father wouldn't care if the house caved in."

"The good news is that it's not a total loss, right? You always wanted a skylight. We can file a claim with our homeowner's insurance."

Momma was quiet.

Selah's stomach twisted. "You let the insurance lapse."

"I had to pay the light bill and we hadn't used that policy for thirty years."

"The money situation . . . It's gotten worse, hasn't it?" Her throat tightened with the powerless feeling that had suffocated her in Shadybrook. Where was Momma's pie when she needed it?

"Just come home. I need moral support."

She watched as Cane left with Shayne and Eva. His jaw was set and his body stiff. Momma was right. Again. There was nothing left for her in New York City.

"You win. I'll be home in a few days. I want to say goodbye to a few of my friends first."

"Your real friends are here, Selah Marie. Shadybrook is your home."

Chapter Twenty-Three

WATER GUSHED THROUGH the roof, surging into a six-foot tidal wave. Selah couldn't swim. She tried to cry for help, but someone, something pushed her head under the black waves. She flailed as Momma, her father, Eva, Shayne, and Cane all stood at the water's edge.

"Please! Help me!" Selah stretched out her hand.

"You will never be enough." Momma shook her head and crossed her arms at her chest. "You can't hold down a job, you can't pay off your debts, you can't lose weight. What does he want with you?"

Eva nodded, slipping her arm through Cane's and pulling him close. Shayne just smirked.

"He'll always hunger for other women. That's just who he is," her father said. "He'll abandon you. Leaving is what we do best."

"No!" Selah sputtered.

"Even God isn't interested in rescuing you. You'll never be good enough." Cane crouched down and let the water run through his hands. "Where's your faith, now, SoaperFan?"

Selah grabbed his hand. He recoiled and gave her that where-is-the-closest-exit look. He dropped her hand and the water dragged her under.

"Save me!" She screamed and sat up in bed, panting, sweating, and freezing at the same time. Recognizing the down comforter, candles, Rubenesque paintings that decorated Dori's place, she slumped against the headboard. Her hand brushed Faith's wiry russet fur and the dog curled up in her lap.

It was only a nightmare, but the desperate, helpless feelings of rejection and drowning clung to her like tentacles of a sea creature. The image of Cane, callous and cruel, sent another chill through her veins. She dressed and wrapped her heavy bathrobe around her clothes.

True to his word, Cane didn't "bother" Selah all weekend. It was better that way. She was all packed to leave tomorrow after giving the news to Julia in person. Waiting until the last minute to tell her would eliminate long, painful goodbyes or an awkward going-away party.

She powered up her laptop to work but found herself drawn to her photo gallery. There was Cane recovering after his surprise kiss from Ada at the cabaret night. Cane laughing with Julio at PieParazzi. Cane posing with every fan who showed up to protest the show's rumored cancellation. Another of Cane at the rally, grinning, with frozen red cheeks and nose, as he dragged Selah into the shot. She was rolling her eyes at him, but her face looked . . . different. Good different.

Her chest grew heavy as she traced her fingertip over

his lips. *I should be angry at you for toying with my emotions, but you've gone and made me worry about you.*

This was craziness, sitting around moping. She snapped shut the laptop and grabbed her keys and purse. He and Julia were working today. Selah had to take action, see for herself that he wasn't pushing himself too hard. Unless the dream was a premonition, they were still friends, and friends looked out for each other.

"I am not kissing *that* stuff. It tastes like sawdust." Cane's protests brought a makeup artist over to change Eva's lipstick.

When her face fell, he knew he shouldn't have said anything. The lipstick wasn't that awful, but it was torture having to kiss her instead of—

Admit it, Ashton. You picture Selah when you kiss Eva.

"Fix the dark circles under his eyes while you're at it," Eva said, standing next to him, stiff as a guard at Buckingham Palace.

She was right though. He'd gotten little sleep that weekend. The few times he did nod off, his dreams were plagued with the same memories he'd had at the church with Selah.

He opened his mouth to apologize and shut it again as he focused on Eva and her new G.I. Jane haircut. No way the Powers That Be at *Winds of Change* had pre-approved such a drastic change. He couldn't blame her for acting out. Her days were numbered.

After the third take, Julia's voice boomed onto the set from the booth. "This is ridiculous, children. I've seen more emotion in a zombie movie." Julia sat in a control room in front of a wall of television screens, keeping tabs on the action on the stage floor and communicating with the director by walkie-talkie.

The director calling the show from the floor nodded his agreement. "Eva, your character's not dead yet, so loosen up and show some affection for the man you love."

Eva looked at Cane and then at the floor.

She couldn't be. She wasn't in love with him. Selah had warned him about it, but he'd brushed it off. He would have a talk with Eva when they finished taping, just to be sure.

"Cane, when you do your tag at the end of the scene, I want to see conflicting emotions. This is bittersweet for him," the director continued. "Remember, Dean might be in love, but he's still riled up at Kelli for lying and marrying his brother. Conflicting emotions. Got it?"

"Got it." An acting coach had once instructed him that, when the camera focused on an actor's face for the tag or parting close-up shot of the scene, the actor could convey the correct facial expression by thinking, 'Did I forget to turn off the stove?' or 'What's that smell?' Today, the bad smell expression would probably work best.

He glanced at Eva. Her scowl matched her severe, blunt haircut. This was going to be a tough sell.

He saw movement and a flash of color as Selah stepped out from behind a cameraman and right into Cane's eyeline. He stayed in character and recited his lines but locked his gaze on her. Her red V-neck blouse showed off her glowing skin and other assets. How he wanted to touch that skin, warm and soft, dragging his fingertips down her jaw and neck, feeling her pulse quicken. He'd gotten a taste, at a church of all places, of how good it felt to have her in his arms. But God and his past would always come between them.

Her emotions shone on her face like a kaleidoscope. The thought that he had caused her pain sickened him, but it had to be done.

"Okay, we're clear and out!" someone called, and he was saved from facing her. He turned and headed for the exit as the crew began to rearrange cameras and sets for the next scenes. The action flowed effortlessly, despite the electrical cords crisscrossing the floor and the boom microphones swinging overhead.

"It's a thing of beauty, isn't it? Like a ballet." Julia descended from the booth and clamped her free hand on his shoulder. Her face radiated pride and passion. If anybody could save this show, it was Julia.

"That was perfect, Cane. I thought I was going to have to get the cattle prod after you two. But whatever changed, it was good. You hit just the right feeling in your tag."

Julia turned her attention to Eva. "*Now* you smile and melt the ice? When the scene is over?" She sighed. "In the future, do it with feeling, and do it on cue."

Of course, everyone knew there would be no future here for Eva.

Julia flitted off in Selah's direction.

Eva intercepted him and threw her arms around him. "What a day, huh?"

"What was that for?"

"I couldn't do this without you, Cane. What will I do when I can't come to work and see your face everyday?"

He watched Selah over Eva's shoulder. Selah was

smiling up at Rick, one of the younger, unmarried cam-eramen, who was standing entirely too close to her. Cane forced himself to take deep breaths as she hugged Rick. He was a stand-up guy, a better match for her.

Cane's vision dimmed and his ears started to ring. This new medication was going to be the death of him if his feelings about Selah didn't kill him first.

Chapter Twenty-Four

SELAH'S BODY WENT cold as she watched Eva in Cane's arms. The smoldering look he cast Selah's way during his scene was nothing more than material for his Daytime Emmy reel.

She knew exactly what Momma would say if she were here. "He's an actor and a man, Selah Marie. He lies like he breathes."

Eva was a better fit for him anyway, since she was an actress, worldly, and skinny. Very skinny.

"Shut up," Selah said, trying to quiet her insecurities. After all this time professing to trust God's plan for her life, her self-doubts were still as twitchy as a gunslinger's finger.

"What?" Julia waved her hand in front of Selah's face.

"Oh, nothing Miss Julia, just muttering to myself."

"I see we've worn off on you, standing around talking to yourself. Split personalities are big around here, on-screen and off." Julia gestured toward Cane. "For instance, while you were bumbling around on set, Cane's demeanor mysteriously changed in an instant. One look at you and magic happens."

Selah's face burned. "I'm not sure what he feels about me right now. In fact, I'm not even sure what I feel about him right now."

"Eh. Forget him then." Julia clucked like a mother hen. "I need to talk to you about something that will directly affect your time here."

"I do too."

"Okay, but me first." She clapped her hand against her walkie. "I've got good news and bad news."

"What's the bad news?"

Chilled from watching Eva and Cane with their heads together, Selah pulled her jacket around herself.

When Julia's pocket dinged, she checked her phone. "Shoot. I forgot about that conference call. I should really break this news to everybody anyway."

She turned to the other actors loitering on set. "Listen up, children. I need you back here in a half hour to give you some news."

Cane walked out alone. He'd warned her to stay away, but she couldn't leave without clearing the air and telling him goodbye.

Cane was sweating from scalp to feet as he emerged from the bathroom. Not the best time to run into Selah in a narrow hallway. He swallowed. Where was Shayne when he needed a diversion?

"Hey." He dropped his eyes and tried to walk around her.

"I don't want to bother you," she said sweetly, using his own words to stop him, "but I'm leaving today."

"You're headed home? Good."

"That was cold."

Bile rose in his throat. If that's the way it sounded, then that was the way it had to be. "Have a safe trip."

"You ain't looking good, Cane." She touched his clammy face and gasped. "You're sick, aren't you?"

He pushed her hand away and growled. "Yep, your hot hunk of daytime just finished puking his guts out. Almost passed out while we were shooting. I told you I will not go down this road with you."

Her eyes misted. "What does the neurologist say?"

"Doc says I'm in a relapse or something and he can't get my meds regulated. He thinks I've got PTSD and depression from this disease and from all the crap I've pulled in my life." *That should scare her off.*

"Let me take you back to your dressing room and you can lie down."

He splayed out his fingers and then fisted them. "Stop being so nice to me, Selah."

"Sure. Right. I'm sorry." She moved out of his path.

He smiled and softened his tone. "You just can't help yourself, can you?"

"I guess there's no helping you then."

Cane heard humming and wondered if it was in his head, until he realized it was Shayne coming down the hall behind him.

"Sounds like Cane's trying to break up with you, corn puddin'. He doesn't want to be your teenage dream anymore." Shayne edged past him and gave Selah a squeeze on the shoulders.

"Stay out of it."

"We're just friends." Selah said flatly.

"How sad for you. Now you have no friend but Jesus." Shayne patted her back and rubbed a tear from his eye with his other hand. "There there."

Selah looked from Shayne to Cane and shook her head.

Cane felt the nausea rising again. "Goodbye, Selah."

Without a word, she turned and walked away. Cane clenched his jaw and hardened his heart.

"Dude, you look like something my dog rolled in."

"You don't have a dog, Shayne."

"Oh right, I'm thinking about that rat I saw in the subway station."

"A rat. That must be it."

"The bad news is that the ratings dropped despite this serial-killer storyline." Julia pulled in Selah, Eva, Cane, and a few PAs and camera operators to hear her announcement.

"Probably *because* of the graphic serial killings." Selah was weary of the negative turn her show and her life had taken. "A lot of fans swear they'll never watch again. What's to watch after the massacre of one beloved veteran actor after another?"

"Be that as it may, I've come up with a way to keep this ratings dip from becoming a plunge." Julia's excitement was palpable.

And then Selah saw Mason out of the corner of her eye. He approached the group like the dark shadow of the Grinch, looming over Whoville.

Julia was so focused on her news that she didn't see him. "The good news is that—"

He walked over and stepped between Julia and Selah. "I was rather enjoying the bad news."

"Why are you always underfoot, Mason?" Julia pinned him to the wall with her fiery gaze.

"Because I am underpaid, underappreciated, and under my quota for getting on the nerves of both cast and crew."

Selah stifled a laugh.

"As I was saying, the good news is that we're pulling out all the stops to save the show. We're doing a *Winds of Change* tour of college campuses on the east coast. We'll film on location on campus and have students audition for speaking parts." Julia took a breath. "We need to talk about you going home, Selah."

At least the tour news saved her from having to tell Julia she was leaving.

"Don't worry. You'll go out in style. The college tour stops at three universities within an hour of your hometown. Any ideas on reasonable dining and lodging? I'm on a tight budget."

"A few come to mind." Her parents' diner for one, and Rendezvous, the lodge run by another childhood friend, for two. She pictured her parents and Chinese Willie arguing over who would provide the vittles for this momentous homecoming. Her heart drummed in her chest. An infusion of business and publicity like this was the kind of lifeblood that could revive Good Company and her family's finances.

"This college tour is a farce, worse than the SoaperFan idea." Mason typed on his phone as he talked. "What a joy it will be to write for yet another no-talent punk."

He raised his head and eyed Cane, who smiled blandly.

"Working with college boys sounds good to me." Eva licked her lips. She wasn't much older than a college kid herself.

"There won't be any characters to write for if they cancel us. I am trying to save our jobs. When you come up with a brilliant plan, Mason, let me know. For now, a brilliant storyline will suffice."

Selah studied her mentor and mirrored her posture, lifting her carriage and head and pulling back her shoulders. How did Julia have such confidence, such poise, in the face of Mason's constant heckling?

"How soon does our plane leave?" Eva yawned and rested her head against Cane's arm. "Tell me Mason's not going with us."

Way to go, Eva. Who knew she could be funny? *Just keep your body away from my man.* But he wasn't Selah's man and never would be. The icy air in the studio penetrated Selah's skin and grabbed hold of her heart.

"This show is a laughingstock, Julia." Mason seemed frustrated that he couldn't get more of a reaction from Julia. "You're just throwing ideas at the wall to see if anything sticks. Couldn't you have picked better colleges than Boondox U. and Hayseed State?"

He waved his hand toward Selah and it came within inches of her nose. "I suppose it won't be so bad with the Hillbilly Whisperer interpreting for us."

"Easy, boy." Cane's jaw muscle clenched. "Isn't there somewhere else you need to be—taking candy from babies, robbing little old ladies?"

Selah's breath quickened. He was defending her again.

In an instant, she was ready to forfeit her liberated-woman card and sing "I Need a Hero."

"Actually, I've come to ask Selah to dinner." Shoving his hands in his pockets, Mason leaned back on his heels. "There's a cozy Italian joint down the street."

"Dinner together? At the same table?" The room got very quiet. Or else she couldn't hear anything for the sound of blood rushing to her head. That was the biggest smile she'd ever seen on Eva's face.

Selah's stomach took a Powerball tumble at the thought of enduring dinner with the thorn in her side. What was his angle? It had to be a setup to suck as much work out of her as possible before she left. She would need to bring her super-sized bottle of Pepto-Bismol.

"You are so . . ." Julia narrowed her eyes at him, making a clicking noise with her tongue. His grin grew wider. This had the makings of a shootout at the OK Corral.

"Lovable? Cuddly?" Selah finished for Julia. Julia laughed and shook her head. Bullet successfully dodged. Would these two ever see eye to eye?

Mason chuckled. He never laughed unless it was at his own joke.

"I'm out of here." Cane kissed Julia on the cheek. "You know I won't be on the tour, but I wanted to wish you a happy birthday. Happy you survived another year and Mason hasn't sent you to an early grave."

When she released him, he walked toward Selah. He bent his head to her ear, so close she could feel his breath on her neck. The heat rippled throughout her body. "Take your mace with you," he whispered.

When he lifted his head, she fixed her eyes on his,

refusing to revert to her practice of looking down so he couldn't see how much she cared about him. There was sadness in his dark, lidded eyes.

As he left the group, his shoulder bumped Mason's. Eva winked at her and trailed off behind Cane.

Selah exhaled, realizing she'd been holding her breath. Her shoulders retreated to their hunched position.

"I have to run to a meeting." Julia pointed her walkie at Mason. "You behave."

"I'll pick you up at seven." He smiled at Selah again. Something was definitely up.

Julia cast a dismissive hand at him and stomped off.

"Farewell, your majesty." Mason slapped his phone to his ear and strode off in the other direction, leaving Selah alone.

Dinner with Mason and then a Shadybrook homecoming, soap-opera style. She held her palm against her chest and willed her heartbeat to slow. She wanted to live to see *The Winds of Change* blow through Mayberry.

The image of pompous Mason in rural Shadybrook was as mindboggling as a parallel universe. If she brought him, fifteen to twenty years her senior, home to meet her parents, her father would get out the shotgun and run him off. When Cane had compared the soap to *Alice in Wonderland*, he'd forgotten to cast Mason as the Mad Hatter.

She hit speed dial on her cell phone, calling the one person who could make sense of her swirling emotions. "Frankie, hey! Guess what? I'm fixin' to come home next week, and I'm bringing a few friends with me. But first, I have a date tonight."

That must have been what they meant by changing in a New York minute.

Chapter Twenty-Five

"A DATE WITH THAT old guy? Not Cane?"

Just the mention of Cane's name and Selah's stomach took another Powerball tumble. Their relationship was over before it started.

"Mason's not *that* old, Frankie." Mason wasn't as awful to her now as when they'd started working together. Maybe they could find some common ground. "He's almost attractive in a menacing, Al Pacino way."

"Al Pacino is pushing seventy!"

Selah laughed so loud it echoed into the phone. The crew members who were attending to actual business on the set looked up at the sudden noise. She waved an apology.

"If you're talking to me again, I guess you've forgiven me for deceiving you into coming to New York for the fan weekend."

"I'm going to pay you back somehow," Selah said in a soft voice. "I can't believe you did all that for me, Frankie."

"I did it for us. And from the sound of it, I'm getting a twofold return on my investment. You're rubbing shoulders with celebrities, dating a head writer, starring as an extra in a TV show. You're having so much fun, you won't want to come home."

"I want to see you and Momma." *Don't I? Just when I'm gaining ground, everything shifts and I'm back where I started.*

"Just wait until Cane Ashton meets me and your parents in person." Frankie whistled. "This is just like that movie, *Win a Date with Tad Hamilton*, where the bumpkin meets the hot actor. Do you think he'll run screaming when he hits Shadybrook?"

"I am not a bumpkin."

"He *is* going to meet us?"

"Cane isn't coming."

When she hung up with Frankie, fatigue spread through her. She felt as lifeless as the studio did without the actors and the lights.

She wandered over to the tiny set that was Cane's apartment. Selah sunk down onto a black leather sofa, warmed by the thought that he had spent a lot of screen time there. Ugh. How had she gotten so attached to this man who bolted every time they got close?

Something crackled. She reached beneath the sofa cushion and recovered a pile of multi-colored scripts, presumably hidden there by actors who needed help remembering their lines.

The first script in the pile was an old scene between Cane's character, Dean, and Eva's character, Kelli.

Dean: "Admit it. You've got it bad for me, darlin'."

Kelli: "You are so full of yourself. Even if I had feelings for you, I've never been in love before,

so I wouldn't know if it's infatuation or the
real deal."

Dean: "Trust yourself. Trust me."

Selah chuckled. Like his character, Cane acted too big
for his boots at times. Other times, his eyes were like those
of a death-row inmate, guilt-riddled about the past and
fearful for the future. Her feelings for him spun in a thousand different directions. But at the heart of the chaos lay
an overwhelming desire to help him past his pain.

Selah turned over the script, found a pen in the bottom
of her purse, and began to write.

Dear Cane,

*Today was the last time I'll ever see you. My NYC
SoaperFan adventure burst like a soap bubble and
disintegrated. I will miss my sidekick, the Shirtless
Wonder (the Eighth Wonder of the World).*

*I apologize if I did or said something that broke up our
friendship. My mouth has been getting me into trouble
lately. I hope this letter makes clear the things I wanted
to say when we were together.*

*Six weeks ago, I had such severe writer's block, I
couldn't work. Part of me closed off, paralyzed by fear
and self-doubt. It was an empty, hopeless place. When
you told me your story during the blackout, I realized
you lived at that same place.*

*I was angry and disappointed with God for not
answering me or helping me to change. I threw my*

Bible across the room just as you threw that glass in your dressing room. I demanded of God, "Where are You? Why haven't You helped me lose weight? Why haven't You healed my parents' relationship? Why did my business crash? Why do I feel worthless?"

He can do all things, but He doesn't do them for me. It must mean He doesn't care about me. I'm not good enough.

She paused and scanned the room to make sure no one was around.

Did she want to share this much of herself and her faith with him? How could she speak to him about God when she was too self-conscious to get up in church and pray or lead a Bible study?

Taking a deep breath, Selah grabbed another sheet of old script and continued.

Two women in the Bible have helped me understand Him: the woman at the well and the woman with the issue of blood. Two women hopeless with sin and pain. God knew who they were, knew their hearts, when no one else saw them. He saw their worth when they were invisible, worthless to the crowds around them, to the other Jews. He knew what they needed, and He stopped in His tracks to give it to them.

All He asks is that we accept His gift, His love, and hold onto it with everything we've got. Look at Faith. A scruffy, three-legged mutt. Somebody neglected that dog and gave her away. But God cared about her enough to lead her to a home with a bottomless bowl of dog biscuits. She taught me about hanging on even when you're broken inside and out.

I hoped to put all the pieces together, to help you to see God in a better light, without being preachy, but I'm still struggling myself. All I know is that God doesn't see you as the bad seed, the screw-up, the sick guy, someone deserving punishment.

Neither do I. As I recall, you asked me not to pray for you. I don't understand. Where did that come from? I've been praying for you since we met, actually since I first saw you onscreen (I know, stalker, right?), and I'm not about to stop now.

I miss you.

Selah.

P.S. I found Tanner. I'm enclosing his contact information. Do whatever you want with it. I just felt you should know.

Selah folded the letter, wrote Cane's name on the outside, and took her final walk down the winding hallways to his dressing room. She would never see this place again, but it would always be a part of her. She hesitated in front of his door as a memory flashed in her mind. In sixth grade, on a field trip, she'd passed an "I love you" note to a boy she had a crush on. An unromantic teacher intercepted the note and had read it—out loud—to a busload of classmates.

This letter to Cane had the potential to go wrong too. Was it worth the risk of humiliation? Her hand trembled as she weighed the issue. Yes, Cane was worth the risk. She slid the letter under his door and prayed for the best.

Chapter Twenty-Six

SELAH SWAYED ON her high heels as she walked from Dori's bungalow to the curb outside. Be happy you have a date, she kept telling herself. *Yay, I have a date.* Then reality set in. *Why me?* On the positive side, after she figured out what he wanted from her, she wouldn't have to see his craggy face again.

Think. Think. What would Julia do in this situation? She would match him insult for insult or refuse to show him the angry or irritated reaction he craved. Mace was always an option. This was going to be a long night.

At seven p.m. sharp, Mason's Mustang screeched to a stop in front of the curb. Selah stepped back quickly. He might be annoyed enough to mow her down. He unlocked her door but did not get out to open it. If this was a real date, he was rapidly losing favor.

"I thought you said this was a rental car." Selah slid into the leather passenger seat, barely able to hear herself over the roar of the engine.

He grinned but didn't say a word until they reached their destination. The "Italian joint down the street" turned out to be a fine dining establishment with a maître d' and live violin music. Good thing Selah had worn a dress.

When they had ordered, Mason opened his briefcase and plunked a humongous stack of files onto the table. "Before you return to Kansas, Dorothy, I want you to research a new story angle I have in the pipeline."

"I knew it! I should have listened to my instincts." Selah tapped the pile with her index finger.

"Well, go on. Take them." He pushed the files toward her. "You've been doing an adequate job on the writing projects I've given you so far. This is your chance to impress me and go out with a bang."

"This is a working dinner? You brought me to this overpriced, high-falutin' restaurant so you could shackle me with more slave labor?" She squeezed her elbows against her ribs, trying to restrain the pounding of her heart.

"Of course I did. What did you think this was?"

She raised an eyebrow and sent a searing look his way, but he couldn't tear his eyes from the door. She turned around. Maybe it was Cane coming to her rescue. Suddenly, it all became clear. Julia made a grand entrance in a form-fitting black dress and a fur stole. As she chatted with her entourage of six women carrying gift bags, Selah recalled Cane mentioning Julia's birthday.

Mason was entranced. Ordinarily, this could have been a romantic scene straight out of a soap opera. In real life, Selah just felt used. "Why don't you go over and wish her a happy birthday?"

"Who? What are you blathering about?" He continued to gaze over Selah's shoulder.

She clenched her fists to keep her hands from shaking. "You have to be the most self-centered person I have ever met. You brought me here under the guise of taking me on a dinner date just so you could spy on Julia—or irritate her."

"Bravo for using 'guise' in a sentence. I have taught you well, grasshopper." His head snapped back and he turned his attention to her. "You thought this was a date? Are you nuts?"

She dropped her voice down to hissing level. "I cannot believe I thought you might be interested in me."

The furrow between his brows deepened into a chasm. "I advise you to stop making such a scene. We have a lot of work to do before you leave."

"And here's my advice to you." She threw her napkin on the white linen tablecloth and grabbed her purse. "Stop jerking other people's feelings around. Between you, Cane, and Shayne, I've taken enough abuse."

She held her head high as she headed for Julia's table. Julia spotted her, stood, and threw her arms around Selah with such vigor she might have popped her spaghetti straps.

"What a wonderful surprise!"

"Happy birthday, Julia."

"Weren't you supposed to go on a date with Mason tonight?"

"I did. It was a working dinner. He was working me."

Selah looked back at the table where Mason scrambled to explain to the waiter where he should put her untouched dinner. Upon seeing Mason's wet pants, she snickered. She must have knocked his water into his lap when she bolted from the table.

Julia nodded. "Happily, that means you are free to join my birthday celebration. I want all my friends around me."

Her dining companions smiled and pulled up an extra chair. She hesitated as she heard Momma say, *Your real friends are in Shadybrook.* She shook the thought from her mind. Turned out, Momma wasn't always right.

"I can't think of a better way to spend the evening." And she meant it.

Chapter Twenty-Seven

THE WINDS OF Change were blowing south.

Selah rested her head against the scratched Plexiglas window, waiting for takeoff, as Faith snoozed in her carrier beneath the seat in front of her. *I wish I could be that peaceful.* Going home to reality after her amazing time as SoaperFan in New York City was like the Space Shuttle reentering Earth's atmosphere after traveling among the stars.

"I believe you're in my seat, ma'am. I always buy an extra one for my ego."

She looked up. And there he was, wearing the same shaken look he had the night the lights went out at the bungalow. Selah fought the urge to yank down an oxygen mask and inhale. "Cane! I thought you weren't coming."

"And I thought you had already gone home."

Selah craned her neck to look over the top of her seat. Julia ducked her head.

"I smell a setup." Cane pointed his finger at Julia. "The

boss put her foot down. In my backside, actually. So, here I am."

"Here you are, with me, on a cramped plane." She watched him stow his duffel bag in the overhead compartment.

"Carrying a camouflage bag." The universe was conspiring against her.

"My buddy, Justus, gave this to me when he graduated from Citadel. Otherwise, I'm not into camo." He slid into his seat.

She breathed a sigh of relief.

"You look especially lovely today."

Smiling a thank-you, she didn't mention how her thighs were sandwiched between the seat dividers. She didn't want to be one of those girls who complains about her fat in front of a man so he'll be forced to give her a compliment.

She handed him his seat belt so he wouldn't have to dig for it, making their seating situation more awkward than it already was.

"So," he said and turned toward her.

"So." She tried to look engrossed in the airplane safety card. Had he read her letter?

He took the card from her hand and returned it to the seat back. "Don't worry. I'll save you if we crash."

"That's comforting." Selah shuddered as the plane's engine roared to life.

"You've been a great comfort to me, Selah. I repaid you by acting like a child."

"Are you sure you want to sit here and talk to me? Shayne said you didn't want to be my teenage dream anymore."

"I deserve that." He groaned.

Her first instinct was to be a doormat, pat his hand, and tell him it was nothing. But she made herself remain silent and wait for an explanation.

"I shouldn't have taken my issues out on you when all you did was listen and be my friend."

His friend. Great. Here we go again. "SoaperFan to the rescue," she muttered.

Regardless of the way their arms and thighs bumped together in the cramped plane, a distance spanned between them. Although he said all the right things, the barrier he erected stood firm.

Faith whined and scratched violently at her carrier. Cane leaned down and stroked her head through an opening in the bag. "Hey, you."

Suddenly, Selah was jealous of a dog. "She goes wild when she sees you."

"I get that from women a lot." Cane grinned boyishly while Selah rolled her eyes. "Except for you, SoaperFan. You never cry or paw at me."

He studied her like a museum curator evaluating a new piece of art. "You just do that little thing with your mouth."

Her hand automatically flew to her mouth. "What little thing?"

"It starts out as a little dimple and smile on the right side of your mouth, but then you bite it back."

"I do no such thing!" She clamped her lips together.

He laughed and relaxed against the headrest. "Trust me, I've played a little poker. I know the poker tells."

At the mention of gambling, her body tensed and she looked away from him and out the window. As the plane lifted off, Selah watched the Statue of Liberty and the skyscrapers shrink and disappear. She put her hand up to the window and waved.

"Are you and Faith excited to be going home?"

She crunched on the airplane snack mix, desperate to soothe her nerves.

"Just as happy as if I had good sense."

"What?" He pulled an index card from his back pocket. "Julio sent this for your mom. You charmed him."

She read it. "A recipe for another pie. She'll love this."

"I can't wait to meet your parents. They sound like nice folks."

"Mmm." She choked on a mini pretzel.

He patted her gently on the upper back. "Now I'm intrigued."

Selah took a long swallow of flat ginger ale. "They're complicated, but they're good people. Wonderful parents. Adored me and worked themselves to the bone at the diner to help me through school. I'm not complaining."

"I've never heard you complain about anything."

"You haven't seen me in my natural habitat. My parents drive each other crazy. They seethe and simmer and make little jabs at each other all day at the diner. Customers love the entertainment. They're like the Honeymooners. Then, behind closed doors, fireworks. It's not so funny anymore."

Cane raised an eyebrow.

"Not that kind of fireworks. It's not physical, just . . . loud and bitter and cutting. 'He's a lazy idiot.' 'She's an old nag.' Then he'll leave and she'll be home miserable and angry and wondering where he is or with whom. Same argument. Different day."

"And you, the only child, are caught in the middle." He

reached for her hand and brought it to his mouth, brushing his lips against her knuckles. Her breath hitched as she gazed into the eyes of the man who made her inner child feel very grown up.

"Tell me more about Shadybrook."

Instant mood killer. She eased her hand out of his and pushed her head back against the seat. "Oh, where to start. Did you know Shadybrook is the name of a mental institution on *General Hospital*? You'll soon discover how ironic that is."

She gripped the armrest as the plane descended over the Blue Ridge Mountains of Virginia. "I think we're about to hit turbulence."

Chapter Twenty-Eight

"That's what's really cool about the places you love. It doesn't matter where you are or how far away you end up. They will always be a part of you. Always."

Brittany Hodges (played by Lauren Woodland),
The Young and the Restless

"WE'VE LANDED IN Oz," Mason grumbled as he led the cast and crew down the airstairs and out to the parking lot.

"This is just like *Sweet Home Alabama*!" Eva clapped her hands like a child.

Selah squinted as her eyes adjusted to the sunlight. What could be so special about the Shadybrook air strip? Mr. Newman had it installed near the speedway in hopes of attracting deep pockets in corporate jets.

A convoy of peach and mint-green antique cars sputtered up to the sidewalk. The Shadybrook volunteer fire department and rescue squad cruised into the airport after them. Frankie must have recruited the entire town to transport cast and crew of *Winds of Change* to their country home away from home.

Surreal was the only way to describe the scene. She whipped out her camera.

"Hey, Southern Fried! Over here!" Shayne Nixon waved at her friend Gina. A founding Hunk O' the Month Club member and local cop, Gina looked right at home driving an antique police cruiser. Aunt Ruby cut in front of Gina, jumped out, and pulled a mortified Shayne into Ruby's pink Cadillac, a shiny remnant from her Mary Kay glory days.

"Southern Fried. I like it." Cane stood so close behind Selah, she could feel his breath on her neck. "Maybe I'll start calling you that, Selah Southern Fried. Or should it be Southern Fried Selah? I've got it, Southern Fried SoaperFan."

Selah pressed her fist to her mouth as Eva settled in beside Selah's grinning father in his 1969 Dodge Charger. That car was the only possession he hadn't tried to gamble away.

"You're tense. Who is that?"

"My father, Russ Morgan."

"And who is *that*?" He motioned toward a black Hummer limousine that screeched to a halt in front of them.

A blonde whirlwind jumped out of the Hummer and wrapped Cane and Selah in a three-way hug. "Hi, Cane! I'm your chauffeur. Wow, Selah was right—you are just as smokin' hot in real life."

"Frankie!"

Cane flashed a cocky smile. He hefted Selah's luggage into the trunk and carried the dog crate as they climbed into the Hummer.

Before taking the three of them to Rendezvous lodge, Frankie drove the long way through the town of Shadybrook. Despite Selah's instruction that Frankie do nothing to draw attention to the cast, a gaudy "Welcome, Winds of Change!" banner waved in the breeze over Main Street.

"This is amazing, Frankie. Thank you for the airport cruise-in and the banner." Cane had chosen a seat beside Selah in the back of the Hummer. Frankie beamed at them from the rearview mirror.

"Selah nixed my idea to have a tickertape parade down Main Street."

Cane laughed. Selah didn't.

"You're too quiet. I thought you would play tour guide."

"I'm tired." Tired of trying to gauge Cane's feelings and playing his game of keep-away. She rested her head against the cool glass of the window and watched the scenery go by.

"The mountains are so green they look like emeralds with the sunlight shining on them," Cane said.

She looked again, seeing her home and its beauty through his eyes. The new growth reminded her of the hope that had blossomed within her in New York.

"Most people come for the fall colors, but May is my favorite month because the dreariness and the ominous wintry clouds pass away and everything comes alive again. In the short time between the dark winter and the spring, I feel I've become a new person."

A new person who didn't know what she was coming home to. *Have my parents separated? Has any semblance of my business survived? Do I want it to? Should I have accepted the offer to teach computer science during the college's summer session?* She'd given up a lot for this trip and didn't have much to show for it.

"Are you happy to be home?" Cane asked.

"Like Erica Kane in an orange jumpsuit, shrieking as the prison bars close behind her."

He nodded and rested his hand on hers. "Mixed emotions."

She hesitated, remembering his scene with Eva at the studio.

He whispered her name.

She stared down at their tangled fingers and then lifted her eyes to meet his. Eyes like brown autumn leaves drifting along in a soft, cool wind. Eyes like pools of melted chocolate she wanted to dive into. Eyes that . . .

"Earth to Selah." Cane's lips were moving, but they were definitely not on hers.

"I'm sorry." And she was—about the distance between them. "What were you saying?"

"I said, let's have Frankie drop us off at the diner."

"Why?"

"I want to meet the Morgans."

Cane pushed open the doors to Good Company and found more of a circus than a diner. A beehived woman stood on the top rung of a ladder, balancing a light bulb, a screwdriver, a hammer, and a flashlight. She looked like a clown juggling batons while riding a unicycle.

"Momma! What are you doing?"

At Selah's shriek, the woman lost her footing and

teetered backward. Her big hairdo likely was the tipping point. Cane lunged forward and caught her.

Setting her down, he said, "Mrs. Morgan, I presume. Pleased to meet you."

"Well, if that don't beat the band." She grinned and patted her hair. "I done been rescued by Dean, I mean, Cane on *Winds of Change*. Welcome!"

Cane extended his hand, and Selah's "Momma" enveloped him in a hug. He felt a twinge in his stomach. If only his own mom was alive to see how far he'd come with his recovery. She would have loved Selah and been so mad at him for breaking things off.

He turned and climbed the ladder to fix the lightbulb.

"I see you Hollywood types have the women of Shadybrook falling for you already." A man with white hair and mustache came over. Everyone had big hair around here. Cane needed a larger bottle of hair gel and a supersized appetite, judging by the huge plates of food on the diners' tables. His stomach rumbled.

"Cane Ashton, meet my parents, Russ and Margo Morgan."

"Now what were you doing up there, Momma?" Selah's voice was rising. "And what were *you* doing, Dad, while she was trying to do an extreme makeover on the diner? She just had surgery."

"You should know by now that Momma is going to do whatever Momma puts her mind to, whether I approve or not."

"My shoulder done healed up now, Selah. We managed just fine when you left us for so long."

Cane climbed back down the ladder and stood beside

Selah. It hadn't taken long for the family dysfunction to rear its head.

"There weren't many customers, so your dad taught me how to play five-card stud," Eva called from one of the booths.

Selah blanched. "I just bet he was."

Cane rubbed his hand against her back.

"He's going to take me to see the racetrack too."

"Have a super-fun time. Bye, everybody." Selah clutched Cane's arm to usher him out.

"Selah Morgan, don't be in a mood!" Momma scolded. "You've been gone for ages."

The muscles in her back tightened under Cane's fingertips. She squeezed her arms around her stomach. He hadn't seen her this vulnerable before, even when facing Eva's venom.

"Just made some chocolate cake." Momma got out a plate, fork, and a large knife that had no place in that woman's hands. "Won't you have a piece with us?"

Chocolate cake. One of many memories he'd like to erase. "Thank you, Mrs. Morgan, but I'm still queasy from the flight. I have to pass."

The look on his face must have been as pained as he felt because both Morgan women tilted their heads at him.

"I want to show them the ins and outs of the kitchen first, Momma," Russ said. "You can fatten them up later."

Margo's nostrils flared, but she didn't say a word.

Selah squeezed his arm. "Go on with them. Momma and I'll be fine. She's dying to tell me something."

Cane followed Eva and Russ into the kitchen. Cane turned to flash Selah a reassuring smile. A giddy feeling spun like a merry-go-round in his chest when she mouthed a thank-you.

After ten minutes of listening to Russ talk about Stonewall Jackson's march through Shadybrook, Cane couldn't hold back a yawn. The early morning flight had drained him. He left Russ and Eva. He needed to get back to Selah. Just being near her energized him.

Make up your mind here. You broke off your friendship for a reason.

He pushed open one of the galley doors a crack but stopped when he saw Selah sitting at the counter, resting her head in her hands. Margo scrubbed down the front counter as if Martha Stewart was coming to inspect it.

"Selah Morgan, you of all people should know better than to have eyes for a man like that. Handsome is as handsome does."

"What is that supposed to mean?"

"You can't trust a man, especially an attractive one. Just look at your father."

"Cane is not my father."

"If he marries you—"

"We're not getting married. I'm his neutral non-Hollywood confidant."

"If he marries you," Momma persisted, "you'll always wonder if he settled when he could be beddin' some skinny floozy like Eva."

"Thank you, Mother, for that vote of confidence. What about the saying, 'Beauty is only skin deep'?"

"He'll eventually wonder if he coulda had both outward and inward beauty."

She cringed and scarlet splotched her face and neck. "Are you saying just because I'm heavy, I'm not beautiful?"

"No, of course not! I know my baby has the prettiest face in Shadybrook." She stopped scrubbing and squeezed Selah's cheek. "Eva looks like the waif child in that movie about the miserable French people."

She went back to her scrubbing while Selah picked at a piece of cake. "Haven't I taught you anything? Don't let your self-esteem rise and fall on a man. You're too taken with him now to see the hurt he can bring down on a sweet girl like you."

Margo's was the same as the warning he had been giving himself. He had inflicted a great deal of misery on his family and most of the women he'd dated.

"I'm not a girl anymore. God gave me the brains to take care of myself."

Margo ignored her. "What man doesn't like chocolate cake?"

Cane chuckled. He had some work to do if he was going to win over Momma.

"He didn't say he didn't like it. He said he didn't *want* it."

"Same thing. Who doesn't *want* a piece of my chocolate cake?"

"That man is chocolate cake personified if you ask me."

Selah looked up to see Cane watching her with a secret smile. How long had he been standing in the doorway?

"Devil's food then." Momma finally plunked the beaten rag down on the counter. "You can be happy without a man."

"You could, but why would you want to?" Her father came up behind Cane and slapped him on the back. Cane grinned.

Selah could read Momma's mind, and it was saying, *I told you so. Cane and Dad are two peas in a pod.*

"I need some air," Selah announced, feeling like her old self. Funny how fast people revert to their worst selves when they're with the ones they love most.

Outside, a black Hummer pulled up to the curb. Frankie met her on the sidewalk. "Your getaway car awaits, Madam."

"You have the best timing." Selah led the way out and climbed up into the bowels of that black beast, huffing as if she'd climbed Pike's Peak. She left the door open while they waited for Cane.

"I dropped off Julia and Mason at Rendezvous and doubled back. It's common sense that you, Margo, Russ, Cane, and Eva in the same place could only have apocalyptic consequences."

"My father and Cane were bonding." Selah made air quotes.

"They're a lot alike."

"Not you too! That's what Momma said."

"It's not a bad thing. They're both attractive and outgoing characters, and people love them."

"'People' meaning 'women.' According to Momma, handsome men like Cane and Dad will never be cured of their roving eye for the ladies and can't be trusted."

Selah heard something knock against the Hummer. Cane pulled himself in with no effort and slid onto the seat beside her and Faith. "Who can't be trusted?"

Chapter Twenty-Nine

FRANKIE OPENED HER mouth as if to explain but closed it when Selah shook her head. "Frankie can't be trusted . . . on the open road, that is."

"Don't worry. I'm on my best behavior." She winked at Cane from the rearview mirror.

Selah turned toward the sidewalk outside the diner. "Where's Eva?"

"Momma is taking her to prayer meeting tonight," Cane said.

"Eva is going to prayer meeting? At a church?"

"Maybe I heard wrong. Maybe she said *hair* meeting."

"Or *terror* meeting," Frankie offered.

If anyone could get Eva to church, it was Momma, Shadybrook's resident prayer warrior. If only she would take Cane to church with her too. But no. Momma was too busy calling him a no-good player.

Frankie stopped at Rendezvous to pick up Julia and Mason.

"I needed that power nap. We've got a lot of work to do tomorrow," Julia said as they entered the Hummer limo. "Where are you taking us for dinner, Frankie?"

"We're going to make a side trip first, if you don't mind. Selah's got a little surprise planned for Mason."

Mason and Julia turned in their seats to face Selah. She batted her eyelashes. "I promise this will get his creative juices flowing, Miss Julia. He'll be a new man."

"I can't argue with that." Julia shrugged.

Mason aimed his furrowed brow at Selah, but the twinge of fear in his eyes said he anticipated payback for the way he'd acted at dinner in New York. "I don't like the sound of this. Can't we stop and get something to eat first?"

"Trust me. You won't want to do this on a full stomach."

When they pulled into the Shadybrook Speedway, Selah was overwhelmed by the beauty, even here at the place her father loved more than his family. The mountains skirting the dirt track were wrapped in spring greenery like the ancient Olympians crowned with leafy wreaths.

Frankie parked the Hummer across three parking spots. She took Faith's leash and they sprinted down to the driving track, leaving Selah, Mason, Cane, and Julia to keep up. Selah was grateful that Frankie hadn't offered to take them through the main building, her dad's home away from home.

When he reached the clay-based track, Mason bent down to touch it. He rose and circled one of two modified cars parked on the track.

"She didn't have a Mustang available, Mason."

"What are we doing here, Selah?" he asked as he ran his fingertips across the hood.

"Taking you on the ride of your life. Suit up, cowboy,"

Frankie ordered. Her blonde mane bounced with her steps, and her face shone.

Miraculously, his furrowed brow relaxed. Mason the drill sergeant fell in line behind Frankie, following her every command.

Jealousy flashed across Julia's face. It sliced through Selah as well, but not for love of Mason. Her envy lay in Frankie's confidence.

"You ride with me, Mason" Frankie said. "For a little healthy competition, Selah will drive the other car."

"Selah's driving?" Cane and Mason spoke at the same time.

Cane paled and Mason smiled. For once, that smile was genuine and, dare she say, attractive. All that work she had done for him in New York without a word of encouragement. No respect, until she took him racing.

"I wish you wouldn't do this, Selah." Cane tapped the hood with his knuckles.

"It'll be fine. Frankie and I raced each other when we were kids." She warmed at the memory of her only rebellion as a teenager. Momma couldn't have known about it or she would have put a stop to it.

"It's just like riding a bike. I was always faster at that too." Frankie cracked her knuckles.

Selah followed Frankie and Mason to the pit to put on their fire suits. The pit consisted of two RVs parked beside the track while Mr. Newman renovated the speedway facilities. Where were the Newmans getting the money to fund his quest to put Shadybrook Speedway on the map?

When they returned, Cane was standing on the track, kicking the tires on Selah's car.

"You're welcome to ride with her, Cane." Frankie said. She looked like a ninja in her solid black fireproof suit. In her white suit, Selah looked like the Michelin Man.

Cane caught Selah's eye and held it. "Too dangerous."

Frankie looked from Selah to Cane and back again. "I'm just gonna shut up and go show Mason how to put on his seatbelt."

After Frankie was out of earshot, Selah said, "I didn't think you were afraid of anything. Why are you so upset about this?"

"Bad things happen in threes." Cane's voice was quiet but firm. "My parents' death. My recent car accident. I'm not ready for a third, especially one involving you."

"Don't put so much stock in old wives' tales." Just fortune cookies. "I'm in God's hands."

Cane stepped back. "Forgive me if I don't take solace in that."

When Selah pouted a little, his stony facade cracked, and his eyes softened. "Go on, then. I'll hold onto Faith."

"What?"

"The hound. I'll hold it for you." Faith jerked the leash out of Selah's hand and hurled herself at Cane's feet. He scooped up the dog and she licked his face as if it were steak-flavored ice cream.

"Now that's unconditional love."

"You look very sexy in that get-up." Cane called over his shoulder as he and Faith walked toward Julia, who was sitting on the bleachers and talking on her phone. Selah gaped at him until Frankie laid on the horn.

Selah hurried to pull her helmet over a giant mound of curls. Squeezing her ample hips through the car's window necessitated some wiggling and sucking it in. She had a brief panic attack, picturing Frankie having to push her in like Winnie the Pooh stuck in a rabbit hole.

When she was finally settled in the car, Mason gave Selah a thumbs up. Frankie stepped on the gas, and his head snapped against the seat.

Frankie let Selah lead for a few laps. In her rearview mirror, all she could see in the other car was Frankie's helmet bobbing, but she knew her friend was laughing as she drafted Selah's car.

Frankie loved racing. This was it for her. Her thing. She didn't need to go to New York for passion. Selah did.

Frankie bumped Selah's car again and passed, leaving her literally in the dust. Frankie always said racing made her feel as if she was dropping off the first crest of a goliath roller coaster. Selah loved roller coasters too, but she didn't feel that rush.

When Frankie and Mason finally headed for the pit, she slowed the car and pulled up beside them.

"You almost beat me today," Frankie hollered out the window. "But you're too careful. Someday you'll learn to trust the car and yourself."

Cane strode toward them, smiling and carrying a snoozing Faith in his arms. Selah's car had come to a complete stop, but she now began to feel the rush. Her heart raced and her stomach plummeted on the death-drop of the super loop-de-loop.

Mason jumped out and punched the air. "That was incredible! Amazing! Let's go again."

Maybe he'd found his roller coaster too.

Chapter Thirty

"I DON'T KNOW HOW you do it," Selah said as Frankie pulled her out of the car. "It is so claustrophobic in there."

"Like it's the oven and you're the turkey?"

Julia dashed over to the parked cars and squeezed Selah and then Frankie. "That was exhilarating to watch."

Frankie rubbed her ribs where Julia had hugged them. "Thanks, but I think my appendix just burst."

Julia moved on to hug Mason. He looked stunned at first but finally wrapped his arms around her and closed his eyes.

Cane threw his arms around Selah and whispered in her ear, "I'm glad you're back too."

On the inside, Selah was doing backflips and pom-pom cheers.

Frankie beamed at both couples. "My work here is done." She popped the hood of her car and poked her head under it, which meant she would be oblivious to what was going on around her.

"Since I survived, can I at least drive you around the track? We'll go ten miles per hour." Selah stepped back and pulled off the suit.

Cane shook his head. "I . . . If you knew the kind of memories this dredges up . . ."

"I would know if you would tell me about them. Why were you mad at me for racing?"

"I wasn't mad, just . . . concerned."

"Does that mean we're friends again? Because I can't keep up." Selah brushed mud from her cheek.

He hesitated for much too long. "I don't want something bad to happen to you."

"I'll take that as a yes, which means that you owe me an explanation and I ain't taking no for an answer."

His eyes searched her face. "You're right. You deserve to know. Let's get out of here and have some fun first."

"Fun?" Her eyes brightened. "I know just the place."

Two hours later, Cane tried and failed to get a read on Selah as they sat atop a Ferris wheel at the county fair. Selah wouldn't look at him, gazing instead at the sun setting over the mountains. Since she'd touched down in Shadybrook, she seemed more guarded than she'd been in New York, and his tantrum at the track hadn't helped matters. He had no idea how he was going to break down her walls. Well, maybe one idea.

He rocked their seat and she half-screamed, half-giggled as she grabbed the safety bar. "You can race a car, but you're afraid of falling off a carnival ride?"

"I have some control over the car. Up here, with you, there's no telling what could happen."

Curling his fingers through hers, he raised her hand to kiss it. He watched in anticipation as her lips curved up on one side and parted slightly.

"Hey!" The chair lurched forward and backward, throwing him off balance, but it was Selah rocking it this time. He clutched the safety bar as the chair began to descend. She grinned with all her teeth.

When they were safely on the ground again and walking the fairgrounds, he continued to hold her hand. Something seemed missing without the dog at Selah's side. She had left Faith with "Aunt" Frankie.

"Don't tell Momma I brought you here." She led him down the aisles of an exhibition building full of quilts and 4-H projects and mason jars.

"She doesn't like the fair?"

"Boycotted it for twenty years." Selah inspected a blue-ribbon pie. "Momma always placed second in the pie contest, no matter what kind of pie she baked."

"And that was bad for Momma?"

"She had a conniption when one judge told her she lost because her pies were too rich, too sweet. Momma said, 'That is impossible. There's no such thing as being too rich or too sweet.'"

He held the door open for her as they exited the building. "Sage advice."

"The judges didn't agree." She shrugged. "That was the last time Momma and I went to the fair."

She talked about her momma's antics but never mentioned her dad. As well as she hid it, it always seemed as if some dark emotion seethed beneath the surface, threatening to spill out.

"Hey, don't frown. Let's eat. All those baked goods made me hungry." He wrapped his arm around her shoulder as they strolled. "Someday soon we're going to talk about what's eating you, Selah."

She looked away. "Nothing worth talking about."

They headed for a row of food vendors in campers and trucks. After making their selections, they sat at a picnic table under a large tent.

"That was amazing. The only foods they sold were fried, chicken-fried, or double-fried."

"I see you managed to find a few things." She eyed the five Styrofoam plates he'd piled on top of each other. "No judgment here."

"I need this on a daily basis. Maybe the vendors will give me a job." He took a bite of fried okra. "Since I'm soon to be unemployed, I no longer need to exercise for those shirtless scenes. I can get away with two-pack abs."

"A cryin' shame. You're starting a job search tomorrow, mister." She waggled her index finger at him.

Cane turned up his nose. "What is that smell?"

"Poultry barn." She snickered.

He laid down his chicken-on-a-stick and pushed aside that plate.

"Try one of those." She pointed to the plate of deep-fried Oreos. "It will take the chicken taste out of your mouth."

He bit into a deep-fried doughball covered in chocolate and powdered sugar and closed his eyes as he chewed. "I done died and gone to heaven."

"Now that I've plied you with food and you cannot move, start talking."

"So, that was your master plan all along." He wiped sugar from the corners of his mouth and set down the napkin.

She was studying him like Oprah or some shrink, waiting for him to spill his guts. His guts were wishing he hadn't eaten five plates of fried food.

"I don't know where to begin. There's no script for this." He rubbed his palms on his jeans.

"Just tell me what is troubling you about your past."

He took a swig of water. "It all blew up a couple years after I quit *Winds of Change.*"

He couldn't tell her about the drug use. That part of his past would stay buried.

"I was a high school senior, all-American, and so in love with myself back then."

Selah raised an eyebrow.

"Even more so than I am now." His courage surged as her grin widened. Then he told her the worst. "It was a car wreck. My parents and a friend from church were killed."

The laughter and music around him grew tinny.

"Oh, Cane." Her face was soft and sweet, full of compassion he didn't deserve.

"Grandma raised us until we turned eighteen. I left for college on a football scholarship and majored in sports medicine. My brother, Tanner, just left, never to be heard from again." He shrugged and leaned back. "That's the end of it. See, I'm not so exciting."

"You walked away and never looked back."

"Until I met you, I did a pretty good job of it."

"I see the pain etched on your face. You couldn't keep it hidden forever." Selah leaned forward, watching him.

"You want more, don't you?"

Her high ponytail of long black curls bobbed as she nodded. "I can see why the accident would make you leery of driving. How did it happen?"

"It wasn't an accident. It was my fault. Mom, Dad, and a family friend had come to see one of our playoff games. We lost by three points—Tanner's missed field goal."

"One loss shouldn't have meant the end of the world."

"A recruiter was there. I was being courted by a few colleges, and I was furious at my brother for ruining that game and possibly my plans for being an NFL star. Our parents were caught in the middle."

The muscles in his face tightened as he tried to keep his voice steady.

"But that's how teenage boys act sometimes."

"Yeah, but I couldn't let it go with him. I never understood why he didn't care about football like I did. All he wanted was to quit sports and be in the math or computer club. Something nerdy." Cane exhaled a jagged sigh. "We were angry at each other over nothing."

He turned away, watching fairgoers stroll by, smiling and laughing. A young boy, hoisting a cone of cotton candy like the Olympic torch, trotted by their table with his mother at his heels. Cane's eyes clouded and he fought back the torrent of pain. How could one mistake, one blip on the timeline of his existence, color everything in his life? Why couldn't he get over it and move on?

"I insisted on driving home so my parents and friend could chat in the backseat. Mom told me to take the back roads so there wouldn't be so much traffic. Tanner rode shotgun."

"You were fighting and driving?"

"I was distracted." *And high.*

He ground his teeth. "A drunk driver crossed the center line as it came toward us. I swerved and the other car plowed through the back half of our car. Both cars went into a ravine. The end. Aren't you glad you asked?"

"Oh, Cane, what a nightmare!" She rose and sat down beside him, embracing him.

"A nightmare I caused." The nightmares he endured after the accident had returned in the past few months, but more vividly now, stealing his sleep every night. He pulled her close as he tried to hold himself together.

"No, the drunk driver caused the accident," she said quietly.

He snorted and released her. "I killed three people. There's no positive spin you can put on it. There's no coming back from that and living a happy life."

"You've probably heard 'it's not your fault' a thousand times. But that doesn't make it any less true."

"Please don't say it was God's will. I've heard that plenty too." He hated it that his sharp tone had caused her face to fall. He reached over to stroke her cheek. "God may be able to heal your beautiful broken heart, but He and I haven't exactly been on speaking terms since the wreck."

"Actually, I was going to say how courageous you are to have survived so many losses and disappointments." She got up and threw their plates into the trash. When she sat down again, it was on the opposite side of the table, and her face was unreadable.

"Now that you mention Him, He has never left you.

He doesn't hold you responsible for their deaths, but I can see you're determined to torture yourself with this forever."

"Grandma tried to get me to believe all that. I told her then like I'm telling you now: if I'm not to blame, then God is."

"It's been a long day, Cane, between the flight, the racing, and the fair." She gathered her purse and keys. "I'm worn to the bone."

The light had gone out of her eyes.

"You're right. We should call it a night."

When Selah dropped him off at Rendezvous that night, she said nothing more than a vague reference to seeing him tomorrow.

He stood on the sidewalk, watching her go. He turned his eyes heavenward, immediately rewarded with a magnificent display of stars that, in New York, had been obscured by city lights and skyscrapers. A calm passed over him. Was there hope for him?

Chapter Thirty-One

Cane's car spun on the road. He tried to straighten the wheels, but the steering wheel was stuck. He pulled the parking brake and threw the stick shift into a lower gear, but the speed increased with the sound of his mother's screaming and the smell of burning rubber and brakes. When he looked in the rearview mirror, it wasn't his mother's eyes that met his as usual. It was Selah's. Startled, he looked back at the road. Now Selah stood in the trajectory of the out-of-control car. When he stomped the brake pedal and his foot hit dead air, he could only cry out to God as the car hurtled toward her.

"No!" He shot straight up in his bed, and the spinning stopped. He blinked, panted, made a mental inventory of the room. A suitcase sat beside the bed and a script lay on the nightstand. Good. That meant he was safely in his room at Rendezvous. He must've fallen asleep when he sat down on the bed to take his medication.

This was the first time the dreams had included Selah

as his victim. He needed to go outside and see those stars, feel calm again.

Cane opened his bedroom door just as Selah lifted her hand as if to knock. He closed his eyes for a moment and exhaled, thanking God, if He cared, that Cane hadn't killed her too.

"Cane." The way she lowered her gaze and half-whispered, half-squeaked out his name made him want to pull her into his arms and kiss her, tasting the sweetness of her lips. Remembering the horror of the dream, the pain he inflicted on the people he cared about, he stiffened and retreated into his acting mode.

He leaned against the doorjamb, eyebrows raised. "That's me. Always imitated, never duplicated."

He'd been pretending to be happy, carefree for so long, it was a part of him. The television star that fans idolized was just a poser, a faker. Underneath, he was a junkie and a murderer.

Selah thrust a thick envelope against his bare abdomen. She needed to invent blinders for humans like the ones they used on horses. *Deliver me from temptation.*

"Sorry for interrupting, but Julia wanted me to deliver these script revisions. You've had a long day with the college auditions and filming, so I'll just skedaddle now."

"Where ya going, SoaperFan? Come on in and set a spell." He did a fair job of imitating Selah's accent.

"Oh, right, sure." Her face blazed, and it only got hotter when she realized how obscenely short his running shorts were. Maybe he was getting ready to go out for a jog. But if he ventured into town in this getup, her mother might throw a blanket over him.

"Julia sent this?" He opened the envelope and pulled out a stack of papers. "Interesting." He grinned when he picked up a sheet with something drawn in red magic marker.

"What does it say?"

"I'll tell you someday." He hopped onto the bed and patted the space beside him. "Have a seat."

Selah hoped her gulp was not audible. "I'm good with standing. I think I'll stand. That'll be good. Great, even."

She backed away from the bed and bumped against a dresser drawer, sending a long white pen to the carpeted floor. She bent and picked it up and recoiled when she realized it was a syringe.

In an instant, Cane was on his feet, reaching for her. "Be careful, Selah. I don't want you hurt."

"Am I going to get hurt, Cane?" Her question was bigger than just a syringe.

"It's not what you think."

"You don't have to explain. I believe in you." Why was he getting so worked up over it? "It's for your MS, right? I've been reading up on it."

"Doc is talking about switching it to medicine in pill form, but until then, I'm stuck. Get it?"

She snickered. "I get it." She was enjoying their banter, relieved that they had gotten past their disagreement.

He picked up the needle pen and placed it in a bag on his bedside table. "It's easiest to put it in my thigh. That's why I'm running around showing as much leg as a showgirl."

"I hadn't noticed."

"That mouth twitch of yours always gives you away." Hearing him talk about her mouth and seeing him grin down at her blew the circuit board in her brain.

"I've been procrastinating on the shot tonight. I sat down to rest a minute and fell asleep. Guess I need to scream at a Packers game or punch a bag to get my muscles pumped up for it, huh?"

"I have another idea." She couldn't believe the words that were coming out of her mouth and the conviction with which she said them. "I'll give the shot to you if you show me how."

"What? No, no, Selah. I wasn't trying to make you feel sorry for me."

"I don't feel sorry for you. I want to help." She stared him down, dared him to refuse. While most things in life felt uncertain to Selah, this felt right. "Now sit down before I have to hog tie you to the bed."

He obeyed and sat back down on the bed. The look on his face was raw and childlike in its pure vulnerability. Selah realized how far gone she was.

After washing her hands, she took him up on his offer to get into bed with him—er, sit on the bed with him.

"Here's the instructions if you want."

She took the scrolled paper he handed her. "No, I'll just depend on you. Wow, look at all these side effects. Behavioral and mood problems. That's a pre-existing condition, so we won't worry about it today."

He laughed. "If you can bear to touch me, here's an alcohol wipe for your hands and you can use this one for my skin."

Wipes. She could handle that.

"Bunch up the muscle a little."

Muscles. She could definitely handle that.

"What's got you smirking?"

"Because I ain't seen this much muscle since the monster truck show at the county fair."

"We'll never get through this if you keep making me laugh."

She would make it her mission to see that grin on his face every day.

He snapped off the top of the pen and fiddled with it. "Hold the pen with the needle away from you like it's a dart and my leg is the bullseye. Jab it against my skin, push the button, and keep pushing the pen against me for ten seconds. Then take it out and hold this gauze against my skin."

"The nurses on *Winds of Change* slide the fake needles in slowly." When she gently placed her hand on his thigh, she wasn't sure whether the trembling came from herself or Cane.

His smile boosted her confidence—a little. "I know, but you're going to do it like a nurse, not like SoaperFan playing a nurse."

"You will never let me live that down, will you?"

"Nah. Your performance will be on the fan club's gag reel next year."

"I won't mess this up." If obnoxious Katie could be in the health profession, Selah could give an injection successfully.

She followed his directions. When she hit the inject button, she flinched, but he didn't. She counted to ten seconds, but it felt like ten minutes before she could exchange the needle with the gauze and then a Band-Aid. He took the pen and dropped it into a plastic container.

When it was over, tears streamed down her face. She tried to turn her head so Cane wouldn't see, but he reached up and took her chin in his hands. He brushed his thumbs across Selah's wet cheeks. His brown eyes, clouded with emotion, searched hers and then fell to her mouth.

He leaned in and whispered a husky "Thank you" before taking her lips in a gentle kiss that awakened every nerve in her body. She slid her arms instinctively around his neck and returned the kiss.

When he finally dragged his lips away, he grinned like a mischievous little boy. "That was much sweeter than a lol-lipop, Nurse Morgan."

She smacked him lightly on the shoulder, and he kissed her again, this time more possessively.

Just as she was relaxing into him, he drew back. He left his hands on her shoulders, effectively keeping her at arms' length.

"What is it?"

"What's what? Can't I just sit here and admire you?"

"Not with that look. There it is." She pulled his hands off her shoulders and pointed her finger. "*That* is the same look you had in your eyes the night of the blackout. At the church too."

"I'm sorry I ran out on you."

"I am too. I was confused. When you confided in me about your MS, I thought we shared a genuine moment and maybe . . . maybe we could be more than friends."

His eyes softened and she faltered for a moment. It

was hard to look at that face and be angry at him for long. No, she would not be swayed by a square jaw and long eyelashes.

"I felt like such a fool when the lights came on in the cottage and, wham, you got that wild-eyed look." She circled her hand in the air in front of his face. "It was as if you'd been sleeping off a bender, woke up in the soft grass, and realized you were in a cow pasture, staring down a heifer."

"You have really gone country on me since you've been home. Even your accent is deeper."

"Don't change the subject. You know what I'm talking about. Am I that hard to look at?" She stood, keeping her back toward the mirror on his dresser.

"Selah, please. You're as easy on the eyes as they come. It's not like what you said at all."

"Then what is it like? Tell me before you give me a bigger complex than I already have."

He ran his hand through his hair and stood to pace the floor. "Ugh. I'm such a terrible actor. No wonder I didn't win the Emmy."

"All this is an act? You're lying to me about your feelings?" She backed toward the door. No way was she opening herself up to him like that again.

"I've been lying to myself. That night during the blackout, we were getting close. When the lights came on, I saw your face illuminated with such innocence and compassion that I froze. I realized you aren't like the other women I've dated."

"Uh, no, not quite. You've heard what Shayne and Eva say about me."

Selah's embroidered capris were straining against her muffin top and the underwire beneath her sassy red blouse was digging into her skin. She would kill for a piece of pie right now. Why was it that, when she felt so uncomfortable and insecure, the very thing that made her situation worse was the thing she craved the most?

Cane punched his hand into his open fist. "I could kill that guy for hurting you. Not literally though. Don't worry."

"He was right. I don't look like any of the women on your show or someone that Cane Ashton would want to be seen with."

"Selah, stop. You are very, very sexy, and the fact that you aren't trying to be sexy makes you even more appealing." He wrapped his arms lightly around her waist. "You're not like the other women I've dated and thrown away. The flings, the one-night stands, the big mistakes, whatever label you put on it. They were the ones I used to help me forget the pain I caused."

She clamped her eyes shut, trying to block out images of him with other women, including Eva.

Cane cupped her face and lifted it so she couldn't look away.

"You matter to me. They didn't. If I had a weird look on my face, it was because I knew in those moments at the church and cottage how easily I could hurt you with my anger and my mistakes. I'm afraid your mother was right when she said I could cause you a lot of pain. I never want to do that. I want to be worthy of your trust."

Please don't let Momma be right this time. "So, what did you know in the moment you kissed me just now?"

"How much I care about you."

He cares about me! This crazy, mixed-up hunk of a man cares about me.

"How scared you are of me." He brushed a dark curl from her face.

"I am not." She bit her lip. Not scared, exactly. Panic-stricken, maybe.

"I'm not the only one who's been holding back, Selah. What's eating you?"

Suddenly, he took a step backward and sat down hard on the bed. "Hold that thought." He dropped his head into his hands.

"What's wrong?" She knelt in front of him and pried his hands from his face, alarmed at how quickly he had deteriorated from perfectly healthy to pale and clammy. Now she was scared.

"I'm okay. Just a little dizzy, probably from the medicine."

Selah rose and dug through her purse to find a handkerchief.

"Don't get up on my account. You can bow at my feet any day."

She rolled her eyes but breathed a prayer of thanks as the color returned to his cheeks. Sitting beside him on the bed, she used the handkerchief to dab beads of sweat on his forehead.

"Thanks for the save, SoaperFan. I'm good to go." He waved off her help and slowly pushed off the bed, favoring his right foot.

"Sorry. I don't mean to hover." Shoving her hands in her pockets, she resisted the urge to grab his arm to steady him as he walked over to his suitcase. *He said he didn't want you to go down this road with him.*

"You shouldn't apologize so much. You haven't done anything wrong." He rummaged around in the suitcase. "I've got to get dressed and check on Shayne. He said he was heading up to the speedway tonight for some action. He's bored out of his gourd here."

"I can relate." She picked up her purse. "I'll drive and you run in and rescue him."

He pulled out a pair of track pants and, without warning, began to pull them over his shorts.

She turned her back to give him privacy. If only she had those blinders.

"What? Oh, my bad." He chuckled. "I forget about your delicate sensibilities. It's not like you didn't just volunteer to put your hand all over my leg."

She turned around and he continued the show, dragging his hoodie slowly over his biceps and wiggling his hips.

"My diagnosis is that you are terminally incorrigible. The medicine aggravated your behavioral problems."

He kissed her on the check. "I am starving. Maybe that's why I almost wiped out."

She glanced at the time on her phone. "The diner is probably closed by now, but I have a key, and I know my way around the grill." She winked.

"The lady knows her way around a kitchen, a racecar, a computer, and a soap star. She's amazing. She's SoaperFan!"

"I can see you're feeling better already."

He clasped his hand around hers, sending a sensation like heat lightning to the deepest part of her. "Much better."

Chapter Thirty-Two

THE "CLOSED" SIGN hung in the window of Good Company, but Momma had left a few lights on. When Cane pushed open the doors for Selah, her parents' voices radiated from the kitchen into the restaurant. It wasn't like them to leave the doors unlocked while they cleaned up.

"This is all your fault," Momma shouted. "You gambled this diner away. Our livelihood. The place we built together."

Selah felt Cane's hands massaging the knots that had snowballed into boulders at the top of her shoulders. They couldn't lose the diner. It was more of a home to her than their house had ever been.

They can sell the diner, Selah. Frankie's words popped into her mind. If her father had gambled it away, they couldn't sell it. Selah tried to steady her breathing, but it picked up speed with the increasing intensity of her worries. How would her parents make it if they couldn't work?

They would have to sell the house, maybe move in with Aunt Ruby or take a reverse mortgage.

She could survive on beans, Ramen, or macaroni and cheese. Maybe Selah would lose weight. She could find another job. Wal-Mart was always hiring. She had a few friends with teaching degrees who worked there.

"I told you. That harebrained deputy cheated. It was a dirty game."

How could Dad be so nonchalant? He had hit a new low.

"Well, he might be harebrained, but he came in again today to inform me he's taking over the place in two weeks. I had to spend my own money to hire a lawyer to get us out of this mess you created."

Poor Momma.

"I don't know what we're going to do. Meanwhile, your daughter is parading all over town with some unbeliever."

Poor Momma nothing. Why would that woman say such a thing? Stress was no excuse for meanness.

"Are you talking about that soap opera fellow? I thought you liked him. He seemed all right."

"You would like him. He's playing your daughter, and she's gullible and needy enough to fall for the first guy who shows her some attention."

Selah sucked in a sharp breath and Cane's hands stilled against her shoulders. Could a person die from embarrassment?

"I'm sorry, baby. I'll fix this mess with the diner, and I'll talk to Selah."

"Don't you 'baby' me, Russ Morgan. Go tell it to one of your young floozies."

"I don't—"

Something metal crashed against the wall. "Get out! I hate you."

Selah had heard enough. She turned and bolted out of the restaurant. Cane was faster. He pulled her into his arms and crushed her to him. "From now on, you and I are going to stop running from our problems."

"I'm fine. It's no big deal. There's always hope that I'm adopted." She pushed at his chest, but he was a solid wall.

"Please let go." Her whisper came out like a growl. "I need some air." She couldn't think straight when he smelled divine and his embrace made her want to curl up and sleep for hours.

"You're standing outside, Selah. The air doesn't get much fresher. Except for the poultry barn. That was fowl."

She couldn't resist smiling. When she was with him, life didn't seem so hopeless. But in two more days, he and the cast would leave Shadybrook for more stops on the college tour. Then she would put all her time into getting the diner back.

"Bad time for dumb jokes." He smoothed her hair. "What I lack in social graces, I make up for in good looks. Ah, I can't help myself."

She raised her head. "Ordinarily, I love your goofy jokes, but we need to get back to the car before they spot us."

He nodded, taking her hand and hustling to the parking lot. They ducked in her car just as her father, driving his Charger, peeled out from behind the diner.

"Won't Momma follow him out?"

"No. She'll be in there another hour, scrubbing and

scouring anything she can get her hands on. But she might see us out the window." Selah slumped over the steering wheel, needing a moment of calm before she could safely drive him back to Rendezvous. "She would pitch a fit if she heard you call her Momma."

"It suits her personality. She's crazy about me, don't you think?"

"Just plumb crazy." Selah snorted. "Why does this bother me so much? I'm a grown woman, but when I'm around them, I revert to a six-year-old."

"We're all six-year-olds deep down." He stroked her hair and began to rub her back.

She sat back, forcing him to pull away. Looking straight ahead, she buckled her seatbelt before starting the ignition.

"What was that about back there?"

"Let's go to the lodge first, I can't think." She knew she might as well head out to Rendezvous because it was highly unlikely she was going to calm down tonight.

"Whatever you need."

Miles went by in silence until she turned the car into the pine-tree-lined driveway of Rendezvous. She took her time easing her car into a space under a lamppost and shut off the ignition.

"Finally! That is the longest you've ever gone without speaking. It was painful." Cane wasted no time taking her hand in his. "No excuses now. Nowhere to run. Talk to me, Selah."

"If I open my mouth to talk about my parents, the explosion will be nasty."

"And it wasn't difficult for me to tell you about mine?"

Cane had opened up to her about his past and his

illness and he was pressing her to do the same. She was a hypocrite, but she couldn't let him see the ugliness in her soul.

"All right. I'll talk," Cane said. "Momma was wrong. Despite the way I've been acting lately, I'm not playing you. Not saying I won't make mistakes and hurt you again.

"Look at me, Selah." He turned her chin toward him. "You're the first genuine relationship I've had in my adult life. I'm going to hold onto that with everything I've got."

"Stop it, Cane. Stop saying such sweet, incredible things to me." She extricated her hand from his and slapped her palm against the steering wheel. "A relationship is a bad idea. You were right to put a stop to it in New York."

"No, I was wrong. I was reacting to my fear the way you are now. We can have something real."

"What you heard at the diner, *that* is my reality, my legacy: a gambling, cheating father and a miserable mother in this miserable town. *That* is what happens to love and trust."

She wanted him in her life so badly, but he was just a perfect fantasy. After surviving her father's messes and her parents' marriage, the thought of opening herself up to a man and having him rip her apart from the inside out made her sick.

"How long has your father been gambling?" Now he looked away. The playful tone in his voice was gone.

"Since I was five at least. Maybe longer. We've tried to get him help. The one time he promised to go to rehab, he skipped out and went fishing."

The muscles in the back of her neck and head had tightened into an ache. "I shouldn't be so angry at him for having a disease. I should be grateful he's not a felon or a druggie."

Cane made a guttural noise and leaned his forehead against the glass of the passenger window. "He's an addict. I never realized—"

"You're pale. Are you dizzy again?" She unbuckled her seatbelt and switched on the overhead light to investigate. "I completely forgot about eating. Wow, never thought I'd say that in my life. We really should feed you though."

"I'm all right, but I have something I need to say."

"You're not all right. And, golly, haven't we done enough talking?" She gasped. "I remembered something. Wait here."

She jumped out of the car and retrieved a pie, spoons, and napkins from the trunk. When she got back in the car, she was out of breath.

"Why was there a pie in your trunk and why am I just now finding out about it?" Cane grinned. "Honestly, Selah, sometimes when I'm around you, my head does one of those 360 spins like in *The Exorcist*. I was thinking it might be the MS, but it's you."

She widened her eyes theatrically and rotated her neck.

"Dig in," she commanded as she handed him a spoon and took the plastic cover from the pie. "I forgot I had a couple of Momma's pies I was bringing you and Julia."

"You saved the day." He plunged his spoon into the pie and took a bite and another and another. "We could take this up to my room."

"No, we couldn't."

"Yeah, you're right." He winked.

She took a few bites, smiling as he enjoyed his pie. It sure beat rehashing the mess at Good Company.

He groaned and put down his spoon. "About your Dad, Selah."

"I wish you had made me lose my appetite *before* I ate so much pie."

"There's something I haven't told you."

More secrets? Her chest constricted.

"It's something that may change the way you feel about me."

While he was speaking, a shadow crossed in front of the car. They both sat up and Selah locked the doors. "You have got to be kidding me."

Her father knocked on Selah's window and waved.

"Would it be okay if I kept the doors locked and pretended I didn't see him?" She laughed, but the sound rang hollow.

He knocked again. "Hey, kid, it's chilly out here."

She sighed and rolled down the window. "What are you doing?"

"I come looking to talk to you."

"He wants to talk? This I gotta hear." As she got out of the car, she pushed the door into Dad's leg. He grimaced.

"Oopsie."

"Passive-aggressive much?" Cane chuckled and followed them to the sidewalk.

Cane could always make her smile, even when her insides were churning. Squinting from the brightness of the streetlamps, she said, "As much as I like you in that five-o-clock shadow, you should head up to your room. You must be dead on your feet."

Her father was mumbling something about Momma, but Cane ignored him. "I'm not leaving you alone. I'll be right over here while you talk."

Cane walked back to the car and leaned against the hood. Her vehicle hadn't looked that good rolling out of the showroom.

"Go speak to Momma for me."

"Why?"

"The deputy sheriff stole the diner right out from under us. I need you to help get it back."

"What would you propose that I do?"

"I don't know, but there's no talking to her. That is the complainingest woman I ever seen."

Selah had heard all this before. He wanted her to choose sides, to be his confidant. She didn't want a buddy, she needed him to be a man, to be a Daddy.

Say something. Yell at him. Haven't you changed since your trip, become more confident, less of a doormat?

But this was her family. She couldn't say no, couldn't hurt them.

"She is going to be the death of me." Dad paced the sidewalk.

Say something.

"I know. I'm sorry." *No! You could have said anything other than that. Oh, Lord, I need Your help.*

"How exactly did you lose the diner, Mr. Morgan?" Cane's voice penetrated the clamor in her head.

Her father looked up as if seeing him there for the first time. "I used it as collateral for a small loan."

"And you defaulted?" Cane's tone was dispassionate, but she knew what he was digging for.

"In a matter of speaking, yes." He smiled at them as if he was the mayor of Shadybrook giving a speech to his constituents, earnest in the lies he had deceived himself into believing.

"How much time did he give us to vacate?"

"Two weeks. But we are not leaving that diner. It will be over my dead body."

Only two weeks. She pressed her fingers against her temples. That way she could keep her hands busy and not strangle him.

"It's late and I'm tired." She fished her keys out of her purse. "You should come home too, Dad."

"I'll be there shortly."

Right.

"Would you keep it down out there? Isn't it supposed to be tranquil in the boonies?" someone shouted from one of the rooms on the lodge's lower level.

"Is that Mason?" She snickered.

"Peculiar little feller, ain't he?" Dad interjected.

"We've worn out our welcome, Dad. It's time to go home." She gave him a quick hug.

Compassion began to break down some of the anger that had fueled her for so long. This was the man who bragged about her at the diner until the whole town knew about every straight-A report card she'd brought home, every funny poem she'd written, every solo she'd sung in the church choir. He'd taught her how to ride a bike, the one her family had to sell to repay one of his "small loans."

She turned to Cane and surprised herself by kissing him on the cheek.

"Thank you," she murmured into his ear, drinking in

the scent of his cologne, which should have been named "The Stuff That Dreams Are Made Of."

"Aren't you going to help me, baby?" Her father's voice cracked.

She opened the car door and looked back at him. *Of course you'll fix things for him. You always do.*

"No." She held her breath as her father's eyebrows went up and a smile flickered over Cane's lips. "You're on your own this time."

"She's an incredible woman," Cane said as he and Russ stood watching Selah's car until it was gone from sight. The pain etched on his face betrayed how torn Russ was between his love for his daughter and his love of the game.

"Well, I'll be dogged." He shifted his weight from side to side, seemingly at a loss as to his next move. "She's never turned her back on me like that before. She's always helped clean up her old man's messes, smooth things over with the wife."

"I've been where you are, Mr. Morgan."

"Where is that?"

"Quicksand. The more you flail around, trying to change, the more you sink and drag down the people you care about."

"I don't know what you're talking about." He dug around in his jacket pockets and pulled out his keys. "Selah will come around."

"You know what I'm talking about. You just don't want to hear it."

Russ frowned and pointed one of his keys at Cane.

"You best take care of my daughter, and I'll take care of myself."

"You can count on that, sir."

Russ glared at him and left in the Charger. In his self-ishness, Russ would let his family's diner go before he'd sell that vintage car.

God, don't let that be me. Don't let me screw this up with Selah. He didn't push the thought of God from his mind as he usually did. Would she hate him when she found out he was an addict too? How could he convince her that he had changed, that he wouldn't cause her the same pain as her father had, when Cane wasn't convinced himself?

When Selah opened the door to her house, the smell of Momma's baked concoctions filled her nostrils. She leaned back against the door, overwhelmed by the scent of vanilla and cinnamon, the rumbling in her stomach, and her feelings. She shouldn't eat in the middle of the night like this, when she was so keyed up. Oh, but she wanted to.

Food was the most dangerous when she used it to comfort and soothe her emotions. She needed a plan: Grab a water or glass of milk from the kitchen. Then run out of there before she could eat the Oreos in the shelf above the oven, the thin mint cookies or chocolate moose tracks ice cream in the freezer, the Mountain Dew in the frig, or the candy in the dish on the kitchen table. *Don't even get me started on the pantry.*

She hadn't counted on Momma waiting up for her in the kitchen. Faith was at her feet, scrounging for scraps. "I got worried when I came home and you weren't here, sugar. Is your daddy with you?"

Selah shook her head and Momma pressed her lips together. "Typical."

Selah hung her jacket and purse on her chair at the kitchen table. Pouring herself a glass of milk, she tried not to look at the cobbler Momma was taking out of the microwave. "When did you get home?"

"A few minutes ago. What can I fix you to eat?"

"Nothing, thanks. I'm going to bed." She took another swig of milk. It needed chocolate syrup. "Anything happening at the diner?"

Momma turned away and rummaged around in the cabinets. "No. I've got everything under control."

Her father had Momma lying to her daughter to cover for him.

Selah's phone beeped to announce a text message. It was from Cane. "Sleep tight. I have a surprise for you tomorrow."

She smiled, thinking of him leaning against her car, watching over her. That image would make for sweet dreams.

"You were with that boy tonight, weren't you?"

"Cane is not a boy, a player, or an unbeliever. He's a complicated man and I care about him."

Momma talked right over her. "I hired some extra help for the *Winds of Change* party tomorrow night. You can have fun tomorrow without worrying about helping me. It's the last day you'll get to spend with those people from New York. Then we can get back to normal."

"Normal," Selah muttered.

To Momma, they were just New York people, strangers. To Selah, they were part of her heart and, after tomorrow's filming and party, they would be gone. Even Mason had been tolerable—still cranky, but respectful—since she put him in his place on their "date" and introduced him to racing. Selah felt herself tearing up. And Cane . . . Saying goodbye to him, tearing out that piece of her heart, would be like separating the eggs and vanilla from one of Momma's chocolate cakes.

Chapter Thirty-Three

*T*HAT FEELING OF impending loss continued to weigh on her chest the next morning. She and Frankie sat on the bleachers of a local university's football stadium, watching the cast and crew. It was a beautiful day for filming and auditioning college kids hopeful for a part on the show. Dew on the green turf sparkled in the sunshine. The white spire on the university's ad building stood in contrast to the azure mountains in the distance.

Frankie sat on the edge of her seat, watching her favorite actors in action. "Let me get this straight. Last night, Cane tried to comfort you about your nutty parents, but you dropped him off at Rendezvous and then bolted?"

Selah yawned. "It was after midnight and I couldn't listen to my father's delusions anymore." Cane knowing so much about her family issues was humiliating enough.

"You two are like a seesaw. He's into you, then he backs off. You fall for him, but then you run screaming into the night when he comes to you."

"I am not falling for him. He's merely providing a gorgeous distraction from the doldrums of Shadybrook."

Selah told her everything about Cane and herself, except his MS, what she knew of his past, and his kisses. Oh, those kisses . . .

"Gimme a break. Didn't we dream of romance with a soap hunk?"

"That was fine when it was all a dream. I'm not up to the reality. I think I liked it better when he was just a fictional character we watched on TV."

Frankie looked at her as if she'd sprouted antlers. "Why? Is he stuck on himself?"

"No. He's very humble."

"He wears a toupee?"

"Absolutely not." She blushed at the memory of running her fingers through his soft brown locks.

"Bad breath?"

"No."

"Aha! Then you've been close enough to notice."

"He's sweet and charming and talented, but he doesn't know God and he doesn't know me. When he takes a deeper look, he'll head back to New York and forget all about me, and I'll be left broken-hearted."

"You just got home, but you've resumed the pity party already."

"It's not pity. I'm preparing myself."

"Why are you down on yourself all the time? I thought you were coming into your own in New York. You're the Christian—don't you believe God loves you?"

"I guess so." She rested her elbows on her knees and

her head in her hands. Beating this low self-esteem thing like a dead horse, she was getting on her own nerves.

"Either you do or you don't. We're back at that little matter of faith again."

"God has to love me. He made me. He loves everybody."

Selah raised up when she noticed Frankie flipping madly through a pocket Bible.

"You're carrying your Bible around? You're reading your Bible?" Selah's eyes filled.

"Living with your mother drove me to it." Frankie's teeth gleamed against her tan.

Thank You, Lord, that she is my best friend and that she is reading Your Word. Even if it is to teach me a lesson.

"Here it is!" She began to recite. "'Every wise woman buildeth her house, but the foolish plucketh it down.' Proverbs 14:1, KJV. You're tearing yourself down, out of fear or anger or whatever, and you're coveting a body, like Eva's, that doesn't belong to you. That makes you a fool." Frankie slammed the book shut.

"Thank you, BFF, for those special words of encouragement."

"You know what I'm saying. You'd better wise up and see the beautiful, kind, forgiving, funny person that the rest of us know and love."

It would have been nice to hear those words if they hadn't been so aggravating and on point.

"It's easy for you to say. You've never had a closet full of three sizes of clothes, most of which end in "X." You've never worried about whether you'll fit on an amusement park ride or in an airplane seat, about your double-chin and non-baby stretch marks, about people mistaking your stomach fat for a pregnancy. You've always been the stunning, slender beauty queen, and I was Miss Congeniality."

Frankie huffed. "You've lost that title."

Her stomach roiled from the harshness of Frankie's barb.

Frankie's cell phone jingled. She glanced at the screen. "It's Mason. Three times in one day! He's been pestering me to take him for another spin around the track. He's got the fever."

"I knew there had to be a way to get that grump revved up. Pun intended."

"A bad pun is no pun at all." Frankie put her arm around her and squeezed, easing the tension between them.

"There he is, over there, lurking around Julia and Cane." Selah pointed at a group standing around a goalpost. Cane approached a few of the kids who had auditioned and shook their hands or patted them on the back. "Wait, now they're headed this way."

"Hide me." Frankie slumped against the bleachers.

Selah's pulse accelerated as Cane, with Mason bringing up the rear, strode across the turf.

"Guess I need to deal with my stalker. I'll see you and Cane at the wrap party tonight." She narrowed her eyes. "Don't mess this up, Selah."

Frankie stood and shook out her hair, looking like Beyoncé working the stage in front of a giant fan. Frankie wasn't trying to make Selah feel bad. Selah was making herself feel bad with all the constant comparing. It was going to stop, regardless of what happened with Cane. She sighed as she watched her friend walk out to meet Mason. It was going to take a lot of work and a lot of prayer to break a lifetime of negative thoughts and habits.

Selah stood and greeted Cane with a hug. Life was better when you left the bleachers behind.

"Top o' the morning, gorgeous." He kissed her forehead and intertwined his long fingers with her small ones. "The sun is shining and I am done for the day. Actually, that was my last scene, so I am done with *Winds of Change.*"

"Welcome to the ranks of the unemployed." Selah cringed. She took complete responsibility for the failure of her business. She remained grateful that she had two very forgiving clients left and she'd been able to change her student loan repayment plan to income-contingent.

"Let's celebrate. Since it's 11 a.m. already, I am taking you to an early lunch," he said. "I know this world-famous diner where you can order chocolate pecan pancakes all day."

When he was grinning down at her, holding her hand, she had the courage to do anything. The world could collapse around them, but she would still be safe. She needed all the strength he gave her to face the volatile situation at Good Company.

"I hear the proprietors desperately need some business." Selah said.

On the walk to the parking lot and drive to Good Company, she couldn't stop thinking of the diner's future. She had less than two weeks to stop Cody from taking over. But first, they needed a new roof on the house. After that, the only thing left to fix was her parents. It was too late to save her parents from themselves.

"How did it go with my father last night? Was he angry?"

"Just surprised that you were abandoning him in his time of need. You did the right thing, you know, by not giving in to his demands. Russ is in total denial."

"He may win the diner back eventually. Even if he does, I'm afraid of what he'll bet next. The stakes keep getting higher."

When they reached the doors of Good Company, she hesitated, reliving her parents' blow-out last night.

"I'm right behind you."

Something warm released inside her. She leaned against him, feeling protected and safe.

Cane's phone buzzed. He frowned when he looked at it. "I should take this, but I hate for you to go in there alone and unarmed."

"Go ahead and take it. I'll be fine." She waved him off and pushed open the doors. "The situation here can't get much worse than it already is."

When she stepped up to the chrome counter, everything seemed peaceful: a few customers nodded their heads to Elvis' "Suspicious Minds," Momma smiled as she cut a piece of cake, her father grinned as he lifted a basket of onion rings from the fryer. They were both smiling? This fight was worse than she thought.

"Come sit down, sugar." Momma set a tall slice of chocolate fudge cake on the counter and slid the plate into the hands of a customer.

"Cane and I are here for lunch."

"Hey, y'all, if it ain't Miss Selah." The customer turned and she recognized him by his smirk.

"Hello, Shayne. I haven't seen you since we flew in." And what a blessing it had been.

He crammed a forkful of cake in his mouth and looked up at her. "I've been bonding with your daddy at the Speedway."

Momma rolled her eyes, a rare phenomenon that only Russ and now Shayne could bring out in her. As Momma pushed a slice of peanut butter pie toward her, Selah sighed and sat on the barstool beside Shayne. He had devoured half of his cake and was checking out her plate. His eyes looked red and glassy.

"Two pieces of pie and a slice of cake. I'm going to have to cut you off before you keel over with sugar shock." Momma shook her finger at him and left to refill another customer's coffee.

"I've gained ten pounds from eating here. I understand now why you look like you do, Selah."

She squinched her eyes shut, willing away the urge to dump Tabasco sauce on his cake. She tried a different tack, laughing at his insult. "Yep, you are in deep-fried, chicken-fried, double-fried country."

The mirth in his eyes turned into daggers as the doors whooshed open and Cane walked in.

When Cane saw Shayne and Selah with their heads together, he had a sickening feeling his future with her was about to blow apart. Cane walked over and stood behind her barstool, his hands on her shoulders.

"Funny story," Shayne aimed the fork at her. "Picture this: your boyfriend, high-test party mix, and a chocolate cake twenty or so years ago."

"What are you smoking today, man?" Cane's voice sounded angrier than the situation called for.

She swiveled her barstool and leaned back, watching them both.

"This golden boy act of yours is wearing thin, Ashton."

"Let's not do this here." Cane lowered his voice.

"I will do this wherever I want. Before you arrived, I was having a lovely conversation with Selah about the good old days, when you knew how to have a good time and you weren't such a hypocrite."

"What's party mix?" Selah interjected.

Ice filled Cane's veins. He should have told her the truth sooner.

"You mix uppers, downers, whatever pills you can find in a big bowl, like Chex mix, and scoop out a handful. Instant party." Shayne inspected his jacket pockets. "I might even have a sample in here if you'd like to try. Live a little."

Selah's eyes widened. Momma was inching along the counter, leaning toward them as far as she could without tipping over. She could probably fit a listening device in all that hair if she tried.

"Cool it. You're in a public place and there's a cop sitting over there." Cane was anything but cool right now. Short of clamping his hand over Shayne's mouth, how could he shut him up and get Selah away from him?

Shayne wasn't listening to reason. He'd given up trying to find his drugs and was eating from Selah's plate.

"You haven't told your beloved about your sordid past, have you? Tsk. Won't she be in for a letdown when she finds out her SoaperMan is human after all?"

Chapter Thirty-Four

SELAH ROSE, HER pale face a stark contrast to the colorful diner. "What is he talking about?"

"Is there a quiet place we can talk without interruption?" Cane turned his back and blocked Selah's view of Momma, who looked as if she was about to sic her flying monkeys on him.

"Follow me." Selah wrapped her arms around herself and led the way out of the diner.

"Have fun you crazy kids," Shayne called.

This was going to end badly. If only Cane had listened to Justus.

Justus had phoned last night, warning him, "Don't you ever watch that soap of yours? If you did, you'd learn the truth always comes out. Tell her, brother. Tell her everything."

Cane followed her next door to a Chinese restaurant that welcomed customers with a koi pond and small red pagoda. Around back were ornate benches and a water garden that would have, under normal circumstances, been romantic.

She knocked on the glass door at the back of the restaurant and waved at a goliath with a buzz cut. The man saluted and returned to his stove.

"This should be private enough. Just Willie and the fish." Trembling, she sat facing him on the bench. He took off his jacket and wrapped it around her.

"Shayne warned me twice, but I didn't believe him. You wouldn't hide something that might hurt me. We're over all that, right?"

He swallowed and ran his hands through his hair.

Comprehension dawned in her eyes and they filled with tears. "Say it, Cane. You aren't a coward."

"I am. A coward and an addict." The night of the accident, as he watched the rescuers pull his parents from the ravine, the feeling of powerlessness had brought him to his knees. That feeling threatened to crush him again.

"When you said you had a surprise for me, I didn't see that coming." She laughed raggedly and looked heavenward.

A light rain was falling, but she shrugged off his jacket and placed it neatly between them on the bench. "Are you on drugs now?"

He stretched out his hand to touch her. "You know I'm not—"

She shrunk back. "The injection I gave you . . . It wasn't . . . You wouldn't—"

"No, Selah. The injection you gave me was for my MS. I've been clean for fourteen years and thirteen days."

"For that, I am proud of you."

"I should have told you sooner."

"Why didn't you? Why did I have to hear about it from Shayne?"

His gut twisted. "I was afraid it would drive you away." Judging from the look in her eyes, his fears had materialized.

"Because of my father." She glanced in the direction of the diner before dropping her gaze to her hands. She nervously rubbed the flesh between her thumb and index finger.

Where was that dog when she needed comfort? She was better off with it than with him. "I didn't realize he had a gambling addiction until you told me a few days ago, after he and Momma had the blow-out."

"When I was looking for your brother, I came across a gossip item about your addiction, but I was hoping they got it wrong. I was so sure it was just Shayne they were talking about."

"You searched for Tanner?" The tight muscles at his temple began to throb.

"I found a phone number for him and gave it to you in the letter I slid under your dressing room door."

"I never got a letter from you. What else did it say?" What could have happened to it?

"I wrote it when you weren't communicating with me. I wanted you to know that I missed you." She looked up at him, her eyes hypnotic. "I don't have the right to demand that you share your darkest secrets with me. We're not dating or exclusive. You said it yourself, we're friends."

"When I'm away from you, I can't stop thinking about you. When I'm with you, I want to kiss you. When I kiss you, I want to be a better man. Am I crazy or does that qualify us as more than friends?"

"Both, I think." She smiled shyly, reaching across the divide to take his hand. "Help me to understand. How does someone so young become a drug addict?"

"While I was on the show, I lived with Shayne in the city. He got me a fake ID and took me to clubs with him."

"Shayne did this to you? He corrupted a teenaged kid?" Her head shot up, eyes blazing.

"I pushed him to take me with him. Both of us thought we could handle it."

"There's no excuse for his behavior. He was supposed to be the responsible adult, a father figure." She shook her head. The rain had picked up, but she didn't seem to notice.

"What did you and your responsible father figure do together when you were fifteen, Selah?"

She bit her lip. He brought his hand to her mouth and dragged his thumb across her bottom lip. Her sharp intake of breath was audible.

"Talk to me, sweetness. I've broken down walls and opened up to you like no one else. Please, let me in."

She sighed raggedly. "He taught me how to count cards."

A tear slid down her cheek. She rubbed it off with swift strokes that left red smears in its place. It was all he could do to keep from reaching out and grasping her cheeks in his hands.

"He showed me how to have a poker face, a skill I never mastered. He brought me along to the track and casinos until Momma found out and threatened to divorce him and take me with her to Canada. I wish she had."

"The thought of Momma in Canada, eh?"

"Scary." Selah sniffed and smiled up at him. "Your

addiction is upsetting, but this is more about his addiction and the junk that's left over in my head and my use of the only drug available—food. He took everything from our family and, even at my age, I feel those childhood betrayals and disappointments like they were yesterday."

Cane's throat contracted as if a poker chip was lodged in it. Watching her hurt was worse than feeling his own. Unable to take it another minute, he enveloped her in his arms.

"It's all right to cry. Heck, I'm on the verge of crying for you, for both of us."

When she buried her face in his chest, he squeezed her tighter. Her shoulders began to shake. She cried quietly with no loud sobs or melodrama. He kissed the top of her head and ran his fingers through her tangled hair.

After what seemed like ten minutes, she moaned. He released her. "Thank you for letting me cry on your shoulder, literally."

She straightened and wrung water out of her blouse.

"Think they'd let us stand under the dryers at Cooter's Car Wash?" Cane asked.

"Now, can we please table this topic of 'Poor me, Daddy's a gamblin' man'? I am horrified at how Shayne contributed to the delinquency of a minor, an innocent kid."

"I was never innocent. I could have stayed home, made the choice to turn him down. But I enjoyed partying. I thought I had it made. I was on TV. I had girls. I had drugs."

Selah looked so stricken, it nearly undid him.

"Word got back to my parents that I was blowing off my tutors and coming to the set wasted. They made me quit the show. The incident Shayne was talking about was the going-away party for my last day on the set. I had a little of his party mix and ended up face down in my 'Good Luck, Cane' cake."

She laughed. "Was it chocolate?"

"When Momma tried to get me to eat her chocolate cake," he grabbed his stomach with one hand and his forehead with the other, "I didn't know what to do."

Her amusement faded and she pinned him with her eyes. She was thinking the same thing he was. He should have come clean with her right there and then at the diner. He could have told her everything at the racetrack or at the fair. Maybe she would have forgiven him.

"What a moron I was." Thunder rumbled in the distance, as if God fully agreed. "I give credit to the show. They tried to get me help, and they kept my problems quiet when my parents took me home. They also did not recast my character."

"They brought you back later."

"Years later, after my NFL career was over. That's when I got clean and they re-hired me."

"You didn't straighten out after your parents brought you home?"

He tried to rub the rainwater from his hands, but there wasn't a dry spot on his body. His clothing clung to him like his past. He knew how Hamlet must have felt, trying to rub out the blood that would never disappear. "I got worse. Being on TV made me popular in high school. That got me back to drugs and girls."

With her arms wrapped tightly around her, she rose and paced the tiny garden. Cane rose too but stood in place, watching her. "We should get out of the rain. Aren't you cold?"

She turned to face him, water dripping from her hair and eyelashes. "It's liberating not having to worry about how my hair and makeup look."

"You're beautiful either way."

Out of the corner of his eye, he saw a flash. Chef Willie was standing at the glass door that separated the garden from the restaurant. Carrying a butcher knife, he looked from Cane to Selah and back again. Cane smiled politely and made a mental note not to cross that guy.

Willie was just protecting her. She had so many people who cared about her. She was the only person who sincerely cared about him, and he had blown it.

"Is all this why you blame yourself for your parents' accident?"

Drenched, he imagined himself in the ocean, drifting out to sea.

"It wasn't an accident. It was partly my fault." He braced himself to confess the truth he'd been trying to escape for nearly twenty years. Or perhaps keeping the secret was his way of holding onto their memory.

"I've never admitted this to anyone. Only Tanner knows the truth. That night, before the game, I took amphetamines. After the game, I smoked a couple of joints. Then I got behind the wheel."

As soon as the words left his lips, the crushing sensation in his chest lifted.

Her mouth formed an "O," but no sound came out.

"I'll never know exactly how much my drug abuse contributed to the wreck. The cops didn't investigate me because I was only seventeen and the other guy was obviously wasted with a 0.19 blood alcohol level."

"The law could never punish you as much as you've punished yourself." Her voice was soft and her face filled with such compassion for him, the loser who lied to her repeatedly. He was in love with her. If he hadn't known before, it was clear now.

He held his breath as he reached for the hand she'd been massaging. She didn't pull away. He let out the breath. There was still hope.

"Did you get help after the accident?"

"You would think so, but no. I tried to party myself to death in college. The only thing that kept me going was football. But it became harder to beat the drug tests."

The rain was pouring now. Even the fish had taken cover.

"When I injured myself, one of my doctors discretely checked me into a rehab facility. It saved my life."

"Thank the good Lord."

"Can you forgive me?"

"There's nothing for me to forgive, except you jerking me around. I need time to process this. It's a shock."

When lightning crashed, she startled and took a wobbly step back. He caught her before she could fall into the koi pond. She giggled. Some things never changed.

"Before I met you, I prayed for passion and excitement in my life," Selah said. "God has more than delivered."

He brushed his thumbs over her cheeks, wiping away tears and rain. Her lavender blue eyes were wide as he bent and kissed her. She returned his kiss as the rain streamed down their faces.

Thunder boomed again. She pulled away. "Don't, Cane."

"Don't what? Don't touch you? Don't care about you? Don't want to spend every moment with you? Too late."

"All of the above. When you say things like that, when you kiss me, it lulls me into believing that we have a future." Her words eviscerated him like Willie's butcher knife. "I cannot go through with you what I've been through with my father, what I'm still going through with him: wondering what you're doing and who you're with when you stay out all night, thinking there must be something wrong with me because I can't convince you to stay and give up your addiction."

She put her hand to her face, stifling a sob. "It would destroy me."

He shook his head. He was determined to get it right this time. "I left that dark part of my life behind. It will never touch you."

"It already has."

"I'm a different man now. I don't plan on going back."

"You can't know that." She clutched her chest with both hands. "I was never enough with him. I have to be enough for you, Cane."

"You are enough. I will always choose you over drugs, over other women." This went so much deeper than his past and his lies, he wasn't sure he could convince her.

"It's not about avoiding the things you've done in the past. It's about who you are. You aren't truly changed if you haven't given your life over to God and asked His forgiveness."

He blinked. "Oh, man. I did not expect an ultimatum

to choose God over everything." Feeling dizzy, he returned
to the bench and put his foot on the seat for support.

"We will never make it if you haven't made God the
center of your life."

"If that's what you need from me, then I will. Anything."

"You have to do it for yourself, not for me. When you
get the urge to use again, who will you run to?"

"God isn't the enemy anymore, Selah, but He's still a
stranger. He's my parents' God, Grandma's God. I've managed to live successfully without Him for a long time."

She didn't speak.

He sighed. "It's that important?"

"It's a deal-breaker."

Selah left Cane standing in the garden, as shaken and
soaked as she was. Everything after that was a blur—walking home, showering, changing into her dress for the party,
praying, crying. She couldn't stop crying. She had always
been annoyed by girls who were weepy and needy, whose
spirits rose and fell with the affections of a man. How had
she turned into one of those girls?

Cane's voice had cracked when he asked, "Are we okay,
Selah?"

The answer would have been a resounding "yes" if she'd
allowed herself to gaze into the chocolate waterfall swirling
in his eyes.

But she kept a level head. "You're leaving tomorrow,
so it doesn't matter anyway." The thought sent her deeper
into melancholy.

"It matters," he murmured.

She'd walked away, feeling partly like an adult who

needed to terminate a relationship that would never come to fruition and mostly like a child. Hadn't she known in her gut that Cane was too good to be true?

She managed to pull herself together by five o'clock, leash up Faith, and walk back for the wrap party at six. She trudged her way up the grassy area and walkway in front of Willie's and Good Company. Guests trickled in as workers set up picnic tables and a buffet under a tent. The rain had stopped, but everything and everybody sank in the wet grass.

The only one who wasn't struggling in the rain's aftermath was Frankie who hiked up her black sundress and sprinted over to her. "There you are!"

Selah hugged her tightly, wishing she could confide in her. Where to start? It was such a tangled mess. "You don't know how happy I am to see you."

"This party is the coolest thing ever to hit Shadybrook. Why aren't you happier about it? Why do your eyes look weird? Did you and Cane break up?" Frankie tilted Selah's chin and looked in her eyes, honing in on the sadness that had to be written all over her face.

Selah batted her hand away. "Leave me be. I'm just nervous. I want this night to be perfect for my parents and for the show."

"I don't believe you, but I have to run take care of a few things, so I'll let it slide for now." Frankie jerked a thumb toward the grassy area. "Cane's over yonder. How can you lay eyes on that dreamboat and not want to fall in love and get married?"

Frankie sighed. A lump formed in Selah's throat as she caught sight of the man who had just torn her heart out.

"Have ya met my parents?" Her body felt so brittle she could shatter and blow away in a gust of wind.

"You surprise me. For someone who was so guy-crazy, you are the most cynical person I have ever known when it comes to love and marriage."

How could you truly know a person until you were deep in the trenches of a relationship, too far down to dig yourself out? You couldn't foresee that he was capable of stealing and sacrificing your childhood and your family business at the altar of a poker game, all while expecting you to be his cook, washwoman, and maid. She realized she was projecting her parents' heartbreaks onto Cane, but this talk of marriage was terrifying.

She responded curtly. "Sixty percent of marriages end in divorce."

"Well, there's a forty percent chance you'd make it. You've always been the oddball."

"You have to account for all those in the 40 percent range who are miserable but don't get a divorce. I think the wild animals at the zoo are beautiful and fascinating, but that doesn't mean I want to take a tiger home, feed it, clean up after it, and be growled at."

Frankie's eyebrows squished together. "Even the animals went into the ark two by two."

"Why does the thought of becoming a couple make me feel as if I'm about to walk the plank?" Selah murmured as her eyes moistened. "Can we please not talk about this anymore?"

"You are messed up right now." Frankie hugged her again. "I wish I didn't have to leave you. Please go work this out with Cane. Tell him if he doesn't treat you right, I will run him down with my racecar."

Selah nodded and Frankie left. She scanned the grounds and found Cane close by, tossing a football to a man who caught it with one hand. His intricately-woven dreadlocks took flight in the wind like a waving flag. He looked familiar, as-seen-on-TV familiar.

Selah waved at Julia and snickered at Mason in his aviator glasses and a new t-shirt emblazoned with the Shadybrook Speedway logo. Cane's next throw grazed Mason's ear.

Julia covered her mouth with her hand.

Cane grinned. "Sorry, man, it slipped."

Mason waved him off like a gnat and continued to talk to Julia. That man had it bad.

When Cane caught sight of Selah, a smile swept across his face. He had changed into jeans, black cowboy boots, a dress shirt, and tie. Thankfully, she had taken extra time with her makeup and opted for a lavender and white sundress and sandals. The guys met her on the walkway.

"What is it about men and throwing the ball around?" She kept her voice light. "Is it an ancient bonding ritual?"

The friend looked Selah up and down. "Dang, Cane, that girl is fine. Are you sure she's into you?"

"Watch your tone in the presence of a lady, Justus." Cane smacked his back and Justus bowed to Selah. "Selah Morgan, I'd like you to meet—"

"Justus Jackson from the Washington Redskins. I couldn't place you at first, but, seeing you up close, now I remember. You made that record-breaking interception in the playoffs last year."

"You are my kind of fan, Selah."

She raised her hand for a fist bump, but he pulled her into a hug. Faith barked until he released Selah and bent to scratch the little rascal's head.

"Hey, where's my hug?" Cane stretched out his arms.

Justus wrapped him in a headlock. Cane's eyes bugged out and he stuck out his tongue. The football player ruffled his hair and released him

"Justus is the real surprise I planned for you."

"I love it. Much more pleasant than your other surprise." She faltered when Cane held her gaze, reaching out and taking her hand. *Stay strong.*

"How do you know each other?"

"Cane is like a big brother. He looked out for me in high school after my mother died. He paid my way through college."

"Most of that was paid for by football and basketball scholarships." Cane beamed at his friend, who spun the football on his index finger. "Showoff."

Cane's phone buzzed. He released Selah's hand and tapped on the screen. "It's my agent. He has a lead on a part."

"Take it. I'll keep your lady entertained."

"Don't talk trash behind my back, kid." Cane pointed at Justus and took his phone to a quieter spot.

Justus watched him go and then turned to Selah. "You've been good for him. He's more relaxed, dare I say, happy."

"I needed to hear that. Thank you."

He motioned toward a picnic table, and they sat across from each other. "He told you about the accident?"

Selah nodded, not willing to speak and betray Cane's confidence.

"My dad was the drunk driver."

She pressed her hand to her chest, tears pricking her eyes. "Oh, Justus."

"I was a little kid, too young to understand. My mother, though, it was rough on her. I do remember that."

Selah reached over and squeezed his enormous hand. He placed his other hand over hers and smiled back at her.

"Cane brought us groceries, did handyman jobs around our house, anything he could to look out for us. When she died years later, Cane stepped in as my mentor."

"He was just a kid himself." Selah sniffed and brushed her fingertips across the corners of her eyes. Justus handed her a maroon and gold handkerchief. She dabbed at her eyes, proud of the gentleman Cane had shown him to be.

"In his shoes, I don't think I could have taken in the family of the drunk driver who killed my family and my girlfriend."

"Girlfriend?"

"She was sitting with his parents in the backseat. They were killed instantly. She was a cheerleader. She'd gotten him into Bible studies, something I've been trying to do for years."

Cane's words came back to her. *I was the cliché. Captain of the football team dating the head cheerleader. My parents were in the backseat with a friend from church.*

She closed her eyes. Another lie of omission. Instead of anger, she felt his pain at her core, understood the weight of guilt and despair he'd carried around all these years.

"You love him, don't you? It's written all over your face. He's very blessed."

No! Love was cruel and bitter, the equivalent of the saying, "familiarity breeds contempt." She had never met anyone who lived the biblical "love is patient, love is kind" model.

"I care deeply for him." Feeling someone watching her, she looked up to see Cane standing a few feet from them. Her words curdled in her stomach. He had to have heard them.

He acted as if he hadn't. Holding up his phone, he said, "I've got a lock on that part."

"That's great." Just great. Super. She felt the walls rising up around her heart. It was fun while it lasted.

"That's good news, man." Justus stood and gave him one of those half-handshake, half-hugs she'd seen other men do. Would a complete hug not be manly? "Since you'll be working, I won't have to support you and pay for you to live in a nursing home."

"Fine friend you are."

"I got to get back to Richmond for minicamp, bro. Keep in touch, both of you."

Selah stood and Cane wrapped his arm around her waist as they watched Justus jog off toward his car. She knew she should push Cane away—they were done, broken—but she couldn't bring herself to do it.

He surveyed the crowd that had gathered. "Wow, would you look at this place? Shadybrook is gonna have a hoedown tonight."

"This isn't a hoedown."

"What is it then?"

"Just a big party. A hoedown entails fiddling and dancing a jig. I've never been to one, though."

He spun her around. "Now it's a hoedown."

She laughed, then straightened. "I just can't quit you." She must have inherited her father's addictive personality.

"I'm never going to stop trying to win your heart." Cane brushed his hand across her cheek.

Momma's voice snuck in her head. *You can do better, Selah Marie. Men like that are only out for themselves.* Selah stood on her tippy-toes and kissed him on the cheek before stepping into his embrace.

"Let's just enjoy the sunset and the time we have left." What Momma didn't know wouldn't hurt her.

Chapter Thirty-Five

*G*OOSEBUMPS RAN DOWN Selah's arms as she watched the cast and crew of *The Winds of Change,* the fans, and the curiosity seekers descend upon Good Company for a wrap party. The party had just begun, but the diner was already crammed full. Patrons also mingled in the street and drank milkshakes under umbrella-covered picnic tables with red checkered tablecloths.

Selah had fallen into Wonderland and then Wonderland had followed her home. God had blessed her beyond her wildest dreams. She'd become friends with the people she'd admired her entire life. Now the business they brought to the diner just might be enough to save it.

Sixty-year-old Aunt Ruby leaned into Mason's personal space, touching his arm and laughing. Mason, despite having been hit in the head with a football and abandoned by Julia, was laughing too, probably thrilled that someone would willingly listen to his egocentric rants. Chinese Willie, in fatigues and white chef's hat, offered Julia a taste of sauce from a serving spoon.

A group of male cameramen gathered around her father, who entertained them with either a hillbilly joke or a dirty joke. When Selah walked by, the group went silent. Yep, dirty joke. Momma was probably slaving in the kitchen, despite the extra help she'd hired for this event. And they said Selah was the predictable one.

All heads turned as a white stretch limousine pulled up in front of the diner. A familiar woman stepped out and took in the scene from behind Audrey Hepburn sunglasses and a vintage hat. She was the embodiment of elegance in a red silk pantsuit and a diamond necklace with so much sparkle it should have come with its own bodyguard and alarm system.

Selah rushed to greet her, but her father beat her to it. "Welcome to Good Company. I'm the proprietor, Russ Morgan."

"Hello, darling," she said to him. "I'm looking for Selah Morgan."

"She happens to be my little girl." He beamed.

She had a flash of him teaching her how to drive a stick shift in the convertible, grinning at her from the passenger seat as their hair made crazy shapes in the wind. She started to get a lump in her throat until she saw him smooth his mustache with his thumb, the motion that was his tell in poker. His eyes pleaded with her. He was still trying to win her over, to get her to help him out of this mess with the diner. He loved her, but his love always came with conditions.

She brushed by him without introducing him to the stunning diva.

"Hello, Miss Dorian." Selah took her hands and received air kisses in return. "I'm Selah and I'm honored finally to meet you."

"The pleasure is mine!"

"I'm surprised you came. After visiting Italy and China, you might find Shadybrook to be— "

"Beneath me? I love visiting exotic locales," she whispered. "But I was born near Petersburg, West Virginia."

"I didn't read that in your autobiography."

"If you repeat it, I'll deny it."

Mason chose that moment to interrupt and push Selah out of the way. "Dorian, you've finally returned." He smiled shyly, seemingly star-struck.

"What is our head writer doing here? Still panting after Julia, I suppose?"

He backed up.

"I'd love to chat about my abominable storylines later, but I want to talk to Selah first, okay, love?" Dorian flicked her hand and Mason was dismissed.

Selah felt a little sorry for him. Just a little.

"That man is as irritating as a horsefly on a hot day, bless his heart."

Selah grinned at Dorian's attempt at a Southern accent.

"Speaking of people who need to be reined in, bravo to you for getting my daughter fired. It was a long time coming."

"I expected you to be mad."

"Dorian Forrester—mad? No, darling. Eva needed a good kick in the pants, and I haven't been around to do it. She's still got a lot of growing up to do."

"She's got talent," Selah politely lied through her teeth. "I'm sure she'll find a new job that's more suited to her, um, unique abilities."

"What that girl needs is to take acting lessons and do theater, anything to loosen up that sour puss of hers. I'm told she uses menthol and has even poked herself in the eye to help with crying scenes." She put the back of her hand to her forehead, like a heroine about to faint dead away. "I can cry on cue, anytime, anyplace."

"Maybe that's the problem. It would be hard to live in the shadow of the great Dorian Forrester."

Sadness flashed briefly across her perfect features before she regained composure. "Speaking of children, look at your little angel!"

She scooped up Faith, who proceeded to lick her silly. "I adore my Chihuahuas, but you can't help but love a scruffy Brussels Griffon."

"A what?"

"She's a Brussels Griffon, a purebred. Show quality, except for the leg, of course, and this dreadful clip that makes her look like a terrier."

She handed the dog to Selah. Faith, panting with her mouth wide open, looked as if she was laughing—laughing at Selah for calling her a mangy mutt when she was actually a princess with a pedigree.

Julia swept in and wrapped Dorian in a hug without waiting for the air kisses. "Dori, I'm glad you made it in time for the big announcement."

"I wouldn't have missed it." She smoothed out her suit. "You still hug like a freight train."

Selah looked around for Cane, then realized he was right behind her.

Someone handed Julia a microphone. "Attention, everyone!"

All eyes turned to the wiry dynamo. "Will someone turn

down the music? Thank you. My name is Julia Whitmore, and I am the Executive Producer for *The Winds of Change*."

Applause.

"Thank you to Good Company and Chinese Willie's for catering this wrap party for the first leg of our college tour."

More applause. As a spotlight beamed on her parents, Dad hooked his thumbs in his apron straps and rocked back and forth on his heels. Momma patted her hair and waved to the crowd.

"As most of you know, the show has been faltering in the ratings for some time now. The network just sent me the final word about our future."

The audience grew silent. Cane massaged Selah's shoulders. Her thoughts and breathing calmed. Oh my, the man was good. He should make that a second career. Wars could be won with those hands.

"The good news is that *The Winds of Change* is not being cancelled."

The cast and crew hooted and screamed. Selah's eyes moistened. *Thank You, Lord, for caring about my friends and their careers and families.*

"The taping of the show will move from New York to Los Angeles. Most of the cast will make the trip. However, the bad news . . . " Julia's shoulders heaved. She took a swig from a water bottle. "The bad news is that our unionized crew at the New York studios will not be coming with us."

She dropped her head and covered her face with her hand.

Dorian stepped in and gently took the microphone from her. "Julia and I are brokenhearted at the thought of losing these talented members of our family, many of whom have been with us for thirty years. However, the winds of change are blowing in a different direction and that means a new beginning for us all."

She punched her diamond-laden fist in the air. "Let's keep this party going until we arrive in LA."

Selah and the rest of the crowd gasped as fireworks exploded above the mountains in the direction of the speedway. Frankie didn't get her ticker-tape parade, so she'd improvised.

Faith whined and started digging at the ground. Her body was shaking when Selah picked her up. "It's okay. The fireworks won't hurt you."

Faith continued to whimper and tremble. Cane took the pooch from her and tucked her under his jacket and against his chest. Lucky dog.

Selah felt every boom of pyrotechnics like a heartbeat. Watching Cane, his eyes wide, as his head bobbed with the movement of the explosions, she caught a glimpse of the beautiful, innocent boy he must have been before he'd become a child star.

He turned and met her gaze and all logical thought evaporated from her mind. Her heart lit up like the rainbow streaks zig-zagging across the sky. The feeling was almost too powerful to stand. It was just as Justus suspected and as she feared. She was in love with Cane Ashton.

Chapter Thirty-Six

*A*S SOON AS the fireworks stopped, Selah excused herself under the pretense of fetching beverages for Cane and herself and checking on her parents. Cane and her new friends were leaving tomorrow. The best way to push that farewell and her feelings out of her mind was an Oreo cheesecake shake with whipped cream. Or a simple Cherry Coke from the fountain would suffice to cool her off and calm her down.

She squeezed through the crowd on her way into the diner. It was like a mini version of Times Square in there, with workers shouting out orders and carrying trays of food in and out. She could make the treat herself. It was one of the perks of having a family diner. Would this be the last party they would host before the foreclosure?

She noticed that waste cans were overflowing onto the floor, so she carried the bags out back to the dumpster. Her veins filled with ice when she looked up to see Cody sauntering toward her.

"What you think yer doing, trespassing back here?" He rested his hand on his gun holster.

"It's still our property, making you the trespasser." She straightened and planted herself between him and the kitchen door.

"Fer the time being. Only 'cause, out of the kindness of my heart, I allowed yer folks a few weeks to prepare for the transition."

"After this party, we'll have enough money to buy it back."

"Not even close, seein' as how I'm not selling. I won it from your daddy, so it's mine to dispose of as I please."

Her heart sank.

"Prepare yourself to part company with Good Company." He ran his hand along the siding and kicked at a drain pipe. "I cain't decide whether to turn it into a bar or sell it to the developers looking to revitalize this town. Whatcha think?"

The back door opened with a whoosh and the smell of grease and fried chicken.

"I think you better step away from my daughter and get your sorry self off this property." Momma stood at the door, holding a rolling pin in one hand and a whisk in the other.

"Margo, are you threatening an officer of the law? Stress makes people go off the rails sometimes."

Momma surged toward him, but Selah held her back.

Selah's nose turned up. "I think you are a disgrace to that uniform."

He chortled and spit tobacco on the grass in front of

them. "In school, you always did think you were smarter than everybody else."

"Smart people get the last laugh."

"You do that. I'll see you girls next week."

Selah blew out a breath as he walked away.

"Lord, don't that man make it a chore to 'love thy neighbor.'"

Selah turned and eyed the kitchen utensils in Momma's hand. "So your plan was to whisk him to death?"

"Paddling would have satisfied me." Momma took the whisk and swatted her lightly on the behind. "In a way, I'm relieved he's going to take the diner."

"You don't mean that."

"I'm tired of all the bills, all the fighting about the bills. We can use the money to repair the house. I'm just tired of the struggle, sugar. Your daddy alone's aged me twenty years."

"Oh, Momma. I am so sorry." Tears filled her eyes as they embraced. "Don't give up. It's not over yet. Have faith that God will make a way. Isn't that what you always tell me?"

"Your Momma is a wise ol' woman. Don't you forget it." Momma squeezed her again and released her. Then she went back into the kitchen and returned with a tray of drinks and fries. "I was fixin' to bring these out to you. Now, go have fun with your friends."

Fun wasn't the first thing that came to mind when she returned to the party. She started toward Cane, who was sitting at one of the few empty plastic tables remaining. He was talking to someone, who leaned over and kissed him. When he pulled back, she could see the person's face under the lights. It was Eva. Of course it was. That girl never gave up.

Selah shrunk back and the drinks teetered on the tray. Her stomach felt as if she'd been tackled by the Redskins' defensive line.

It was a misunderstanding. I misinterpreted the scene. He wouldn't have kissed Eva voluntarily. He wouldn't lie to me. Well, he would, but only about his past. He doesn't seem like a sociopath.

She looked up from the tray as Eva turned and left, walking toward the street. Cane spotted Selah and motioned her over. Standing, he bumped his head against the lopsided umbrella covering the table.

He kissed her on the cheek. "I missed you, sweetness. Where did you run off to?"

Her pulse throbbed in her ear as she set the drinks on the table. "I had a run-in with Cody."

He stiffened. "If he hurt you, I—"

"No, just running his mouth. Momma came out to rescue me, and I had to save her from being arrested for assault with a deadly whisk."

Chuckling, he took a swig of a shake. "A whisk?"

"And a rolling pin, but he didn't budge about giving the diner back."

He sat down beside her. "Even if you buy it back?"

She nodded. "He'd rather let the developers bulldoze it. When it happens, Dad will probably be at the track."

Surely, Cane would explain what just happened. She waited for him to tell her he had just been with Eva. That her pouty lips had been on his. Selah dragged the back of her hand roughly across her mouth.

But he didn't speak. He just frowned and scrutinized a stranger walking down the street.

"Who is that? Is something wrong?"

"I don't know." Cane smiled tightly and rapped his knuckles on the table. "It's nothing."

She strained her neck to see what he was watching. "You seem edgy, as if you're casing the perimeter here. I'd like to be prepared if I'm going to be invaded."

"Do you ever get the feeling you're being watched? Like somebody's breathing down your neck?"

"Sure, sometimes, but there are a ton of people here, most of whom are looking at you and trying to see what the hot soap star is like in real life." And trying to kiss him.

"Yeah. You're right. I'm sure that's all it is." The creases in his forehead smoothed.

"For example, see that girl there?" She tried to point at her without pointing. "She has seriously been checking you out. She's nice-looking, huh?"

Selah couldn't believe the words spilling out of her mouth. She was pushing him into the arms of another woman. What was wrong with her?

Cane glanced at the leggy and very slender blonde, who waved coyly in return. "In a post-breakdown Britney Spears kind of way, I guess."

The more the woman ogled him, the more inadequate Selah felt. "I should go help my parents. I'm sure you've got other people you'd like to hang out with. I don't want to keep you."

She peeked at her phone but saw no text or message notifications. Where was Frankie when she needed advice and an excuse to leave?

He eyed Selah curiously. "I'm good, right here. With you. Unless you're trying to get rid of me." He sounded a little hurt.

"No, of course not." She was now officially a dating moron. Why couldn't she just be happy he was here with her and not be paranoid? "I love being your friend and spending time with you, but—"

"Enough with the "just friends" bit. We passed that a long time ago, and you know it."

Just then, the blonde hoochie in question "accidently" bumped Cane's chair. "Pardon me. Oh, hi, Cane!" she said sweetly, ignoring Selah.

Cane gave her a charming smile.

Selah rubbed at her eyes and groaned. She'd been so distracted by Cane, she hadn't realized who the blonde was. "I take back everything I said."

"I'm Katie, your biggest fan. I love *Winds of Change*."

"Well, thank you." He extended his hand.

Her cream skirt was so tight, Selah couldn't tell where the fabric ended and her skin began. Katie asked Cane to autograph her shirt in a location as close to her chest as possible. Unbelievable, the nerve of that woman.

Selah marveled at how easily he interacted with the countless fans who interrupted his meals, his workouts, and his conversations. He seemed to have eyes for only that one fan he was speaking to. Now that he was looking sincerely at Katie with those eyes, it sent a surge of jealousy like a cold knife blade through Selah's chest. She was still the same sixteen-year-old fattie fawning over the homecoming king and bullied by the head cheerleader.

Katie obviously didn't feel the chill and seemed in no

hurry to leave. "So, Cane, some of us girls—" She nodded in the direction of her equally half-naked friends. "We're going into the city after the party to hit the bar scene. They have some great bands downtown. We'd love for you to join us so we can show you some Southern hospitality. We're nurses, so we would take good care of you."

Selah choked on her Cherry Coke. *That is definitely my cue to leave.* She tried to slide quietly out of her chair, but Cane caught her wrist and held it. "Wow, Katie, that sounds like fun, but I've got an early day tomorrow. I want to spend some time with my girlfriend—and your husband is probably waiting up for you."

Katie's eyes followed Cane's to her wedding ring. She shoved her left hand in her waistband.

A thrill shot through Selah. *His girlfriend! And he put Katie in her place.*

For the first time, she noticed Selah and shot her a thanks-for-ruining-my-moment look. "Selah, wonderful to see you as always. You haven't changed since high school."

Selah gave Katie her most sickening smile in return.

When Katie finally left, Cane pulled Selah back down into her seat. "Thanks for trying to leave me here alone with her. What was that about?"

"I just thought maybe I was in the way."

"Did I give you that impression?"

"No. I'm sorry I said anything. Forget it." She fiddled with a button on her blouse as he studied her. Tears pricked at her eyes. She drew a deep breath and summoned them away. *Tears are not going to happen again in front of Cane.*

"Help me to understand you, Selah. Did you think

I'd be happier hanging out with Redneck Barbie than with you?"

"Well, yeah. Look at the hot bodies you work with and the fans like Katie who fling their room keys and their heaving bosoms at you."

"Heaving bosoms?" He laughed. "I do get a lot of bras to sign. So? Girls like that are a dime a dozen."

"Take an honest look at me." She gestured toward herself. "If I lost every pound on my body, something I haven't been able to attain in thirty-some years, I couldn't wear a size zero."

Cane leaned forward, his lips pursed, his eyes narrowed. "Do you think I'm that shallow? That I can't care about you because of your weight? After all the stuff I shared with you, and after all we've been through together . . . Have I said or done anything to make you think that?"

"You kissed Eva."

His eyebrows shot up. "Eva kissed *me* and then I rinsed my mouth out with that water bottle. She's in a bad place."

"Even so, that's just the way things are. A guy like you just doesn't care about a girl like me in real life. And if he does, it doesn't last."

"*That* is not real life, Selah. *That* is all in your head." Cane's eyes were blazing.

Suddenly, a familiar voice bellowed above the music. "I am the son of Shadybrook!"

Shayne Nixon was frolicking in the koi pond in front of Chinese Willie's. "I am the stud of Shadybrook!"

He cupped the water and poured it over his head. Apparently, Shayne had a little something stronger than cherry in his cola. He stumbled and sang again, oblivious to the lily pads hanging off his body and Willie's imposing figure charging at him.

"Is that a parrot on his shoulder?"

Shayne sang while the bird squawked, "Let's get ready to rumble."

"I have to take care of this," Cane said matter-of-factly. "We'll talk later."

"Cane, wait. I'm sorry."

He jogged off to rescue Shayne. Selah stood unmoving, watching him. What had just happened here? What had she done?

The hand on Selah's shoulder jolted her out of her funk. "There's my girl."

She whirled around. "What do you need now, Dad?"

"I'm certainly in no position to give you advice about love, but . . ."

She kicked the leg of the table. "You're right. You're not."

No advice could fix this, fix her. How had she reverted to her old ways of thinking so quickly and sabotaged herself?

"I've learned a few things about taking risks and rolling the dice. Dice are for rolling, not eating."

"That is the dumbest thing you've ever said." Selah drained her syrupy drink as fast as it would go. A piece of Momma's pie would taste good, too.

He shrugged. "When you're handed a pair of dice, you take the opportunity and you throw them. You don't think about the fear of losing, you just play. But you've been handed dice, baby, and you're trying to suck them down with a straw."

She coughed and gazed down at her straw.

"Take it from one who knows. Someday Cane will begin to wonder whether you've got a point, whether you're unworthy of love. I'm afraid you'll drive him away with your insecurities."

"Is that what happened with you and Momma? Did she drive you away, into the arms of other women?"

"Selah, I admit I've cheated on your mother with cards, poker, horses, cars, anything I could place a bet on. But I've never cheated with another woman."

Momma stood a few tables away, chatting with Dorian, of all people.

"How is it possible to care about two people so much and be equally driven crazy by them at the same time?"

Suddenly, she was a child again, clutching her Pound Puppy to her chest as hard as she could, trying not to cry. *If I hold onto it, the lollipop man won't take it.* He took Momma's wedding band and Selah's boom box, and her father just stood by with his hands in his pockets, letting the guy steal their possessions away.

Nothing to worry about. He would win it all back with the next race. He was on a winning streak.

Dad's voice interrupted her flashback. "Have you heard a word I've said?"

Selah looked up from her empty plastic cup. Her tears bubbled up like the BP spill of vile, black oil gushing into the ocean.

"Selah, honey?"

She threw the cup at him. He put up his palms.

"Don't talk to me about taking risks when you risked

your family's future, everything you worked for, over a poker game, and you lost."

"See that woman over there?" She pointed to Momma. "She sacrificed her life for you. She prides herself on a clean house. The roof of that house is patched and hanging on by a thread because she can't afford a new one."

She pointed to herself. "See this woman here, insecure and incapable of love and trust? When I was a kid, I needed you. I spent more time with your bookie's enforcer than with you."

His face fell and he reached for her. She stepped back. "No. Before you hand me any of your fatherly pearls of wisdom, you need to consider the cost of your addiction, the toll it has taken on your family."

She grabbed Faith's leash, and they power-walked out of there, away from Dad, away from the drama, and away from Cane.

"Pool's closed for the night, buddy." Cane shoved his arms under Shayne's armpits and pulled him, fully clothed, out of the pond. Selah's Aunt Ruby and Chinese Willie rounded up the parrot.

"Aw. Already? You were always a party sport, a spoil pooper. A party pooper."

"Not always." Sometimes he was the life of the party, and other people got hurt. Cane stripped off Shayne's coat and wrapped his own jacket around his friend's wet shoulders.

Shayne cocked his head from side to side to shake the water from his ears.

"Here, let me help you with that." Cane smacked Shayne on the forehead. "What were you thinking?"

Shayne's bottom lip trembled. "I didn't want to think anymore."

The snark and the sneer had fallen away, leaving behind red, dilated eyes, swollen cheeks, and pain that was so raw, Cane had to look away. He had been in Shayne's place and never wanted to go back. *There, but for the grace of God, go I.* His dad said that often when pastoring his congregation.

"Understood. Let's get you some help." Cane groaned as he tried to move forward with Shayne leaning on his shoulder.

Shayne limped along, waving and pulling toward the twenty or so onlookers watching the water extraction. "My people, my people."

Julia and Mason pushed through the crowd and looked from Shayne to Cane.

"Need some help?" Mason asked.

"Please." The flashes of cameras and cell phones were giving Cane a headache.

Julia got on her cell and started giving orders.

Mason walked over to the crowd and held up a hand. "Thanks, everybody, for your concern. Shayne's fine. The performance is over, although you can probably catch it again on YouTube in a few minutes. Please go enjoy what's left of the party."

"I'm going viral tonight," Shayne whooped.

"Appreciate the assist, man." Cane shook Mason's hand as the bystanders dispersed.

Mason nodded and propped up Shayne's other arm. Cane had fallen into Selah's wonderland, a place where people weren't always who you assumed they were.

"It's time we get you back to rehab." For the third time.

Cane's throat constricted. He knew first-hand the loneliness and the emotional warfare that lay ahead for Shayne. He wouldn't wish it on anyone.

Julia strode over and handed Cane a piece of paper. "I contacted a local facility. They're ready to admit him into a program. Frankie and I are going to drive him in the Hummer."

"I'm s-sorry," Shayne said as they stumbled together to the parking lot, with Julia leading the parade.

"You should be. This was my favorite shirt."

"Seriously, dude. I turned you into a juvenile delinquent when you lived with me." His eyes filled with tears.

"I forgive you."

Selah had forgiven Cane. His parents would have forgiven him. God had promised to forgive him. It was time to let it go.

"I was so messed up then and here I am putting all this on you again. I regret it, more than you know." Shayne wasn't as wasted as he let on.

"I do know."

When Frankie arrived with the Hummer, Cane heaved him into the backseat and buckled him in. Throwing a blanket over Shayne's body, Cane said, "The best thing you can do for everyone is to stay sober. You're going to come out of this clinic a new man."

"A do-over," Shayne closed his eyes and leaned against the headrest.

Cane shut the door and waved to Frankie and Julia as the SUV pulled away. "A do-over. Everybody deserves one or two."

Chapter Thirty-Seven

"Being in a coma is no excuse for bad hair and makeup."

You Know Your Life is a Soap Opera If,
by Gerry Waggett

FAITH TOOK HER sweet time sniffing and marking every mailbox and shrub along Main Street. It was late when she and Selah reached the house.

They mounted the front porch steps, setting off a motion light. Someone moaned nearby, and Selah jumped. Faith began to bark at the porch swing. As Selah fumbled for the mace on her keychain, a blanket on the swing moved. Her breathing quickened with her heartbeat.

"Why'd you turn on the light?" The intruder sat up on the swing and rubbed her eyes. "Oh! I know we're not friends, but mace? Really?"

"Eva, what are you doing here?" Selah lowered the weapon and pressed her hand to her chest.

"Watching fireflies." Eva clapped at Faith, who held her ground behind Selah's legs. "Come here, doggy. It's just Evey Weavey."

"Fireflies. In a black couture mini dress." Selah turned the doorknob. It wasn't locked. "Have you been inside too?" In her living room, her bedroom?

"Your dad gave me a key. He said I could rest here."

"Tsk. Of course he did. He rarely uses the place." Selah set down her purse inside the door. "Why don't you come in?"

"Uh-uh. That carpet and wallpaper gave me a psyche-delic seizure. How do you people live like that?"

"It's a struggle." Selah snickered. She sat on a rocking chair facing the porch swing and lifted Faith onto her lap. The dog eyed Eva. Selah did the same. What in the world had possessed Eva to come to her archrival's house to "rest"?

"Your momma was looking for you, Eva."

"The Queen Mother summoned me? A pity that I missed her." She sniffed.

"Is that why you're here? To avoid Miss Dorian?"

"I can do without Miss Dorian's drive-by advice."

Selah frowned, reminded of her father and his drive-by advice, 'Dice are for rolling, not eating.'

"She's all, 'Dahling, do let your hair grow. You're begin-ning to look like Peter Pan.'" Eva made sweeping gestures in the air. "'Chin up, stomach in, smile, that's how a lady holds herself.' 'I'm off to Hong Kong. Kiss, kiss.'"

"That is exactly how she sounds. You nailed it."

Eva rocked back in the swing and turned her head toward the yard.

"You're always welcome to borrow my momma for advice. Anytime. Please."

"Thanks. She's been busy the last few days. Besides, with her, it's always, 'Selah did this or that' or 'Selah is so thoughtful or sweet' or whatever."

Really? Selah's heart warmed. She'd been a little jealous, believing Eva was Momma's new best friend.

She didn't know what else to say. The minutes ticked by. The only sounds were the creaking of their chairs, the chirping crickets and birds, and Faith's snoring.

Finally, Eva sat up and dug around in her purse. She pulled out a lighted compact, probably the same one she'd used on Selah in New York.

Selah said, "I couldn't help noticing that your eyes and nose are a little red."

"Allergies," she said, swiping the foundation across her nose.

Sure.

One side of her mouth curled up. She looked directly at Selah. "You hate me, don't you?"

"Where did that come from? We were having a perfectly civil conversation."

"Your eyes are cold whenever I'm around."

"I've never hated you, Eva." Selah forced herself to breathe deeply and not react.

"Even that ferret of yours hates me. You hate me because Cane is still attracted to me. And because I'm a model and skinny."

In her mind, Selah heard the old "Don't hate me because I'm beautiful" commercial voice.

"You live a double standard. You want everyone to be nice to you and love you, even though you're fat. But you don't like me because you don't look as good as me."

This bashing was over the top, even for Eva. "Enough with the fat jokes. You and Shayne need to find something or somebody else to gossip and giggle about."

But Eva wasn't listening. She was crying.

Selah picked up Faith, retrieved her purse, and fished out a handkerchief for Eva. She would treasure the maroon and gold Redskins one Justus had given her. "What in the world is going on with you? Let's get you back to the party."

Eva sniffled as she stood. She was so wobbly, Selah had to take her upper arm and help her down the stairs. There was such a thing as being too thin.

"Whatever's bothering you, maybe we can find your momma or mine, or even Cane, for you to talk to."

"Cane loves me, not you." Eva's voice cracked.

He was right, this girl was deeply troubled. She stopped and looked Eva in the eye.

"Cane has told you repeatedly that he doesn't love you. He cares for me. You and I may not understand why, but it's a fact." Saying it out loud made it real, gave her courage. "You're a beautiful woman. You can have any man. Why can't you let it go?"

Eva's crying intensified. Selah patted her back as they continued down the driveway and out to the road.

"Because Cane is loving and a gentleman." She swayed. "And I . . . I'm pregnant."

"You're pr—" Selah's mouth stopped moving while her

mind played catchup. "*You* are going to have a baby? A *human* baby?"

"I know, right? I can't even get your dog to like me, let alone a kid," she blubbered.

Selah's head and stomach felt like five hot dogs and five turns on the scrambler at the fair. *It's not Cane's. They're not together. Eva is not having his baby.*

"What should I do, Selah? I don't know what to do. I don't want to get fat or change diapers or be a drive-by mom."

"I don't know, I—" She stopped when she heard someone cough. A tall man emerged from the shadows on the other side of the street. Selah reached for the mace again. The characters that trickled into town from the speedway were bad news. This one, however, gave them a friendly "hello". Under the streetlight, he looked like Cane.

Faith saw him and jerked her leash from Selah's hand. "Faith! No!"

She ran to catch the dog as she darted out into the street. "Come here. Come. C'mon, girl."

The rascal continued on its mission without a backward glance at her master. If only Selah had enrolled Faith in one of those expensive obedience courses. Her heart slammed against her ribcage as the roar of a car's engine filled her ears.

By the time she grabbed the leash, they were in the middle of the road. It sounded as if the engine went into overdrive, and the car accelerated. She didn't know who was panting harder, she or Faith. She yanked the leash and hurled herself at the stranger, who was running toward them.

"Look out, Selah!" Eva called from behind her.

Selah felt a rush of wind against her face. The last thing she saw was headlights and a flash of color as the sickening smell of tar and rubber filled her nostrils.

She awoke looking into Cane's brown eyes. "Hi, handsome," she said to the clean-cut hunk standing over her.

Oops, no, there were two Canes, and they were fighting. She waved at the second Cane, who had scraggly hair and a goatee and a scar on his neck. "If I'm dreaming, this is the hottest dream ever."

The Canes laughed. Suddenly, Momma stood between them.

"Thank you, Mother, for ruining that fantasy."

Clean-cut Cane was at Selah's side in an instant, clutching her hands in his. She blinked and blinked but still saw two Canes. With her free hand, she traced the bandage on her forehead, which felt as if an anvil had been dropped on it. "What happened to me?"

This must be the hospital, since the walls were a sterile, blinding white, and her rock-hard bed creaked when she moved.

"You're in the ER. You had an accident." Momma stood on the opposite side of the bed than Cane, smoothing and tucking in the sheets.

The goopy edges of her memory began to congeal. "They put me on a stretcher and I rode in an ambulance. And just now I had an x-ray, right?"

"That's good, sugar." Momma smiled reassuringly, but her tousled hair and the dark circles under her eyes suggested that she'd nearly worried herself to death.

Selah closed her eyes as Momma's Pearls and Lace perfume wafted over her nose. An accident. She hadn't been in her car that night. Had she fallen? The last thing she could remember was holding a leash. That was it. The dog had run out in front of a car.

Her eyes flew open and she pushed herself up in the bed. "Where's Faith? Is she okay? Was anyone else hurt?"

"She's fine. She's with Frankie. You were the only victim. It was a hit-and-run."

"You saved your dog." The scruffy Cane stood near the door, peering out the windows. The room seemed too small for him. "This might be your doctor coming. Finally."

Selah blew out a breath and leaned back. She closed her eyes again. Even though Faith was safe, there was something else she couldn't remember, something she needed to remember. Whatever it was, it was making her stomach feel like hospital Jell-O.

"Don't fall asleep, darlin'," whispered the Cane clutching her hand. "Let me see what we can talk about to keep you awake. Oh, yes, Julia and Mason were by earlier, while you were in the MRI. They sent flowers and a giant box of chocolate."

"At this time of night? She is amazingly efficient," Selah said.

Momma stuffed two pieces in her mouth.

"Don't look at me like that, Selah," Momma said, chomping on the chocolate like Lucille Ball. "You know I got sugar, and it dropped low waiting on you to finish your tests."

The door swooshed open. A woman in a lab coat strode in, her straight brown hair grazing her shoulders. She nodded at Momma and the Canes and patted Selah's shoulder.

"I'm Dr. Hardy. I'm going to examine you to see how your brain and body have responded to your concussion. We treat head injuries very seriously."

Selah struggled to keep up as the doctor questioned her about her vision, pain, and memory and tested her reflexes and her head and arm strength and motion.

"Your vitals and responses are normal. Your MRI was clear. We'll give you a prescription for pain medicine." She turned to Momma. "Call me if you notice severe headaches, dizziness, nausea, or memory lapses. A concussion is nothing to mess around with."

"Can I go home now?"

"Since you're still foggy, I'd like to be on the safe side and monitor you until morning." Dr. Hardy checked her watch. "What am I saying? It's one o'clock in the morning. We'll monitor you for a few more hours, then you can go home."

The doctor frowned as she patted the pockets on her coat and then on her pants. Finally, her hand settled on the glasses perched on her head. "I apologize for being so frazzled. The ER has been a madhouse."

"It's the full moon," Momma said. "It brings out the crazies and sends the pregnant women into labor."

Selah groaned. That was what she was trying to remember. Eva was a crazy and she was pregnant.

"Selah, are you feeling okay?" The doctor took her pulse and inputted something in her iPad.

"I'm OK." Selah looked at one Cane, at the other

Cane, and back again. She blinked rapidly. "But I see two of Cane. Is this double vision going to last?"

"Unfortunately, the double vision is permanent. Meet Tanner," clean-cut, hand-holding Cane said. He gestured to the scruffier version of himself. "My twin brother."

"Your brother is a twin? Is he the evil twin?" She rubbed the back of her neck, which was beginning to ache.

Another secret. Secrets and lies make good soap opera, Mason had said. In real life, they didn't make a solid foundation for a relationship.

Cane shot him a look of contempt. Tanner smiled tightly. Twins were supposed to think alike, be tuned into each other's emotions, but they couldn't be more different.

"Frankie is going to love this." She needed her best friend. She would help Selah make sense of her feelings.

Tanner held the door open for the doctor as she left. His voice was more gravelly than Cane's and more controlled, but his eyes radiated the strength that drew her to Cane. "I'm partly responsible for your hit-and-run accident, Selah."

Momma patted Tanner's arm. "No, sugar, it wasn't your fault."

"I'd like to know whose fault it was." Selah's friend Gina, the county sheriff's deputy and former Hunk O' the Month Club member, poked her head in the door.

"You're on the case?" Selah motioned her in.

"State police gave us authority on this one."

"That's great." Except that her new partner or trainee was Cody Buchanan, Selah's grade-school bully.

Selah's head began to feel woozy. *In this town, you can never escape your past.*

Chapter Thirty-Eight

"ARE YOU UP for a few questions about last night? That is, if you're not too distracted by your visitors." Gina gave Tanner and Cane a once-over and smiled her approval. Cody stood behind her, looking everywhere but at Selah.

Selah rubbed at the bandage taped on her forehead. "The last thing I remember is that stunt-woman job I was doing for *The Winds of Change*. Amnesiac stunt women can never catch a break in this town. Even on their deathbeds."

"Don't joke. This could've ended a lot worse." Gina slid a pad and pen from her pocket. She was old school. "Besides, the only people who get amnesia are soap opera characters, so spill it."

Cane moved so Gina and Cody could stand at Selah's bedside. He "accidentally" elbowed Cody in the ribs on the way out. Cody grimaced and held his side. She had never loved Cane more than at that moment.

"Tanner and I will be right outside the door."

"Momma, why don't you go down to the cafeteria and

bring me something with a gallon of caffeine in it? I wish you would go home and rest, but I know better than to ask that."

"I ain't leaving this hospital without you, but I'll go and give you space to talk."

Momma pushed out of the chair, stretched her back, arms, and neck, ate another piece of chocolate, and shuffled out the door Cane held open.

Selah, suddenly aware of her thin hospital gown, pulled her sheet up to her armpits. She glared at Cody. He was sweatier than usual.

"I was walking with Eva down Main toward Good Company. We saw a man on the other side of the street. I thought it was Cane with a fierce five-o'clock shadow, but it must have been Tanner."

Gina patted Selah's arm. "I understand your confusion. We don't have one guy in Shadybrook who looks that good, let alone twins."

A vein bulged in the middle of Cody's forehead.

"My dog must have been confused too because she ran across the street toward him. I ran after her, and a car came flying around the corner. It was loud, like it was accelerating."

Gina's voice changed into a serious official tone. "Did you see a license plate or get a look at the driver or the car?"

Cody fiddled with his keys.

"I wish I had. All I remember were headlights and how fast the car was coming at us."

"Tanner and Eva stated the car had no plates and was traveling in excess of sixty-five miles per hour in that thirty-five-mile zone."

"I don't know if the car hit me or if it forced us off the road."

"How do you feel?" Gina closed her notepad.

"My entire body aches. My brain hurts."

"Good thing your head's as hard as a rock."

Rocks. The car's tires had thrown rocks—no, gravel in her face and against the car. Selah had a sudden flash of memory—the gravel striking a crystal-blue bumper. She closed her eyes to concentrate on the image. Something about that car set off alarm bells, but she couldn't quite piece the fuzzy images together.

Gina handed Selah her card. "If you remember anything else, call me. Better yet, call me just to let me know how you're getting along."

As she and her partner left, they walked into Eva. She batted her eyes at Cody. Eww. Selah wouldn't wish Cody on anybody, even Eva.

"Oh, good, Selah, you're awake!" Her chipper voice rattled Selah's skull. "Those bruises and cuts on your face look terrible."

She sank down on the chair beside the bed and pulled it as close to Selah as possible. Cane and Tanner filed in behind her and stood at the end of her bed. Selah squirmed. With all these eyes on her, she needed Eva's compact and mirror, a brush, and her own clothes.

"I couldn't take that waiting room any more—people hacking and bleeding and kids crying. It was a nightmare." Eva shuddered.

"I thought you were supposed to leave with the others today."

"Eva's been here since the accident."

Eva smiled up at Cane, a little too long for Selah's liking. The girl was painfully transparent. *Maybe I am too.*

"I was so worried about you, I couldn't leave. Besides, I'm unemployed. What else do I have to do?"

"Thank you." *I think.* Selah couldn't help but smile encouragement at her.

Eva was still wearing her mini dress and stilettos. No scratches or bruises. No baby bump yet. "I take it you and the . . . I take it you are feeling all right."

"The car swerved and missed me by a few inches. If it had hurt the baby . . ." Eva's voice trailed off as her eyes filled with tears and her hands rested on her belly.

Selah reached over and squeezed her hand. "You're going to be a good mom."

"Really?" Eva wrinkled her forehead.

"Really." Selah nodded, feeling the tears well up in her eyes.

Eva looked at her feet. "The baby's not Cane's. Cane and I were never together."

Thank You, Lord. Selah sagged against the pillow. Cane caught her eye and held it.

"Then whose baby—it's none of my business." Selah stopped herself.

"Shayne is the baby daddy. I haven't told him yet."

Selah touched her throat. Shayne and Eva together? That poor child. She tried to picture it but could only come up with images of the offspring of the Joker and Cat Woman.

"Is Shayne all right?" Selah asked. "The last time I saw him, he was performing a song-and-dance routine in Willie's koi pond." That story would live in infamy in Shadybrook.

"He's safe." Cane answered, pulling a chair beside Selah on the opposite side of the bed as Eva. If only everyone, especially Eva and Tanner, would leave so he could be alone with his girl. "Julia got him into a local rehab. We hope the third time will be the charm."

Tanner stood at the window, watching and listening, his face betraying no emotion. Cane didn't get that guy. He never had.

Selah was saying, "He'll have a happy surprise when he gets out of rehab. It will be a new beginning."

Shayne was screwed up, but he would step up and care for that kid. He wouldn't let it suffer as Shayne had during his childhood.

"Maybe." Eva shrugged.

Selah sat up to adjust her pillow. Cane stood and did it for her. He brushed her hair out of her eyes and kissed the bandage on her forehead.

"Enough with the goo-goo eyes, you two. This is a hospital. People are sick enough." Eva made a gagging noise. "I should get going. Selah looks pale and tired."

"Always quick with a compliment, Eva." Selah stuck out her tongue.

"Wasn't there something you wanted to confess to Selah?" C'mon, Eva. Cane sent her a meaningful look.

"Um, right, I do. I kind of stole your letter to Cane." Eva fiddled with the hospital call button attached to Selah's bed.

"The one I slipped under his dressing room door?" Selah crossed her arms at her chest. "The one that was clearly marked 'personal'?"

"I just popped in to run lines with him, and it was there, and I was curious."

"You mean nosy and jealous?"

Eva cast a plaintive glance at Cane. He nodded to prod her on.

"Yes, but when I read all that stuff about Jesus and faith and your dog, I cried. Real tears," she whispered, seemingly amazed by her own emotions. Her face was childlike in its earnestness and desire for attention. The same emotions had played out on Shayne's face. Cane's throat closed up.

"Then, when I met Momma, she took me to prayer meeting and church. And guess what they talked about in church?"

"What?"

"The story of the woman at the well. That story was in your letter. Crazy coincidence, right?"

Selah's eyes were soft and forgiving. "The letter ended up in the right hands."

"God's been talkin' to your heart, hasn't He?" Momma had slipped in. She beamed at Eva.

Eva tucked her chin, looking suddenly bashful with all these eyes scrutinizing her personal relationship with Jesus. "Since I'm being honest, I might as well tell you I brought Tanner here."

"You?"

"You mentioned him in your letter. I had to know who he was, so I called him."

"She didn't ask me to come. I came on my own," Tanner said.

"What a gift that was." Cane's said drolly, his grip tightening on Selah's hand. He was grateful Tanner called 911 and tended to Selah after the hit-and-run, but, if he hadn't been lurking in the shadows, the accident wouldn't have happened.

The door opened and the doctor entered the room, muttering about Grand Central Station. After a brief examination, she pronounced Selah ready for discharge.

Momma jumped up from her chair and clapped her hands. "Boys, go work out your aggressions somewhere else and give Selah privacy. She'll be on the mend tomorrow. You can see her then. Go on now, y'all."

She motioned Tanner, Cane, and Eva to the door. "Shoo!"

Cane opened his mouth to argue, but the look in Selah's eyes warned him against tangling with Momma. He had a better strategy, one that had never failed him. He winked at Selah and kissed Momma on the cheek.

Well played, Cane Ashton. Momma underestimated you. Selah smiled at Momma's bewildered expressions as she shoved her three visitors out the hospital room door.

"Goodness. I thought I'd have to pry those two men off your bedside."

Selah threw off the sheet, stood, and bent to get her clothes from the bedside storage area. A dizzy spell propelled her back onto the bed.

Momma grabbed her arm and steadied her. "Hold your horses, young lady. No sense in getting another goose egg on that pretty head of yours." She tenderly helped Selah put on her clothes.

"Thanks, Momma, for being here. I'm sorry I wasn't here to take care of you after your shoulder surgery."

"Oh, sugar. You're my life." She started getting weepy then blanked the emotion as she scurried around the room, gathering Selah's things. "But that father of yours could have shown his face for once. He's about as useful as a steering wheel on a mule."

I'm tired of running away from the problems in this family. It's time I stayed still and faced them head on.

"Be honest with me, Momma. Are you and Dad getting a divorce? Because if you are, it's okay. I mean, it's not okay, but I understand."

Momma threw a collection of Styrofoam cups, napkins, and candy wrappers into the trash. "A divorce? Where'd you get that idea?"

"From you two constantly being at each other's throats, that's where. And I saw the package from that lawyer before I left for New York."

She paused a moment from her task of making the sanitized room even cleaner. "That lawyer is trying to help us avoid foreclosure on the diner. Your father gambled away Good Company—to Cody, our resident Barney Fife, for cryin' out loud."

"Everything's going to work out."

"No, it's not." Her quiet voice was laced with anger. "Let this be a lesson to you. This is what happens when you put your heart out there for a man to stomp on. You lose yourself and everything you hold dear."

It was too late to heed the warning. Waking up to Cane's worried eyes and his hands holding hers felt so right. She could hear Frankie reciting their Hunk O' the Month Club motto:

"We put our hearts on the wire for the men who light our fire and ignite our desire." At last, Selah was ready to put her heart on the wire and risk everything for that man.

Chapter Thirty-Nine

"If you love your life, you have to fight. If you believe in life and progress and possibilities, you have no choice."

Michael Zaslow (late veteran soap actor and warrior in the fight against ALS)

"*B*ETTER SIT. You look like death eatin' a cracker." Momma set down a ginger ale and a plate of saltines for Selah's consumption as Selah paced the diner.

A day after the hit-and-run, the residual trauma and pain had faded like a bad dream, but Momma still hovered.

"You just got back from the doctor. I need to keep an eye on you. Take it easy and enjoy a little TLC." Momma flitted along the counter, refilling drinks and clearing plates.

To appease Momma, Selah sat down in front of the snack. Then she picked up her phone and texted Frankie to see if she had made any progress on finding out the owner of the crystal-blue bumper.

Frankie answered: "Have a lead on it. You should use any means necessary to get home." Cryptic, but solid advice. Selah considered the best way to evade her eagle-eyed momma. She scribbled a note and tucked it under her plate. Then she waited until Momma went out back with the trash. She took the opportunity and jogged out the front door.

The pain relievers the doctor prescribed for the giant knot on her head made her feel as if she was high-stepping in a marching band and the road home was rising up to meet her. She shaded her eyes from the bright sunlight, sweat running down her back. Momma and the doctor were right—this concussion was nothing to mess with. She grew heavy-hearted, thinking of Cane with his MS and the pain he had suffered and what lay ahead.

When she finally reached her house, she blinked and feasted her eyes on the figure stretched out on her front stairs. *Please don't let this be a hallucination.* It was Cane, the country version, complete with tan cowboy hat pulled down over his eyes. His hands rested on his stomach, his blue jean-clad legs and cowboy boots crossed at the ankles.

Selah laughed and clapped her hands like a girl. "My first shipment from the Hunk O' the Month Club has finally arrived, twenty years late! Maybe next month I'll even get a guy from *Y&R* or *General Hospital*. They're much hotter than the guys on *Winds of Change*."

"Hey!" Cane, who must have been asleep, sat up and slid off the steps. He ran to her and crushed her to himself with one arm, cradling her bandaged head with the other.

His heart beat against her chest like the boom of the

sound system at a rock concert. When he finally pulled back to look at her, air filled her lungs again. She breathed him in. His dark eyes were misty.

"What's wrong? You look like death eatin' a cracker." She stroked his cheek with the back of her hand, hoping Momma's humor would calm him down.

"When Eva called the other night, hysterical and saying you'd been in a car accident, I thought—" His voice cracked. "I thought I'd lost you."

He embraced her again. "It was my fault. I gave you such a hard time and left you alone at the wrap party."

"You must have relived your parents' accident."

"Can you believe I *prayed* that you would be okay? Well, more like demanded that God not take you away from me."

"See? He answered your prayer. I'm here with you, and the doctor said I'm going to be fine."

He wrapped his arm around her waist to support her and led her to the front steps of her house. Now that was the kind of TLC she could handle.

When she sat beside him on the stairs, he tipped back his cowboy hat to look at her.

She giggled. "I cannot take you seriously in that getup."

"Hey, little lady." He attempted a Southern drawl, which sounded like Fargo meets Elvis. "I needed to do something to keep up with the competition from these other soap hunks. I guess I'll have to woo you with my turkey calls and cowboy campfire songs."

"The turkey calls will do. I'm all ears."

Cane threw back his head and hollered. "Chick, chick, chickeeeee! Sooeeyy!"

A neighborhood dog howled. Selah covered her mouth with both hands.

"I've been practicing! Did it work? Did I woo you?" His lips pursed together, and his eyes widened hysterically when he said "woo."

"That was amazing, redneck, I mean Cowboy Cane." She batted her eyelashes. "What will you ever do for an encore?"

"Cowboy trade secret," he whispered as he pulled her into a kiss that would make any cowgirl blush.

Remembering where they were, she pulled away. "As much as I'm enjoying your company, the front porch is not the appropriate venue. Shadybrook sees all and spills all. We may have already given my neighbors heart attacks."

She pointed at the white rockers across the street. They were empty.

"Oh, no, something must be wrong with my neighbors! They're not out on the porch and there's a sign on their front door."

"You mean the Wallingfords?" Cane asked.

"How do you know their names?"

"They're gone."

"What? You don't mean— That's awful. How did it happen?" A tear streamed down her cheek.

"Calm down, Selah. They're not dead."

She realized she was clutching his chest with both hands. "Don't scare me like that."

He took her hand and led her across the street to their front porch. "See for yourself where they went."

Selah read the sign aloud. "Off to celebrate our fiftieth wedding anniversary. Bon voyage!"

"I ran into Mr. and Mrs. Wallingford earlier. Nice couple. Said they were going on a cruise."

"A cruise! But they haven't left this house in years."

"They said you inspired them to get off their rockers and follow their dreams."

"Me? What did I do?"

"You honestly don't know, do you?" He cupped her face in his hands and then rested them on her shoulders. "Where do I start? You won over Julia and got a job as SoaperFan on a daytime television show. Even though Eva treated you like dirt, you got her an audition with another show and, because of your letter to me, she's *almost* nice. You rescued a three-legged dog from a shelter and nearly killed yourself trying to keep it from being hit by a car. You arranged a trip to the Speedway for a grumpy writer. You rallied the entire town of Shadybrook around a soap opera. You . . ."

"All right, thank you, Cane. That's enough for now. You don't want me to get nauseated so soon after my hospitalization."

"Since you don't believe me, I'll show you." He turned and marched back across the street to her front porch. She followed.

He stopped at her door. "Aren't you going to invite me in?"

Selah hesitated before sliding her key into the front door lock. "I was hoping you wouldn't figure out that I still live at home with my parents."

"You're a failure to launch. I can work with that." Cane grinned wickedly. "As long as your parents don't come barging in on us."

He traced one finger softly, lazily down her arm. The

simple gesture caused a chain reaction. Her breathing shallowed and her cheeks filled with the heat that also radiated through other parts of her.

When Cane saw how quickly his touch affected her, he gave her a knowing, sexy smile. "Take me to your bedroom."

She blinked, waiting for the punch line.

"Trust me, Selah." His eyes shone with the same earnestness as the night she tried to push him into the arms of another woman. He held out his hand.

Selah stood unmoving, fighting back the fear rising in her stomach. *I am not going to fall in love with him. I cannot fall in love with him. Lord, help me, I am so completely in love with him.*

She drew a deep breath and reached for his hand. She led him down the hall to her "apartment" and stopped at the doorway. Maybe he wouldn't notice the dust bunnies tangled with dog hair rolling like tumbleweeds across the hardwood.

"Well, come on then." He pulled her inside and into a kiss.

"Whoa there, cowboy."

"Sorry. I got ahead of myself." He looked around the room and behind her dresser.

Thank heavens she left her "Hunk of the Month Club" book in her office. "Can I help you find something?"

"Where's your mirror?"

"My mirror?" *You mean the shiny object that fills me with dread and makes me want to hurl it against the wall?*

"Aha. I knew you'd have a full-length one in here. It was hidden behind the door."

For good reason.

"Step into the looking glass. You're about to see a whole

different world." Cane said as he stood behind her, his hands on her shoulders, and turned her to face the mirror. "My acting teacher used to make me do this exercise."

She looked away. "I look like the Michelin man with all those rolls of fat or that thing at the end of the Ghostbusters movie—the Stay Puft guy made of marshmallows."

He grimaced. "I want you to really look at yourself in the mirror."

She rolled her eyes and then glanced at her reflection.

He waited. "There it is. That smile. Do you know why I remembered you from the fan luncheon?"

"The camera debacle?"

"I have met thousands of fans. Some scream. Some want me to sign their unmentionables. Others want to touch my unmentionables. You threatening to club me in the head with your camera was nothing."

"So . . ."

"The reason I remembered you was because you were beautiful, even with all that blushing and stumbling. Your curls shone under the light. Your smile shone even brighter. You make me laugh like no one has before."

He smoothed her hair with the back of his hand. "I want you to see what I see. Your skin is soft and clear. Your violet eyes hold no guile and show your every emotion. Your curves drive me to distraction."

She exhaled an "oh."

"Your lips are full and pink and kissable."

He dragged his thumb down her cheek to her mouth.

She swallowed hard. "You did this exercise with your acting teacher? Exactly how close were you?"

"I have learned to ad lib." He lowered his eyebrows.

"Don't change the subject. Tell me, who's your favorite female character on *Winds of Change?*"

"Dorian's character, Leanna."

"Why?"

"Because she's strong but feminine. She breaks all the stereotypes about women. She's funny and alluring in a real way. I'd love to be like her."

"You don't want to be her. You are her." He turned her to face him. "The reason you like her so much is that you see yourself in her, and deep down, you know it."

Her eyes filled with tears. The intensity of her feelings for him overwhelmed her. She reached for him and kissed him on the cheek. "Thank you for seeing in me what I can't see in myself."

That's when she felt it. Passion. It was like dark water, warm and soothing until she realized its depth and what an inexperienced swimmer she was.

"I've been holding my breath all my life. With you, I can finally breathe," she whispered as his mouth claimed hers.

He let out a low moan. "You feel so good, Selah."

His kisses became more urgent. She could think of nothing else but his hands in her hair and his lips against hers. She ignored the alarms in her head, that is, until his finger traced a path down her throat and chest toward—

Startled out of her trance, she pushed him away.

"What's wrong?" His eyes were still languid, his breath warm against her cheek. She looked down and at the ceiling—anywhere but at the face that had seduced soap ingénues onscreen for a decade.

"I can't. I mean—wow!" Her words were breathless and

ragged. "We can't. This is too fast. We just moved from simmer to fire."

"We can take it slow, stoke the embers awhile," he offered, cupping her cheek in his hand.

"No, what I'm trying to tell you is . . ." Her kiss-swollen lips couldn't seem to get the words out. "What I'm trying to say is that I'm still . . ."

"Mmm?" He kissed her lazily on the shoulder. "I know."

"I want to wait . . . until I'm married." *I cannot bring myself to say "virgin" in front of him.*

He smiled tenderly. "I know."

"How could you know?" She choked against her embarrassment. "Do I have it stamped on my forehead?"

He laughed and shook his head. "I can see it in your eyes." He kissed her burning cheeks and forehead. "And in the way you live out your faith."

She waved her hand in a circle around them. "So, if you knew, what was this just now?"

Catching her hand, he intertwined their fingers. "I got lost in you. In that moment, I forgot about my past and my illness. All I could think about was us and I didn't want it to end."

"That was the sweetest thing anyone has ever said to me." She wiped at her eyes.

He eased toward the door. "Maybe we should get out of your bedroom before—

The doorbell rang.

Chapter Forty

"Daytime drama should make 'em laugh, make 'em cry, make 'em wait."

Agnes Nixon
(soap writer and creator)

SHE STARED AT him, wide-eyed, "No, no, no. It must be Momma! Maybe she forgot her keys. She cannot catch me alone in here with a man or—"

Cane paled. "I'm guessing they still have public hangings in the south, and your mother will be the one holding the torch and the noose."

"You have to hide." Selah pulled him out of her bedroom, down the hall, and into the living room.

"Hide? We're not sixteen-year-olds."

"Here, hide in Dad's study."

"His *study*? Who is he, Hercule Poirot?"

Selah tapped her foot. "Duh, it's his game room. Poker, pool table, bathroom—"

"And a plasma and a Donkey Kong arcade machine! Nice."

"Focus, Cane."

"Maybe you can sell all this stuff and stop the foreclosure on the diner."

"Great idea. Now, git!" She pushed the door closed and shut him in the den. "Enjoy that TV while it lasts."

When she opened the front door, she did a double-take. "Tanner. Thank goodness you're not my mother."

"Not sure how to respond to that." He presented her with a quivering brown ball of hair and drool.

"You brought Faith!" She grabbed her with one arm and hugged Tanner with the other. "Thank you, Evil Twin. Thank you."

She kissed the dog's head and set her down in the living room.

"Frankie sent her over."

He'd been talking to Frankie. Hmm. That presented some interesting possibilities.

"What kind of dog is that?"

"I'd say part Ewok, part Muppet."

"Good call." He brushed fur from his faded jeans and short-sleeved black t-shirt that hugged his muscles.

"Frankie wanted me to give you this note. She said something about Operation Blue Bumper being a success." He crammed his hand into his jeans pocket and pulled out an envelope, then he arched one brow. "Is this something I should be concerned about?"

Selah just smiled sweetly. "You should know that

Frankie has a flair for the dramatic. Don't just stand there. Come in."

Tanner ducked to clear the doorframe. His eyes darted around the living room as if he was looking for escape routes.

"Selah, I wanted to make sure you're okay. I wish I could have gotten a good look at the driver, but it was dark and the windows were tinted."

"That's considerate of you. I—"

"Are you stalking her, man?" Cane emerged from the study and wrapped his arm around her shoulders. "Haven't you caused enough trouble already?"

Tanner's jaw tightened but his face was emotionless—a totally different man from his twin.

"Stand down. Tanner was just checking on me and bringing Faith home." Her eyes implored him.

Cane grunted, stepping back so Tanner could come in.

Selah excitedly clasped her hands together. "Hey, let's sit so I can get to know your brother."

Selah sat close to the arm of the sofa so Cane and Tanner were forced to sit beside each other. They crossed their arms at their chests.

"Isn't this nice? Yay, family reunion." She was met with silence.

Faith jumped up and stretched out between them, her head on Cane's knee and her back paws on Tanner. Clearly, Selah had rescued the smartest dog in the pound. She retrieved her phone from her pocket and snapped a picture.

Tanner startled. "What's that for?"

"For me and Frankie's enjoyment. Identical twins are so cute. I bet your mother dressed you alike, right?"

Tanner didn't smile. In fact, his face didn't move at all. How did he do that without Botox or something? She tried to set her face like his, hard and emotionless, but it was hopeless. Her feelings for Cane had to be plastered all over her face.

"Watch it with the camera." Cane chucked her chin. "Mom did dress us alike. She loved anything silly. She got a kick out of embarrassing us."

Tanner nodded slowly. Everyone stared at their shoes until Selah couldn't take it anymore.

"Momma told me you paid my hospital bill, Tanner. That's very generous."

"It's the least I could do for putting you in harm's way."

"What were you doing out there at night? Better yet, what were you doing in Shadybrook?" Cane demanded.

"Eva called me and it piqued my interest. I came to see how you were living."

"How I was living? What is that supposed to mean?"

"I was scoping you out, bro, to see if you had changed and given up drugs. To see if you were still a narcissistic actor."

Cane put his fingers lightly over Selah's lips. "Don't say a word, Selah, not even the truth."

Selah giggled and kissed his fingers.

Tanner shifted on the sofa. "She and Eva were walking alone after dark. I wanted to make sure they were safe."

"She was obviously safer without your help."

They glared at each other for a moment, then Tanner's eyes softened. "How are you feeling, Selah?"

"Great, thank you."

"And you, Cane?"

Selah cut her eyes to Cane, who looked away. "Are you feeling bad? Why would Tanner think you are?"

"He collapsed at the hospital after your mother took you home."

"Why? What happened?"

"Thank you, *bro.*" Cane punched his fist into his hand. "I told you not to say anything. My priority was Selah and her concussion."

Tanner shrugged. "I'm done keeping your secrets."

Cane laid his hand on Selah's and looked her in the eyes. "I have no more secrets. You've seen all my ugliness."

"If that's the case, she'll wise up and stay away from you."

He turned back to Tanner and pointed a finger at his chest. "Stop interfering in my life."

Tanner mimicked his body language. "Stop screwing it up then."

"It always comes back to that night, doesn't it?"

"You mean the night you blew our family to hell?" Tanner's eyes blazed, the first time he'd shown genuine emotion.

🎬

Cane opened his mouth to defend himself or spew something that would wound his brother, but something held him back. The truth. "You're right. I did ruin everything. I was reckless and cocky and stupid. For that, I am sorry, more sorry than you will ever know."

"Boys! Please." Clutching her head, Selah left them and sank into an adjacent recliner.

Cane jerked to attention and woke Faith, who jumped

off the sofa and headed for her dog bed. "What's wrong, sweetness?"

"All y'all's fighting is making my head hurt. It feels too familiar, and I don't like it one bit."

Cane folded his hands in his lap. "I promise to behave."

Tanner held up his palms. "Ditto."

"See that you do." Selah frowned but returned to the couch. "It is scary how much I sounded like Momma, giving you a tongue-lashing."

Cane pictured Selah turning into Momma as she aged. He gulped and shook the thought from his head.

"Now that we've rehashed an accident that happened twenty years ago and was caused by a drunk driver, tell me why you collapsed."

"I was dehydrated and insanely worried about you." Cane was feeling stronger today, gaining energy every time he looked at Selah. He was going to beat this. He couldn't give up when he had so much to live for.

"The doctor explained that it might be a side effect of his medication," Tanner said.

"So you know about Cane's illness? Could you have it too?"

"I'm fit as a fiddle, as you say here in the South."

"Thank God for that." Cane meant it. His brother still hated him, but he was grateful that Tanner was alive and well.

"How did you get your unusual name, Tanner?"

Both brothers chuckled.

Cane loved to tell this story. "Mom hadn't picked out a name for him when we were born. I came out of the gate looking a little pale for the doctor's liking. Little brother came out with Mom's coloring. She had Native American blood."

Cane paused for effect. "Dad looked at my little brother and said, 'Hey, that one's tanner than the other.'"

Selah groaned and smacked his thigh. "That's a terrible joke, Cane."

Tanner smirked. "Cane's jokes are notoriously dreadful, but this one happens to be true."

"Oops!" She covered her mouth with her hand. "Momma should've named me Grace."

Both brothers grinned at her. Maybe there was hope for healing and reconciliation.

Tanner studied the room, his gaze moving from the TV to the mirrors to the growing water spot on the ceiling.

"Sorry you have to look at that and endure the moldy smell." Selah's face flushed and she wrapped her arms around herself. "A bad storm damaged the roof. We're patching it until we can get it replaced. That is, when we procure ten thousand dollars."

She pushed herself off the couch. "Why don't we go outside for some fresh air? I'll fix up some sweet tea."

Tanner stood. "Thanks, but I've got to get going."

Cane jumped up to get the door. He held it open wide and followed Tanner and Selah out onto the front steps. "When are you leaving for home, wherever that is?"

"I like it here. I might stay a little longer."

"You do?" Selah and Cane said at the same time.

"Maybe I'll check out the action at the track."

Selah's eyes turned icy. "More power to you."

Cane didn't need a therapist to tell him how a person's parents and childhood could scar their future.

"What do you do for a living?"

"Odd jobs, here and there."

"A jack of all trades?" Selah asked.

"More like a drifter," Cane muttered.

"I prefer to think of myself as a Renaissance man."

Cane snorted, but his agitation dissipated when Selah slipped her arm around his waist.

His phone rang, the theme song from Sunday Night Football. "It's my agent. I can call him back later."

That's what was really bothering him, more than his frustration with Tanner: the fact that he was under the gun to make a decision about his career and his future with Selah.

Cane bent and kissed her lips. "I don't want to leave you alone."

"I'll be fine."

"Your eyes look weak."

"Go, get a job! I'll be available for further kissing this evening." The corners of her mouth turned up and it left him breathless.

"And that is my cue to go. Feel better, Selah." Tanner strode out to his black Escalade, a nice ride for someone who did odd jobs.

"Better doesn't cover how good I'm feeling."

Cane kissed both cheeks before taking off to catch up with Tanner. "Look at that, the patient is cured."

Chapter Forty-One

WHEN CANE WAS gone, the warmth of his fingers and the faint scent of his cologne lingered on Selah's skin. Worn out from the brothers' intense reunion, she fell asleep on the couch. When she awoke, she stretched and smiled, feeling safe, content—emotions she'd never experienced in this home. Maybe she should call Cane and tell him so.

She looked around for her phone and found it under the note Frankie sent about the accident. When Selah opened the envelope, a jagged piece of orange plastic fell out. She speed-dialed Frankie.

"While you were recuperating, I did some investigating." Frankie sounded breathless with excitement. "I found a piece of the car's headlight at the site of the hit-and-run. A friend at the auto parts store sold a headlight replacement kit today."

"What did you find out about the bumper?"

"I remembered seeing a crystal blue Trans Am like

that years ago. Custom paint job. They must have had it in storage."

"Do you know who it belongs to?" Selah rubbed at the goosebumps on her arms. Could they actually crack this case on their own?

"You're never going to believe it."

Stunned, Selah let the name of the driver sink in. When she ended her call with Frankie, a plan formed in her mind.

"Let's go for a walk, girl," she said as she leashed up Faith. "We've got to get to Good Company. This could be the key to saving it."

As she approached the site of the hit-and-run, a police car sat parked by the side of the road. A familiar figure crouched down at the spot where her head hit the pavement.

Selah rubbed at the bandage on her forehead. The plan couldn't wait. She would have to execute it now.

"Looking for something, Cody?" Selah treaded carefully, remembering he carried a gun.

Cody jerked around and clambered to his feet. As she got closer, she could see his eyes were wide and bloodshot.

"I'm investigating your accident." He put on his hat and aviator sunglasses. "This is police business. You and the tripod need to move along."

She took a step back. Maybe this wasn't such a good idea. If only she'd brought along Frankie or Cane or, even Momma, she wouldn't feel as if her knees could buckle at any second. Like David with stones for a slingshot, she had no earthly weapons except a jagged piece of headlight and a ten-pound dog, who stretched out on the shoulder of the road and fell asleep. Like David, she had a supernatural secret weapon.

Taking a deep breath, she asked, "How is that investigation going?"

He chewed on a toothpick as he glowered at her. "There's no positive ID on the car or driver. No physical evidence. I'm going to close the file on this case."

"You can't do that without Gina."

He threw the splintered toothpick on the ground. "I do what I want. Haven't you learned by now, Selah? I own this town."

He might own this town, but she had the Master of the Universe behind her. *Lord, help me defeat this bully.*

"How do you find the time to run the town, do your job, and race too?"

"Racin's just a hobby. A man's got to make money."

"Is that why you're taking the diner away from its rightful owners? To make money?"

He sucked his teeth against his lips. "I told you and Margo that I'm selling it to the highest bidder, and I've had offers from developers. Your boyfriend even offered to buy it."

"Cane offered to buy Good Company?" Her heart swelled. *Cane went up against Cody for me.*

His radio crackled and he turned toward his car. "Like I said, I'm going back to work and mark this case unfounded."

She nudged Faith and walked her over to the car. "I think I can help you, Cody. In fact, we can help each other."

She leaned against the car and displayed the piece of

headlight Frankie had sent. "This came off the vehicle that ran me and my dog down and then fled the scene."

Cody grabbed for the headlight. "Let me see that. It would make my day to arrest you for obstruction of justice."

She put it back in her pocket and glanced down at her purse to make sure the voice recorder was still hidden there. "I'm going to show this piece of headlight to Gina. I'm going to tell her the car that hit me—and did not stop—had a crystal-blue bumper like the one on your old Trans Am. One of the high-heeled shoes I was wearing that night has a bit of blue paint on it. That paint will match your car's custom color."

Finally she'd gotten her money's worth out of those constricting shoes.

"You're just like your old man, and I'm going to call your bluff, like I did his'n. You cain't prove my car was the one that ran you down." He took a step toward her, his hand resting on his gun.

"Don't come any closer." Selah stood tall. Faith rose to attention and growled. "Even if I didn't have a trail of evidence that led back to you, Gina's such a good cop, she'll figure out your car was missing an identical piece of headlight, a light that was replaced the day after the accident."

Cody rubbed his hand over his mouth and stared at her.

"She might be interested in your backroom poker games as well. If she isn't, the local TV stations love to report police corruption."

She smiled, amazed at how calm she was. "What, no fatty names to call me?"

He took off his shades and pointed them at her. "I wasn't the one who ran you down."

"Deny it all you want, but I can prove . . ." She stopped, trying to decipher the wild look in his eye, the waiver in his voice. It wasn't guilt.

The car flashed in her mind again. The driver was a woman.

"You weren't driving. It was Katie, wasn't it? No wonder I heard the car accelerate as she came toward me." She shook her head. Eva was catty, but she had nothing on Katie.

"I will do whatever it takes to protect my sister." He let loose a torrent of expletives. "What do you want from me?"

"For starters, an apology."

"Why should *she* apologize? You were the idiot who darted out in front of her car in the dark."

And now Selah had a taped confession.

"An apology is off the table then?" She snickered at the extent of his delusion. "Here's the deal. I'm willing to forget about this piece of headlight, your sister's crime, and *your* obstruction of justice, *if* you forgive my father's debt. You leave my family alone forever. But if you take the diner, I'll have you and Katie arrested so fast, no racecar could keep up."

"This is nuts. *You* are nuts." He stamped the ground and kicked the tire of his car.

Selah's spirits plummeted. She had underestimated him. The longer he remained quiet, the more frenzied her thoughts became: Cody operating a giant wrecking ball and Katie driving the bulldozer that would crush her family's future.

Finally, he spoke. "For my sister's sake, I'll take your deal. That dump is a money pit anyway."

"True, but it's my family's money pit. You obviously understand the concept of family." A smile spread across her face and lit up her insides.

He tipped his hat, jumped in his cruiser, and sped off.

"Yes!" She punched her fist in the air. "See that, Faith? God still performs miracles and rights wrongs in His own time."

Chapter Forty-Two

CANE SAT IN a booth by the window at Good Company, mulling over his friend's advice. "Forgive yourself and make peace with God and with the past. Then you can focus on your future with Selah."

They had talked on the phone for the last twenty minutes. Justus ended the call with a prayer. Cane felt awkward and raw, but he vowed to follow his friend's example. His friend had all the things Cane never knew he wanted—good health, a wife, kids, a satisfying job—until he met Selah.

Cane took a swig of Momma's strong coffee. She had been watching him since he walked in. He lifted the mug in her direction and smiled. The corners of her mouth moved, but her eyes had the look of someone who had laced his coffee with arsenic.

She thought she had his number. *Game on, lady. I will win you over. Right after I convince your daughter to run away with me.*

His phone rang again. "Howdy, darlin'." Cane's attempts at a Southern drawl sent Selah into a bout of giggles.

When she recovered, she said, "Hey, cowboy. Please tell me you're not out somewhere disposing of Tanner's body."

"We parted on civil terms. I have some big news though. Can we meet tonight?" No more secrets.

"Sure. Do you want me to come to Rendezvous?"

"That sounds tempting, but the giant bed in the middle of my hotel room might be a distraction for me." He grinned. "I wish I was there to see you blushing. How about the speedway?"

"That's Frankie's playground, not mine. I'm outside Good Company. Want to meet there and go for a walk?"

"I'm at the diner too."

He jumped up on the seat of a booth in front of the window, grinning and waving both arms like a manic Tom Cruise on Oprah's couch. She laughed at the spectacle. Faith's tail wagged at turbo speed.

Cane jogged out to his two favorite girls, Momma on his heels.

"Guess what, Selah!" Momma called. "Cody just came by. He's halting foreclosure and permanently cancelling our debt. It's a miracle."

That creep had laughed in Cane's face when he offered a substantial amount of money to buy the diner. What changed his mind?

"Indeed. It's an answer to prayer." Selah hugged Momma and peeked at Cane over Momma's shoulder.

The first thing to pop into Cane's mind was an expression he'd heard Margo say, "Well, slap my head and call me silly!" Selah had something to do with this. Anxious, self-conscious Selah had somehow gotten the upper hand with Cody. Cane's chest swelled with pride.

Selah released Momma and sidled up to Cane. "I guess Dad's relieved too."

"Who knows? He's not here, as usual. Why don't you stay and we'll celebrate?"

"Sounds great, but Cane and I are going to take a walk first."

Margo's face dimmed. "Don't stay out too long. You're still recovering."

When Selah had her back turned, Cane blew Momma a kiss and put his arm around Selah's shoulders. She rested her head against him. Taking Faith's leash, he led them away from Good Company, toward Selah's house.

"Let's go check on the Wallingfords' place while they're away."

She knit her eyebrows together. "I just came from my house, but I'll go back if you want to."

"You didn't seem surprised by Margo's news about Cody and the foreclosure."

"Oh?" She played it coy.

"You're a terrible actor."

She stopped, stood on her toes, and kissed him on the lips. Well, well. That was a promising development.

"But, lady, you got mad skills as a kisser, and in public too. You made me forget what we were talking about."

Her eyes danced as they connected with his. He couldn't look away. He never wanted to look away. A thrill shot through his jaded heart.

"Thank you for trying to buy the diner."

"I would do anything for you, but it appears you didn't need my help. What did you do to change that jerk's mind?"

"I promised not to expose his sister, Katie, as the hit-and-run driver."

He scratched his head, trying to place the name. "Redneck Barbie ran you down?"

"I remembered that the bumper was crystal blue. Frankie did a little digging and found out that Cody owned a Trans Am in that color and let Katie drive it. Turns out that his sister is his Achilles heel. She was worth more to him than the diner."

"I wish I'd been there to see you in action. This new confidence of yours is fetching."

"Momma would not approve of my methods."

"Momma can't control everything."

Selah stopped as they reached her driveway. "Someone's standing on my roof!" The figure waved.

"Is that Tanner with a hammer and tool belt?"

A Ford-F150 pickup loaded with materials, ladders, and coolers beeped and veered around them and into the driveway. Another truck pulled up in front of her mailbox. Six men and two ladies emerged from the vehicles.

"Hey, y'all," she ran over to hug one of the ladies. "Brenda, what on earth is going on? Why are our best customers taking over my driveway?"

"We're fixin' up your roof, hon." Brenda squeezed her cheeks and left to help unload.

Selah's face was glowing as she turned to him. "Did you do this?"

"I merely got the ball rolling." Cane's eyes grew misty as he took her in his arms. "I told you I would do anything for you."

He cleared his throat. "The added bonus is sitting back and watching Tanner, the Renaissance man, do all the work."

She took his hand. "Thank you, more than I can ever say. I was afraid the house might fall in before Momma and I could scrape together the money to repair it."

They climbed the stairs and stood on the Wallingfords' front porch to watch the construction.

"I have more good news. I got a callback."

"Well, of course you did. What's a callback?"

"An audition. For *Days of Our Lives.* I'm also auditioning for a pilot."

"That's—whoa—that was fast."

He lifted her and spun her around, a feat she didn't think humanly possible.

As he set her down, she hesitated. "*Days* is in Los Angeles, not New York, right?"

"Right."

"But LA is a lot farther away than New York."

"Right again. I love a smart woman," he teased. "We are going to have a blast in California. I know it will be an adjustment from rural Virginia, but . . ."

"We?"

"You're coming with me." He pulled the Wallingfords' rocking chairs together. She took the hint and sat beside him.

"You want me to go with you to Los Angeles?"

"We leave tomorrow."

"But we're just getting to know each other."

"I know all I need to know, sweetness. I want you by my side on this new adventure. Don't you want to be with me?"

"You know how I feel about you."

"I want to hear it from those pink lips of yours." He

leaned over and kissed her. "Mmm. Like strawberry ice cream on a summer day."

She rested her cheek against his while she traced the stubble along his jaw. Cane shivered.

"You are the best thing that's ever happened to me." She still couldn't look him in the eye and articulate her feelings. "But *me*, in Los Angeles? They don't eat there, do they?"

"You are beautiful, smart, funny. You can survive anywhere. Besides, we don't have to live in Hollywood with the starlets. We can get a place by the beach. There are normal people out there, I think. Say yes."

She pulled away from him and began to rock her chair. "I can't go livin' in sin with you. My mother would spontaneously combust."

"We'll get a duplex then or two townhouses side by side or homes within walking distance. I just want you near me. Say yes." This talk was not going the way it had played out in his head.

"I can't leave my parents. They'll kill each other. I have no job, no friends out there."

"You have no job here either. Frankie and Tanner can referee with your parents."

She continued to rock.

"We'll work out the rest. I don't care about the logistics. I just want you with me."

"Why?"

He retrieved a white sheet of paper from his jeans pocket. "I guess I have to pull out the big guns."

He unfolded it, holding it up so she could see that Julia used Sharpies to draw a big red heart with the names Cane and Selah inside.

"That's what she had me delivering to you so late under the guise of script changes," she said. "I knew she was up to mischief."

"See. Even Julia realized I was falling hard for you. I want you with me because I love you."

She shook her head, releasing the tears she'd been holding back.

"Yes, I do. I love you, hardhead." He pretended to knock on her head.

She didn't say it, didn't return his love. His stomach felt as if he'd eaten his brother's roofing nails.

"What will we do if we get tired of each other? We'll fight. We might turn into my parents—stuck in one constant circle of arguments."

"My parents never fought in front of me, so I don't know what the proper protocol is for successful relationships and disagreements." He did remember Dad kissing his mom's hand and helping her into the car. Her smile lit up that night. All these years, he'd been so tangled up in the darkness of the accident, he'd forgotten that perfect moment.

"We are not our parents," he pleaded. "This is our chance to be different, to do things better. I even talked to your pastor today."

"Really?" Her eyes lit up.

"He and I are going to try counseling and Bible study by e-mail, telephone, or Skype, whatever we can squeeze in, depending on our schedules."

"I'm so proud of you."

"So, we're on for LA?"

She sighed.

"I'm scared, too, but you've got to trust me. Have faith

in my love for you. Remember the letter you wrote me. Change your focus. Look at me."

"Lord, help me. I do trust you, Cane."

"Then tell me yes."

🎬

"I told him no." Selah said. The day after Cane's proposal, she called Frankie to her house to show off the new roof and report the news.

"Are you sure the accident didn't knock a few screws loose?" Frankie, who was stretched out on the sofa, leaned toward the recliner where Selah sat.

No, but Cane's goodbye kiss might have. When he finally dragged his lips from hers, he whispered, "I miss you already. I'm going to find a way to keep us together."

Selah swallowed. "As much as I wanted to get on that plane with Cane, I cannot go to Los Angeles with him right now. This will give him time to get adjusted, settle in, and see if absence makes the heart grow fonder."

"Out of sight, out of mind." Frankie countered.

"If you love someone, set them free."

"While the cat's away, the mice will play."

"Enough." Selah put her hands over her ears. "Falling in love always seems effortless on the soaps."

Frankie smacked her arms down. "You are being too logical about this. What are you not telling me? Why on earth would you let a man like that go?"

"I just told you. It's complicated."

"No, you're complicated. The situation is simple. He loves you. You love him. Love and marriage. Baby carriage. Blah. Blah. Blah."

"I can't shack up with him. He needs to find his own

way, and so do I. He's praying again." She was so excited that he sought out her pastor's counsel. She hadn't realized how badly she wanted a man who turned to God first in all things, not to the ponies or the next hand of poker.

"I don't want him to confuse his feelings for me with his feelings for God. His relationship with God shouldn't depend on our relationship."

"So, while he's finding himself and God, what do you plan to do? Wait by the telephone, light candles, and write love sonnets until your conquering hero returns?" Frankie rolled her eyes.

"It's funny you should mention writing." This idea had felt so right when it was just a dream. But in the light of day, she wasn't so sure. "My writer's block is gone. I want to pursue it fulltime."

Was she crazy to believe she could pull off this kind of career change?

"Freelance writing? What about your computer business?" Frankie looked as if Selah had scrambled her brains with a side of grits.

"I hate computers. I'm sick of them."

"But your degree is in computers. Your business is computing."

"I know! How misguided I've been. I'm terrible at running a business. I hate trying to fix computers and outwit them, wondering when the hard drive will crash. Is my data backed up? Do I have enough firewalls, virus protection, encryption? They're like Dr. Jekyll and Mr. Hyde, loveable when they work, diabolical when they don't. I want to throw the computer out the window. I feel freer saying that. It's freeing. I'm free!" Selah raised her arms up in hallelujah. "I mocked the computer, and nothing happened. Not like in *Space Odyssey*."

"Slow down. This is crazy talk."

"I'm perfectly sane. Never been saner. When I was shadowing Mason and writing about *Winds of Change*, I realized how much I enjoyed it."

"You know writing involves a computer, right?"

"As long as I remember how to write in longhand and Staples doesn't stop selling legal pads and ballpoint pens, I'll be okay. I'll use the computer for social networking and promotion."

Frankie frowned and scratched her head. "What about money? Aren't writers poor and prone to drinking?"

"Don't worry, Frankie. It doesn't suit you." Selah was going to let God worry about the long-term details. "I'll find a way to pay my student loans. I don't know what we'll do about the overdue bills for the diner. But I've applied to teach online classes. If all else fails, Willie is looking to hire a delivery person."

Frankie laughed out loud.

"Think of all the free Chinese food!"

"What will you write? How about a torrid romance novel nobody expected?"

"That is an intriguing idea. First, I want to write a biography, if the subject will agree to it."

Chapter Forty-Three

*I*N THROUGH THE nose. Ooowwwtt through the mouth. Repeat.

Selah felt her chest rise and fall. Two days at home alone without Cane, and she was not as well-adjusted as she led Frankie to believe. She waited for relief from worry and loneliness, but it didn't come. Nope. Nothing. Total waste of oxygen. Now she was yawning

It was all over now, and she had to face the facts. *Winds of Change* was becoming a fond memory. Her fantasy trip to New York, her fantasy job, her fantasy man—they were all over. Her man left her behind for greener pastures. The doubting voices screamed at her. She couldn't compete with the women in LA.

I think I'm supposed to be happier or more satisfied knowing I took the risk, I braved the unknown, I gave it my all.

She hummed Whitney Houston's "One Moment in Time." And then she started writing and didn't stop until morning. She pushed "send," catapulting her work into an inbox three thousand miles away. If only she could transport herself that easily.

Cane called within minutes of her e-mail. "Selah Morgan, you amaze me."

"The sound of your voice is pretty amazing."

"I didn't know you could write like that." He wasn't as peppy as usual. "You should explore that talent, but I want you here with me, not writing about me."

Selah was silent. She wanted to ask him how he was feeling, if he found a house, if the weather was balmy. *But if he tells me how happy he is, I'll cry.*

"Are you okay with me writing your life story? I'm basing it on what you've told me about your experiences, but you'll have to fill in the gaps."

"Just change the names. Make it fiction. Better yet, make it our love story."

"Could you be any more romantic?"

His voice dropped. "Oh, you have no idea."

"You are incorrigible." She pictured his chocolate brown eyes crinkling up at the corners and a grin sliding across his face. "I want to hear more about the grandmother who raised you."

"Grandma wasn't old enough to be a grandmother. We called her that because she didn't want to take our mom's place. After our parents died, we were placed in foster care. Grandma was a neighbor who stepped in and became our foster mother. She wanted to adopt us, but—"

"But you and Tanner left."

"It must have broken her heart." Cane cleared his throat. "Speaking of leaving, I am going to be out of touch by e-mail or phone for a few weeks."

"Did you get the part on the soap?"

"Yes. They want me, but in a different role that hasn't started taping yet, so I've got a bit of free time."

"What will you do?"

"Travelling, soul-searching, repairing the bridges I've burned. I'll be out of touch for a few weeks, but my girlfriend will always be on my mind."

"Girlfriend." She repeated. "Hearing you call me that will never get old."

For a few moments, she heard only his breathing and it calmed her.

"Keep going with your writing. I can't wait for the happy ending."

Neither could she.

Cane didn't call or e-mail again for three and a half weeks. He had said he would be out of touch for a few weeks, but "a few" meant one or two to her. She didn't want to interrupt his soul-searching, but what if something had happened to him while he was travelling?

She looked around Good Company to make sure Momma wasn't in earshot. Momma would say she was better off without him. Good riddance.

Dialing his number, she got voicemail. "Hello, Shirtless Wonder. I'm worried. I'm peeved too. At you for not calling. At myself for caring so deeply. If you don't respond soon, I will call your book 'MIA.' I miss your silly jokes and the way you slip Faith treats when you think I'm not watching. I'm always watching. I'm sounding like a stalker again, aren't I? Just let me know you're safe. I cannot believe

I'm saying this to an answering machine, but I love you, Cane Ashton."

The machine cut her off. She had always been in love with him, even when he was just playing a character on TV. She sat in her booth at the back of the diner, gazing down at the wallpaper photo on her cell phone. She and Cane at the rally, laughing so much their tears froze to their faces.

Someone coughed. She looked up and Tanner was standing over her. Her heart lurched and then dive-bombed when she realized it was not Cane.

"I was afraid you'd leave town before I got to thank you for repairing our roof."

"I decided to stay a bit longer." He glanced out the window. Frankie was coming up the walk. Tanner's mouth turned up, but then his face went hard and serious again, as if he'd slipped on a Halloween mask.

"Your dad just hired me on."

"At the diner?" Hope Tanner wasn't expecting a paycheck in the near future.

"I make a mean meatloaf. Cane does too."

She raised an eyebrow.

"Grandma taught us both to cook." He backed up, as if he'd shared too much of himself. "So, I'll be seeing you around a lot more."

"Super."

He scooted out to meet Frankie before Selah could put her next thought together. His presence left her vaguely unsettled. But he was Cane's brother, and he had Frankie beaming, so that was enough for now.

"Let the writing begin." She clapped her hands and picked up her pen. The goal was to get through a half hour without thinking about Cane, no easy task when the story was about him.

All the endings she brainstormed left her unfulfilled.

She welcomed writer's block now, because she finally figured out that she conversed most with God when she hit a wall. Maybe that was part of His plan all along. He was sneaky that way.

She leaned forward and shifted her paper and her body to the left, then to the right. How did anyone get comfortable in a chair that was bolted to the floor? It was even harder to get comfortable with Momma standing behind the chrome counter, watching her like the nuns at a Catholic school.

Her phone vibrated in her jeans pocket. Cane must have called while she was talking to his brother. She pushed play on his message and let his voice drift over her like thunder in the distance.

"Sweetness, I'm safe. Sorry I've been out of touch. But if that's what it takes to get you to admit you love me, I'll leave more often. My TV interview with SoapChat will air in two days. After that, I'm all yours. I love you, Selah Morgan. Believe it."

When the message ended, she played it again and held the phone over her heart. Momma walked over, inspecting the other tables as she went. "You all right? You've been sitting there with your eyes closed and a funny look on your face."

Selah gathered up her belongings and stood. "I was feeling a little dizzy."

Over a man. A man she couldn't live without. God had

brought him into her life. Now she needed to do her part and find some way for them to be together.

"I'm heading home to write." She didn't give Momma time to ask more questions.

When she reached the house, she glanced over at the Wallingfords' front porch. They were gone again, this time on a cruise to Alaska.

She climbed their steps and sat in one of the rockers. The day Cane left, he said, "That will be you and me thirty years from now, holding hands as we look out over the water from the deck of our ship. We'll be waiting for our next adventure to begin."

She swallowed the lump in her throat. Reaching out, she pulled the other chair beside hers until they touched. That's more like it. The tension went out of her body, and a sense of peace took its place.

Her phone vibrated. She looked at the caller ID. So much for peace.

"Hello, Mason. Oh, how I've missed you."

A pause at the other end. "Yes, well, that was inevitable. My charm is legendary."

She laughed at his joke, but he didn't.

"I'm calling because the move to California has presented several challenges. I need an assistant."

"I thought writers worked alone."

"A protégé then."

"Who have you hired?"

"I want you to do it."

Selah laughed, but again heard no laughter on the other end of the line. "You're serious? You want me to be your assistant? Did Julia put you up to this?"

"Julia suggested it because, in her words, I was more moody than usual, and my storylines needed pep."

"She still calls the shots?"

"Nobody calls my shots but me." He sighed heavily. "I need an assistant, not a therapist."

"But why me? Was I the only one who didn't run when you summoned?"

"I like to keep my friends close and my enemies closer."

"Are we friends or enemies? Maybe frenemies?"

"Your grammar is atrocious. We'll work on that."

"Can you guarantee me the respect I deserve?"

Another sigh. "Now that the SoaperFan project has been laid to rest, and my babysitting duties have terminated, we can co-exist peacefully. Yes or no?"

"I'll think about it."

"What's to think about? You'll be working with me again. It's every woman's dream. You have until next week to decide."

He hung up.

She smiled, rocking her chair with a vengeance. *Well, now. This changes everything.*

Chapter Forty-Four

"Stay tuned for scenes from tomorrow's episode."

The Winds of Change closing credits

OMMA MET SELAH at the door of Good Company and enveloped her in her warm arms and the smell of grease and vanilla. "You've been holed up in your room so long, I figured you'd written at least three stories by now."

"Just one so far. It's a novel. I'm still working out the ending."

After Mason called, she spent the next few days writing and mulling over his job offer. The best part of writing was that she could spend hours wrapped up in her characters and not think about working out her problems with a giant piece of pie.

"That's great, sugar." Momma said. "Help me take all

these mason jars of flowers out to the patio and set them on the tables."

Cream eyelet tablecloths covered the picnic tables and the booths in the diner. Red ornamental globe lights hung from the roof. In the twilight, the place looked elegant, classy.

"What's going on? Somebody having a party?" She fingered the daisies and red roses, remembering the daisies Cane sent her in New York.

A yearning for him came over her, so strong that her chest constricted.

"Some lady with a funny accent rented out the diner for an engagement party," said the woman with the thickest Southern accent this side of the Mississippi. "I made three chocolate treasure pies, and Tanner made cookies and other goodies."

Speak of the devil. Tanner came out with an apron around his waist and a giant punch bowl in his hands. Frankie trotted behind him.

"Hey, Selah." He set down the bowl to scratch Faith's bearded chin. "'Sup, Dawg?"

He did have a sense of humor.

He turned to Selah with a twinkle in his eye. "It's almost time for Cane's show. Still can't believe that people willingly tune in to see my brother on TV."

Cane had given a pre-recorded interview to SoapChat, a weekly reality series that focused on the personal and professional lives of daytime's hottest stars. Cane was overqualified.

"Stay and watch it with us on this big-screen TV." Frankie hugged her and cooed at Faith. "It's set up for the party. The couple is going to show pictures from their romance or something sickening like that."

"Watching it with you beats sitting at home alone, crying in my Mountain Dew because I miss him so much."

Frankie squeezed her hand and they settled onto a booth seat. Tanner turned on the giant TV and fumbled with the five-hundred-button remote until he found the correct channel. Her parents shuffled around inside the diner, acting as if they were busy preparing for the party, but when the show started, they stopped in the doorway to watch.

Selah's fingers drummed the table as they waited through commercials. "Tonight on Entertainment Unplugged, a child star's latest antics and celebrity spouses who cheat."

Selah hugged Faith a little closer. "Mason offered me a job as his assistant." She whispered to Frankie. "And before you ask, I'm taking it."

Frankie squealed. "Watch out Hollywood, here comes Selah Morgan."

"Thank you for helping me get there, for helping me to shine."

Frankie and Selah were both blubbering messes by the time the show started. Jack Lavery, a veteran soap actor and musician, filled the screen with adorable dimples and soulful eyes. But when the camera focused on Cane's face, everything else faded away.

Her decision was sealed. Those LA ladies better watch out, because Selah was coming out there. Faith woofed and wagged her tail. She couldn't know Cane was on TV. Could she?

"Cane," Jack said as he shook her man's hand, "congratulations on snagging a new role. The buzz is that you're already a shoe-in for an Emmy based on the work you did for *Winds of Change*."

"Thanks, Jack. I hadn't heard that rumor. I'm humbled by it." Cane said. *"Winds* helped me turn my life around. As for my new job, what an honor to play a legacy character who is rooted in the show's history. I plan to give the fans everything they want and more."

The camera panned out and revealed how lovely and warm Cane's home was. He had three skylights, and the bay windows looked out onto palm trees and a fenced-in yard. He didn't have much living-room furniture other than a comfy-looking sofa and two rocking chairs.

"You've had some major changes in your life this year, haven't you?"

"To put it mildly. Those changes knocked me for a loop, man." Cane ran his hand through his hair, a tic that Selah knew was more nerves than vanity. "Earlier this year, I was diagnosed with multiple sclerosis."

"Wow!" Jack sat back in his chair, reveling in his scoop. "One would never know by looking at you."

"I've hidden it well. Being an actor comes in handy, and my doctors are excellent."

"Would it be weird if I ran up and kissed the TV screen?" She whispered to Frankie.

She put her arm around Selah's shoulder and squeezed. "You knew about the illness, didn't you?"

Selah nodded, brushing tears from her eyes. They turned their attention back to the screen to hear Cane's answer to the question, "Why did you decide to make this news public now?"

"I kept quiet because I was afraid people would think I was weak, and I would lose my job. I believed that, if I went public, the disease would become real and powerful. Turns out that I am more powerful when I talk about it. I'm tired of hiding and running from the pain. I'm going to face this head-on."

"See, Selah," her mother sputtered.

Selah startled as Momma sneaked up behind her.

"If the two of you had gotten together, you would have spent your life playing nursemaid to an invalid."

Frankie and Selah shushed her at the same time. Tanner shot her a hard look, but she kept talking. "He ain't right. A man who won't even eat chocolate cake. That ain't normal."

"No worse than the gambling addict you've enabled for thirty-five years," Selah said as Momma opened her mouth and shut it again.

Frankie whispered in Selah's ear, "Is Cane going to be okay?"

"It looks that way."

Jack continued the interview. "Cane, you have a rep as a ladies' man. Is there anyone who can tame the beast and get you to settle down?"

Cane laughed. "Funny you should mention that. One woman has captured my heart. I've made many mistakes with her, but I'm determined to make her mine."

Selah's stomach did a Tower of Terror plunge. But it was the kind of plunge where you laugh and get back on the ride again once you get your bearings.

"See? He's got another woman already." Momma would not be silenced. "Love ain't no soap opera."

Even Tanner joined in the shushing.

"If she'll have me," Cane continued from his California pad, "I'd like her to be my permanent date to the Emmys for the next fifty years or so."

Jack leaned forward in his seat. "Are you asking this woman to marry you?"

Cane looked into the camera. "Let's just say I'd like her to start working on another album—a wedding album this time."

Jack and Cane grinned at each other before doing the one-armed man hug. "Good luck to you both."

Selah's heart rallied. Was he talking about her Hunk O' the Month Club album? Could Cane be asking her to marry him? *Trust me.* He'd said it over and over.

As the pre-taped interview ended, Frankie clicked the remote to turn off the TV. They all stood staring at the blank screen: Frankie, Tanner, Selah's parents, and Selah. The only one who hadn't stopped talking was her mother.

"I'm sorry I was right about him. But you know what I've always told you: handsome is as handsome does."

"What does that mean, Mother?"

"Love ain't no soap opera."

"Stop it! Stop saying that." This time, Selah didn't react to her mother's drawn face and pleading eyes. Instead, she felt that overwhelming sense of peace again. She knew exactly what and whom she wanted.

"You have to face facts. The woman Cane is in love with is *me*." She lifted her chin. "He wants to marry *me*."

Momma caught sight of something over Selah's

shoulder and blanched. Selah turned to see what had shut up her mother.

Cane stood behind Selah, most likely listening to their entire argument.

She ran into his arms and he crushed her to him, his cheek pressed against hers. Selah pulled away and ran her hands hungrily through his hair and over every inch of his face, like a blind woman seeing him for the first time.

"Momma is wrong." He kissed her with feeling. "It's you. It's always been you and only you. I'm sorry I left you behind when I should have stayed where I belong."

"Where have you been?" She rested her hands against the soft lapel of his dark brown suit.

"I went to Minnesota to see Grandma. She's still living in the old house and asked me to help her move. Turns out, Tanner has been visiting her and sending her money all these years."

Tanner's jaw twitched.

"I'm sorry, bro." Cane offered his hand to Tanner. "I accused you of being a loser, and I'm the one who lost out. Grandma taught us the importance of family and God. When our parents died, I ran from that and never looked back. I don't want to do that anymore."

Tanner took the hand, and the twins embraced. Selah looked over at Frankie, who was as teary as Selah. Her father put his arm around Momma, who didn't murder him. There was hope for them yet.

Cane pulled away. Waving his arms, he shouted, "Let's have us a hoedown."

"The place is already booked for a party, son." Dad said gently.

Comprehension dawned on Selah. "Wait, is all of this—?"

"It's all for you, SoaperFan." Cane grinned. "Welcome to your engagement party."

Frankie screamed and clapped her hands.

Selah tried to take it all in. "Who was the woman with the strange accent who booked the party?"

"Grandma, right?" Tanner answered. "Nobody speaks 'Minnesooota' like Grandma."

A smile crept across Selah's face. "If this is our engagement party, then are you asking me—?"

"You ask too many questions. Let me do the asking this time."

She laughed and cried as he dropped to one knee.

"Selah Morgan, would you do me the honor of becoming my wife? Will you marry me, SoaperFan?"

"Yes! Yes! Cane Ashton! I will marry you, Shirtless Wonder."

He reached into his pocket and pulled out a fortune cookie. He offered it to her. "Frankie told me all about your *Winds of Change* marathons. I hope Willie won't be too jealous."

"You open it, Cane. I tend to get the defective fortunes."

He broke it open and displayed a diamond, a marquis cut, she thought, accented by amethysts.

Who cares what cut the diamond is? I'm totally marrying this guy. Thank You, God, for bringing me all around Robin Hood's barn to this perfect moment.

Cane slid the ring onto her left finger and kissed her hand. Applause erupted from their audience, which had grown considerably. She turned and saw Aunt Ruby and a few of her friends, including Gina, still in uniform.

She helped Cane up, and they fell against each other, laughing. When they'd finally righted themselves, he took her face in his hands and kissed her as if it was forever.

"I know this is strange thing to say while I'm kissing you," he whispered, "but something is scratching my ankle."

"Maybe it's a ball and chain," Momma muttered as a tear ran down her cheek. Everybody laughed.

Cane kept one hand around Selah's waist and picked up her wriggling dog with the other. As Cane kissed her, Selah realized this was how it was going to be from here on out. Cane and her together, with Faith in the middle.

Dear Reader,

Thank you for investing your time and emotions in *Love Ain't No Soap Opera*. When I read, I seek heroines I can identify with. Unfortunately, I don't see myself in many books. Not just because I'm goofy and weird, but because few heroines are plus-size, full-figured, curvy. Most plus-size characters only find happiness upon losing weight. You won't find them on book covers either. No evidence of ladies of size being held, kissed, loved.

Isn't that sad? That message makes me feel less than human, unworthy, unlovable. And that couldn't be farther from the truth, especially in God's eyes, because true beauty isn't found in the mirror. Cane and Selah feel unlovable, broken. They come from very different backgrounds, but, as the story unfolds, they realize how similar they are in their struggles and how much they need love and acceptance from each other and God.

This book is also an homage to daytime drama. The soaps kept this latchkey kid company and they still draw me in. I got a taste of Cane's world when I attended the Daytime Emmys and visited the set of a soap in Los Angeles, highlights of my life.

Dreams come true, no matter how large your size or your insecurities.

Love,

Connie Kuykendall

Corrine Kensington Photography

P.S. The Shadybrook Series continues. Keep reading for a sneak peek at the next book, *Love Ain't No Fairy Tale*.

Connect with the Author

Sign up for Connie Kuykendall's newsletter:
http://eepurl.com/bBmiRT

Join Connie on Social Media:

TWITTER
@CurledCrusader
@SoaperFan

WEBSITE
www.CurledCrusader.com
www.ConnieKuykendall.com

FACEBOOK
www.facebook.com/CurledCrusader

Read on for an exclusive sneak peek at the upcoming sequel in the Shadybrook Series.

Love Ain't No Fairy Tale

By Connie Kuykendall

*W*ALT DISNEY ONCE said that a kick in the teeth could be the best thing for you, to strengthen you. Lark McKenzie had been kicked in the teeth so many times, she needed a mouth guard or dentures. Logically, it followed that she should have super-human strength, strength enough not to have a breakdown over bubble wrap.

Please not today. Someone had bubble-wrapped her desk, right down to the telephone, stapler, and paper clips. Despite the tinsel and Christmas cookies making their way around the office, this wrapped present was not from ol' Saint Nick.

She sighed and tried to ease quietly into her chair, but it was no use. Every move against the plastic cued a symphony of cracking and popping that resonated to the other cubicles.

Lark heard their snickers before she saw the perpetrators. It was the same trio who placed antlers and a red nose on her motorcycle last week and a life-like spider in her lunch bag at Halloween. She had nicknamed them the CGI Stooges or animation's version of the Nerd Herd. Three grown men in white shirts and skinny black ties who were huddled in a corner behind her, giggling. This was an animation studio, for Pete's sake, not a frat house.

"Oh, Alvin!" She called sweetly through clenched

teeth, summoning their ringleader. Everybody called him A.J. for Alvin Jameson, but his naughty Chipmunk namesake suited him.

"Yes, Lark?" He was beside her in an instant.

She concentrated on his hair, so as not to be beguiled by those Persian green eyes. Reddish brown hair splayed out in every direction. He must've tried to tame it with gel and given up.

"Did you have anything to do with this," she waved her hand over her desk, "this attempt to render my desk in 4-D?"

"No. Nooooo." He crammed a tape dispenser into the pocket of his black slacks. "My specialty is computer-generated imagery. Do you love it though? It's like snow in Southern California."

She blinked.

"Embrace the bubbles, Lark." He snapped the plastic covering her computer mouse.

"OK, then." Lark took her cell phone out of her blue jean jacket. She pointed it at the plastic winter wonderland.

"What are you doing?"

"Taking pictures. Duh."

"Why?"

"For my sexual harassment lawsuit, silly."

A.J. paled and his co-conspirators made a speedy exit. "You wouldn't—"

"Gotcha!" Lark snapped a picture of his bewildered expression.

His mouth lifted into a slow grin that widened into laughter. The don't-mess-with-me look she had given him was not supposed to be hilarious. Lark didn't do funny. It was a leave-me-alone-or-die glare. An I-pity-the-fool-who-messes-with-Lark-McKenzie stare.

But he was still laughing. Ugh. Men were so overrated.

Acknowledgments

Thank you

God, the author of my life.

Mom, the friend who has encouraged and put up with me.

Beta readers, the ones who kept on reading even when it was rough: Andy Howell, Elizabeth McEnery, Jennifer Deasaro, Dena Reynolds, Heather Fleshman.

Christina Miller, the editor who reigned in this story and will help your story blossom with proofreading, copyediting, and substantive editing services at

http://www.mentorspeneditorialservices.com/

Alisha at www.damonza.com who created a breathtaking cover that captured the novel's essence.